Open your mind to an exciting but creepy paranormal thriller. Ken Hughes breaks into the genre promising to transcend suspense to a whole new level.

It is refreshing to see an author's debut transcend the genre of fiction, adding to it a fresh, new perspective of a paranormal thriller. SHADOWED is compelling, suspenseful and irresistibly entertaining. Hughes proves beyond a shadow of a doubt that he can create a spine-tingling thriller with gutsy twists and page-turning suspense. You will not be disappointed.

—Ace Antonio, author of
THE CONFESSIONS OF SYLVA SLASHER

Paranormal thrillers are a dime-a-dozen these days, and they more often than not involve handsome, brooding undead heroes, but SHADOWED is refreshingly different. Author Ken Hughes has created in Paul Schuman a protagonist who is very much human, despite a superhuman ability, and it is his very humanity that makes him so believable. He may have the gift to enhance his senses at will, but it's plain old-fashioned courage that ultimately proves his most effective attribute. Written in a clear, straightforward style particularly suited to this genre, from the first page, I was pulled in, wanting to know more about Paul's and Lorraine's abilities, and equally important, the backdrop of intrigue and scandal that the story plays out against.

Fast-paced, well-plotted with a likable protagonist and an ending that leaves the story open for a sequel, SHADOWED is a helluva fun read, and won't disappoint fans of either normal or paranormal-genre thrillers.

—Leslie Ann Moore, author of the award-winning
GRIFFIN'S DAUGHTER Trilogy

He can hear a whisper across the block… and can't remember why.

Open your mind, to a city where mystery chases up and down office back stairways, turns brother against brother, and plays out on frozen sidewalks where lives may be shattered if the enemy even looks at the ragged man passing by in the crowd—and even that man cannot guess what memory will be next to batter his mind.

Paul was no detective, no thief, only a student trying to get some distance from his father and brother. When he found himself marked by the power to enhance his senses, he had only that treacherous gift and what few tricks he dared to teach himself, to search for some explanation—or at least the chance to give it meaning by exposing a few petty corruptions.

Paul thought if he lived in poverty to keep his existence secret from the world, at least nobody could force him to use that gift as a weapon against others. But just when he thought he was untouchable, the last thing he expected shakes his world and drags him into the perils of his family, his power, and two women who each have a different claim on his life.

As Paul begins to play cat and mouse with enemies he can't even name, he must break every rule that's kept him alive, in every frantic chase and every gamble he makes to break his family free. And all the while, he knows his greatest enemy may still be what lies behind his own secrets.

If you think you know everything a paranormal thriller can do, take a closer look.

About The Author

Ken Hughes has been living for storytelling since his father first read him The Wind In The Willows, and everything from Stephen King's edge to Hayao Miyazaki's sense of wonder has only fed that fire. He has worked as a technical writer in Los Angeles at positions from medical research to online gaming  to mission proposals for a flight to Mars. For more about his stories, songs, and his Unified Writing Field Theory, see kenhughesauthor.com.

SHADOWED

SHADOWED

Ken Hughes

Windward
Road Press

North Hollywood, CA

Windward Road Press
13029-A Victory Blvd. #335
North Hollywood, CA 91606

This is a work of fiction. Names, characters, places and incidents either are products of the author's imagination or are used fictitiously. Any resemblance to actual events or locales or persons, living or dead, is entirely coincidental.

ISBN Paperback: 978-0-9850484-0-2
ISBN E-book: 978-0-9850484-1-9

Printed in United States of America

Library of Congress Control Number: 2012931298

Hughes, Ken, 1964-

    Shadowed / Ken Hughes. -- North Hollywood, CA : Windward Road Press, c2012.

        p. ; cm.

        ISBN: 978-0-9850484-0-2
        Book 1 in the Whisperers universe.

        1. Paranormal fiction, American. 2. Extrasensory perception--Fiction. 3. Suspense fiction. I. Title.

PS3608.U364 S53 2012   2012931298
813.6--dc23   2012

Book Consultant: Ellen Reid
Cover & Interior Design: Ghislain Viau

*To we five Hugheses, for forming so happy
and honest a family I had to look this far afield to break
my hero's heart. Thank you, for everything.*

Too loud, too many voices inside talking and jostling to be heard, battering at his Opened hearing… Paul flinched back, couldn't keep himself from a gasp, and that thundered in his senses too.

But it's in there, somewhere.

And he couldn't start hesitating, outside the grand old house in the twilight. Instead, he refocused his power on its second story, finding the half-sheltered region that lay one ceiling above the party. He stepped forward as he did, his feet awkward with most of his will reaching forward. But the echoing in the air ahead, a few footsteps and so many sounds spilling upward through the floorboards, all shifting and mingling and drumming within the rooms and inside his mind…

He broke off the connection and felt the air's chill seeping into his face. The cold felt too deep, as if he'd been standing there for whole minutes instead of mere moments.

I couldn't have been lost in it for that long—could I? Still, even now, he couldn't be sure.

Paul glanced at the people drifting past on the path to the door. *I don't need to do this; the real work here will be late at night, anyway. I could be back reading in bed in half an hour.*

But crowds had their uses too, and he couldn't let fear hold him back. Squaring his shoulders, he shifted onto the path and headed toward the door.

As with most buildings, his first glimpse from inside neatly fleshed out the impressions he'd already formed. The converted mansion was filling up slowly; one young couple lingered in the foyer to wind up their conversation before they reached the main rooms where eager, cynical, young, old, and middling visitors milled about.

First things first. Paul paused at the outer door, looking like just another scruffy young man, perhaps more hesitant than some to join the bustle beyond. Fiddling with his coat to stall, he glanced back at the door and Opened his sight.

From three paces away, the outer face of the lock sprang into his vision, showing him every trace of the plate's shape and size, enough to compare to the types of locks he knew—

The door lurched around, swinging his *self* with it for an instant before he let the connection go. Paul kept the wave of dizziness from showing on his face and waited for the visitor to walk by, thinking ruefully of how movie spies could always pick any lock at a glance.

He focused again. The old brass shape wasn't right; its style might be a Weismann, or at least it looked more like the older models—

"You in or out?" a voice bellowed.

Paul jumped, his trance shattering.

An older man, with thinning hair and a caged dog on his shirt; he spoke again. "Can't just stand out here. You only here to impress your girl, or you want the lab to get away with it?"

Paul allowed himself a grim smile. "No, I'm here about LifeLab alright." *But how much do the people around here know?* He added "I still can't believe they'd do that."

"Of course they did! They think they can do anything as long as it isn't on baby bunnies." But instead of saying more there, he went on "But, do you think it all just started with one lab's experiments, like everything was okay before then? You know how many unwanted dogs are in this city?"

As the activist kept talking, less and less about LifeLab and its secret, Paul could only steal another glance past him to throw his power at the door again. The lock's contours filled his sight again, with a view closer than it would have been through any magnifying glass. The shape still didn't seem like a Weismann, and the size was wrong for…

"…we may never get them all. But we'll shut that lab down, count on it!" the man finished.

No, you really won't. Paul felt himself scowl and turned away to partly hide his face as he muttered, "Bet you will. I'll go take a look," and headed inside.

"…blog all you want, they won't…"

"…ever since Jackie had…"

"…sure, I used to eat…"

The conversations flowed around him, pulling at him under the vaulted ceiling's echoes as he made his way through the main room. As he'd thought, the Animal Alliance—or at least its crowd tonight— seemed to be a mix of young dabblers, longtime believers, partisans of all types, and all the random curiosity-seekers that had come for drinks in plastic cups and an earful about the group's sudden accusations against LifeLab.

Not that Paul had expected the Alliance rank and file to know much about what had really happened with it.

As he passed a grand stairway, his eyes wanted to follow the deep, stained wood of the banister upward, and the blessed quiet there. But that floor was still far from empty, and wouldn't even give him this crowd to blend in with. At this hour, the best he could do was stay down in the thick of it, and plan his approach for searching the place later.

And I'd better not Open my sense of smell—not with this many bodies!

Paul moved toward the next of the several rooms, staying near the wall to slip around one older woman gesturing with her drink. The front door had probably kept the same stiff, ancient lock since when the group's benefactor had lived here; but judging from the newer, gleaming chairs and tables he passed along the poster-covered walls, much of the place had been modernized so some of the back doors might be less trouble.

The rooms weren't really full, either. There in the center, and there toward that side and that corner, a few loud or angry voices rose up and drew more of the people into eddies around them. In other areas, the space was clearer and the people murmured more quietly. A burly young man lumbered past him with an oversized TV screen in his arms, and Paul couldn't help noticing the rasp and wheeze of his struggling breath. Paul half-turned, tempted to help him, but then made himself move on.

Maybe it's just their youth. So many in the crowd were in their early twenties too, still trying to argue out what they'd decide to believe in, even at this cause's own recruitment drive. *I might have been here with them, if things had been different.* And he'd been one year away from being one of the journalists who could report stories like this himself...

But, no point in wishing things were simpler. Or that he could leave this sincere, well-meaning crowd to fight it out with LifeLab's lawyers after what he'd done.

He reached the kitchen. A few people—all women, despite the group's noble ideals—were busy setting up fresh plates of snacks. Beyond them, through the back room, he could see the outer door.

A moment's focus showed him everything he needed about that lock: it was an Ames 50, one he could probably have worked with just the selection of keys he carried with him, even before he returned with his more obvious lock picks.

Now, the hard part. He snatched a couple of flyers from a table and moved to stand in a corner, camouflaging his stillness behind their images of animal abuse and neglect.

Then he closed his eyes and Opened his hearing.

Not to focus on the babble of the crowd; instead he linked his sense to the wall behind him. Beyond the noises echoing back from the room, between the simple paths of wires' steady pulses, he listened for the irregular squeals of electronics or other alarms or cameras.

It had taken most of a year to learn to distinguish those from the sounds of basic wiring—that he could do it at all almost made Paul wonder if he were sensing more than enhanced sound.

This end of the room was clean. Still holding the flyers up to ward off attention, he strolled toward the next corner. As he moved, he focused on the wall again, struggling to make his connection with the sounds within it—despite all the noises around him.

"We should just break in and *get* their rats out," someone said. "And get some real proof, too!"

Paul froze, but even as he did, he knew the tiny woman to his right was only wishing. One of the two men with her was already saying "And how far do you think we'd get, against a labful of guards and all?"

Right, Paul thought as he moved on. *Of course, I slipped in and out without a trace, alone.*

He worked his way to the far corner of the room, and knew he'd studied enough of the layout to be sure he could get in later; if there were any alarms beyond that, he'd find them then. *So… time to go back, maybe rest up for later?*

Still, he looked around at the crowd. Of course a wide-open call for recruits like this would be the *least* likely time for whoever was responsible to let their guard down. There'd be no "Don't talk so loud about how all the evidence against LifeLab is fake."

But all the same, he picked out the smaller knots of people, the isolated twos and threes that just might be muttering about actual secrets, and carefully extended his hearing toward one.

Control, control was everything. Like picking out a distant face while never meeting other people's eyes, he struggled to reach the first corner without his attention drifting away. But no, that couple was only talking about who else they'd seen here, so Paul withdrew his link and steadied his breathing as he looked around for his next choice.

These three were farther away, and hearing them was like finding one current within a lake of sound—but he found them, to share and listen in on their talk about the turnout and the drinks and the presentation…

Something bumped his shoulder. His muscles went limp, his balance eluding him even as he knew he was toppling forward. He broke the last of the trance an instant before he stumbled against a table, and fell.

Pain tore through him, most of it fading in a moment as his nerves settled. Behind the pain were the voices, the whispers, and the circle of staring closing in around him. *Smooth, Paulie,* he thought viciously as he got his feet under him. His knee burned.

One middle-aged man stepped forward, half out of the crowd. "You alright?"

"Fine, fine…" Paul muttered as he lurched upright, trying to look as if he had only ordinary embarrassment to worry about.

But the man didn't move. He said, "Look, are you sure?"

And something in the man's intent gaze set off alarms, not from any flicker of power but from Paul's endless looking over his shoulder.

I wasn't that zoned out, and this guy's not just another visitor, he's a cop! Or a reporter, or someone else who noticed too much.

"Really, I'm fine," Paul said as he waved the man away and turned to walk. He fought to move smoothly, showing nothing to suggest that his slip had meant he was drunk or worse, nothing that would need a second look. His knee throbbed with each step.

He didn't risk Opening now, and for an endless instant, his ordinary hearing couldn't catch any sound of the man turning away, as if he were still watching Paul.

Possibilities flashed through Paul's head—the cop dragging him to a drunk tank as a lesson to the activists, then his control of his power breaking down until he moved to a psych ward and then the attention of anyone ruthless enough to believe someone could have such useful abilities… None of those were likely, but he'd taught himself that there was no moment that the worst *couldn't* happen.

Then he heard him turn and walk away.

And Paul found himself locking his hearing onto the investigator's footsteps before they melted into the crowd. It took a second for his wits to catch up with the instinct: even with his control fraying and the risk of this man noticing him, there was more at stake than being sure the "officer" wasn't still watching. The real question was, *Why is someone like this here at all?*

The man was already two knots of people ahead of Paul, moving with a smooth stride that sounded purposeful even at a modest pace. Paul held his focus on that stride, then weakened it a moment to free his attention to take a few paces after him, and then back to refocus on the footsteps again.

Those footsteps provided a good rhythm, and rhythm was one of the better ways he'd learned to stay in motion while keeping his connection from going deep enough to lose himself in. Besides, he could keep partiers between them to act as a screen, since he didn't need his eyes to track his quarry.

"Can you tell me where James Koenig is… James Koenig…" the man was asking. He sounded more like a cop each time he spoke.

A name… just those two words that might save Paul from hours of searching… He pushed harder to be sure he didn't miss another word, and then drew back at the first muzzy sensation of losing control again.

He knew he was still being careless, when he didn't even know if this man was looking into the activists' frame of LifeLab at all. *And if the police are preparing to expose things, do I even need to get involved?* –But that only made it a race for him to get the truth out first.

With a steadying breath, he slid behind a trio of students and paused to focus more tightly. But as he did, a drunken voice beside him said, "How 'bout *you?* I bet you don't tell *your* family about coming to these things, do you?"

Family? Paul couldn't keep from spinning around at the thought, but he clamped down on his reaction. He managed to give the boy in the college shirt a noncommittal, "Well, not really."

He turned away as if it hadn't been two years since he'd seen Dad and Greg, one more thing he'd left behind forever as he tried to cope with his power.

His connection to the cop's footsteps was gone.

It figures. As he glanced around, another row of people blocked his view. He took a quick step around them, but put his weight squarely onto his hurt knee and barely caught his balance. Gritting his teeth, he used his will to extend his hearing out in a quick sweep—but he still couldn't catch the investigator's voice. Instead, he moved another probe more slowly above the floor, snaking through the echoes of the different footsteps.

After one endless moment, he caught a rhythm that seemed like the cop's steady stride. Paul dodged around another partygoer and at last spotted the back of the cop's head—a tangle of sparse hair over a rumpled coat—walking away.

Almost gasping aloud in his relief, Paul set his focus on him and edged back behind cover again. He could never let anyone notice him—especially not with this case and what was at stake.

"Can I have a word, Mr. Koenig? My name's Reid." And something rustled in Reid's clothing, as if he were taking out…

"About what, Detective?" The other voice sounded almost calm at what had to be the sight of a badge.

Then they both began walking, and Paul could picture that Detective Reid had motioned his suspect to step aside with him. *Is he trying to talk with him, or just rattle him by letting his friends notice him with the police?*

Paul edged to the side and Opened his vision long enough for a good look at the man across the room with the cop: thirties, plump, with reddish hair already starting to gray.

"So," Reid began as they reached the corner. "It looks like this group's claims against LifeLab may not be as true as they seemed."

He let the words hang there, as if waiting for a response. But James Koenig didn't give one.

Reid went on. "That's the weird thing. Even if LifeLab wasn't doing those experiments, the photos were so ugly, and they were so close to the way the lab does work… and then, we have to wonder just how that reporter got those photos out of the lab…"

He can't think Sarah Gomez stole the files herself, can he? I never thought they'd blame her …

Paul pressed his focus closer on Koenig, not watching his face now but following his breathing. Still steady, no signs of nervousness.

When Koenig didn't reply, the detective added "One odd thing might not be noticed. But, to get both just the right dirt, and get it at all despite their security… anyone who looks would think it was someone who knew all about the lab."

Koenig didn't answer at first, but a moment later, he must have reconsidered: "What are you saying? I never even worked in Trials when I was there."

"I know."

And again the cop waited. Paul didn't need to glance over to know he was staring at Koenig's face, searching for any trace of his nerve breaking.

At last Reid said, "Well, one way or another, the truth is going to come out. It's still more a civil matter than a proven criminal one, so far. And I'm sure you'll call me if you think of anything else."

Paul could just make out the snap of a business card being handed over before Reid began walking away. This time, Paul let him go, keeping his hearing locked on their mutual suspect to see how he'd respond.

Is this it, a simple ex-employee from LifeLab who'd faked a couple photos to attack the people he'd parted ways with? Except, the detective had no idea what those lies had set in motion. *And I have no excuse, for rushing off to dig up more dirt the moment I heard the press was interested, never mind if there was any truth to it.*

It had seemed to be just the latest chance to bring one more truth to light while earning a few pennies… but instead Paul had crippled the lab and risked a good reporter's career.

Paul kept still, watching James Koenig from the corner of his eye and Opening his hearing again and again, always carefully letting it drop. He couldn't risk losing himself in his senses now, but he had to know if the detective's warning would make Koenig do anything that would lead him to new evidence. And yet Koenig just stood still as the crowd began shifting and slowly clearing a space around one wall.

Then an older man wearing one of the better suits in the room walked up to Koenig. "What was that all about, James?"

"Just some questions. Nothing important."

"The video's almost ready."

Paul watched them move into place near a big screen that some of the others were setting up. Gradually, the crowd quieted and waited for the video to start. Paul glared harder at Koenig, not studying him but just trying to accept that a disgruntled lab worker had outwitted him without knowing he existed. The plump man still showed no sign of worrying.

Opening his hearing again, Paul cast around the room, trying to catch whispers from the people who seemed to be the other Animal Alliance leaders gathered near the screen, and then just to search tidbits from random conversations, but still found nothing about Koenig or their frame.

Finally, he moved a few steps closer to an older, sophisticated-looking woman in a fine gray dress and muttered, "You think they've really got the goods on the lab?"

"Shhh," she replied. "It's starting soon."

Paul drifted to the back of the room near the broad staircase. A few more people were coming down it now, but a moment's frustrated probing still picked out one or two witnesses moving around above. Of course.

"Have you seen what that lab is doing?" a voice called to the crowd. It was the man who'd checked on James Koenig after the detective left.

As the people began roaring their angry answers, Paul clenched his fists. Whatever they could let the crowd "see," it was his fault. Not Koenig's, not Sarah's…

When they dimmed the lights and every eye turned to the big screen, the old thought came to Paul again, and he slipped up the stairs as the crowd blinked in the sudden dark. Because, *I still know* nothing *about why I have this power, but it has to be for a reason!*

His knee hurt with the first step, and by the time he reached the top of the stairs, he was well aware how reckless he was being, when he could have simply come back after the people had gone anyway. Even if nobody here thought he was out of place, only two things had ever protected him in his work: his senses and his determination to stay clear of risks. *Only stuntmen jump out of windows to escape.*

The upstairs hall was almost empty, decorated with only a painting here and there from the old mansion's past and a few water-stained boxes stacked in one corner. Lights shone from a doorway as two young men walked out of that room.

Paul kept going, barely glancing at them, and his bluff worked: they did the same.

He was still being reckless, he knew. But he strolled from one room to the next as if he were just a curious recruit, looking for a sense of what they kept up here. And what they kept seemed to be mostly empty space, with boxes and posters and other publicity props scattered here and there.

Downstairs, he could hear more angry rumblings that sometimes rose to shouts as the video went on. That raw anger was different from his last few cases, and all the little lies of city officials and double-dealing businesses.

To his relief, the two men he'd passed soon headed downstairs. And he saw another good sign in the corner: file cabinets, not computers. He's never had much luck with passwords, but those cabinets' locks would be easy to bypass later.

He Opened his hearing to catch more of the crowd below, just to be sure they weren't planning to storm the LifeLab gates that night. Not that they'd go that far, but he'd done so much to fan those flames—*and bringing out bits of the truth,* the truth, *is all I have.*

Somewhere below, someone said, "Koenig." Paul started, and cast around for the source. The voice was Detective Reid's again.

"And you never met him before then?" Reid was whispering. A woman began gushing about how recent a convert Koenig was and how hard he always worked, but she said little that would help Paul before the conversation died down again.

And I stuck my neck out up here without even thinking that the detective would stick around after he tried leaning on Koenig. Paul kept an ear on him now, but the only voices he heard down there were the video and the reactions to it. And at least Reid seemed to be staying down there; Paul glanced at the oak tree beside the window and tried not to imagine having to climb out. *I'm taking too many risks just to vindicate Sarah from what I—*

Sarah? Paul frowned. *Why am I thinking of the reporter and not that I helped a liar attack the lab?*

He steadied his focus on Reid, who was still not moving, and considered. Sarah Gomez was just the latest reporter he'd sold anonymous information to. And he'd only toyed with the notion of ever contacting her again, if he did want to do work that was more like an ordinary journalist, at least before his tip to her had gone all wrong.

But no, the thought of contacting her had been crossing his mind more *after* the story had gone bad. After he'd glimpsed how brave she looked when she refused to talk about her elusive source, with her job on the line. Brave and… attractive, not that he…

"Schuman and Son."

Just a whisper, a ripple that barely reached Paul's hearing, where it was still focused on the detective. Paul searched frantically through the echoes of the angry crowd, trying to locate the source of that name—*my own name*, and that voice couldn't be…

"…admit, we're always interested in possible clients," the voice was saying, and now Paul knew it was Lorraine speaking. "But mostly, I was curious about all of you."

"I'm afraid our movement doesn't usually hire PR firms," someone replied. It was the group's leader again, who had so recently been shouting to the crowd.

"I suppose not; my work's done then." And it was Lorraine's laugh: easy, friendly.

Not the same way she'd laughed with them, though, never like she'd laughed with the joy of being Greg's wife, or to make the whole family laugh in return—

Paul's knee twinged in midstride. He hadn't even realized he was moving, but he pulled up short at the top of the broad staircase.

"*Unnh*, did you have to show *that* one?" Lorraine asked, and the rabble-rouser sounded almost embarrassed as he began whispering about bringing different animal-rights causes together.

The voices weren't so far beyond the stairs. Paul edged forward, just enough to peep over and down. The shifting wash of colors from the video screen gave more than enough light for him to spot them—even if she hadn't given a sad little sigh just then.

He saw the top and back of her head, and the even paler silver-blue gleam of a fine silk blouse. The kind of outfit she'd seemed uncomfortable wearing once. *But she's had years learning to be a Schuman now…*

She started to glance around, and Paul ducked back before he came into her view. *Why am I watching her now? She probably hates me.* And he'd tried, he'd been sure he'd kept Dad's and Greg's names out of the exposé about what they'd tried to cover up—of course he couldn't remember who'd dragged them into it, not with his first night's rush of power twisting his mind into knots…

"Are all farms really like that?" his sister-in-law was asking.

"That's one of the milder ones," her guide said.

Paul peeked down again. She was distracted now, watching the screen. He tried to stop staring, but he couldn't pull his gaze from that blond head, or how far away she was, his whole family was, the whole *life* he'd thought he had, *and I can't*—

A tremor went through her; Paul ducked back again as her hands started to clutch at her head. His hearing sharpened and he heard her moving, stumbling away. He peeped around again but she was already out of view.

"Ms. Schuman? Are you alright?"

"I… don't know…" she said weakly, her voice sounding choked with hesitation. No—with *fear*.

Paul crouched down lower on the stairs. He had to move, had to help her, but one voice after another was stirring around her, closing in to watch. *It couldn't be, this can't be happening…*

His hearing focused beyond the others, and filled with Lorraine's ragged breathing. He heard her say one word, the faintest, most fragile whisper.

"Paul?"

Good God, it's impossible—She couldn't have seen him, let alone… But what he'd heard was all too real. He stood up and glided down the stairs like moving in a dream.

The crowd was still mostly watching the video, bathed in the images from the pound and the room's half-light. It took him a moment to pick out her shape behind one knot of figures.

He still couldn't believe it, but Lorraine was huddled there, leaning against the wall, hands pressed over her eyes. Four, five, seven people had turned halfway toward her, even though she'd barely made a sound.

He could see the detective was still on the far side of the room. He wasn't looking over, but no doubt he would soon. *And somehow it's my fault.*

Paul slipped forward, using every advantage he had among people slowed by the weak light, ignoring the throbbing in his knee. He slid around them, past them, he had to move faster…

When he got close, he reached right between the gathered onlookers to grip her shoulders and lean in next to her still-covered face. As softly as he could, hoping the faintness itself would draw her attention, he said "Let it go. Let it go… it'll pass…"

"It… you…" she gasped.

"I'm here. Just let it go."

It was all he could think to say, but through her shoulders he could feel her trembling ease. Her breath steadied, and she drew her hands down and looked back at him, shock still glittering in those blue eyes. Slowly she turned away.

Then, in an almost normal voice, she said to the others "I'm alright… I guess I need some air." And she pulled herself up and started walking for the door.

Paul fell into step behind her, not glancing at the faces that followed them. *Let them think the explanation is something simple. Something possible.*

Lorraine walked steadily, except for a tiny falter in one step, when she stopped at her chair to grab her coat and purse. She didn't say a word until they were outside.

"It's so cold!" She shivered and hugged the coat to her, but didn't put it on. Instead she turned around to him. "Paul… how did you…?" Her voice faded away.

"Keep your eyes moving when it starts. Back and forth, don't focus on one thing. That should usually keep you from…" *God, how can I put it into words…* "being pulled in. Can you do that?"

"I…" She swung her head to one side, then another, more slowly. Then she turned and stared right at him. "But, *how?*"

Her words were still quiet, but they seemed to hang there in the cold air.

"I know what happened to you. Somehow, it happened to me two years ago. I'll try to show you… how to handle it," he added weakly.

I'll try. Even though I've just destroyed your life. And Paul knew he still didn't actually *know* much more than what he'd just told her about the power.

"I need your help," she was saying, insistent.

"Right. I said I'd try." As he watched her, his vision blurred. He began to understand how much he was risking. "But please realize, I haven't seen Greg or Dad in years…"

A hopeless protest rose in him, for her not to tell her husband she'd seen him. Everything he'd tried to do, all the secrets, the dangers… Now *he* was the one who couldn't seem to breathe. It would be so easy to admit he'd told her everything he knew and then just slip away. *But could I leave her to face what I've been through, alone?* Just seeing her gain the power had shown him more than he'd ever known about it…

His head was spinning. "Two years," he said again weakly.

"Are you sure?" And she took a step toward him.

"What?" He shook his head, trying to clear it. Why was she *looking* at him so intently, as if all her doubts a minute ago had just been pushed aside? "I don't think…" he began awkwardly. "I mean, I ran away from you all. I don't think I can ever go back."

"Paul!" Lorraine caught at his arm, and he barely jerked out of her reach. More gently, she said, "Paul. Greg asked me to go out tonight, but… he's been in the hospital, for days. And someone broke into our home."

aul couldn't say a word.

"It was the night after his car crash—and he's fine," Lorraine added, just in time for him to feel the stab of guilt for not asking at once. "Mostly bruises. They wanted to keep him for observation, but he should be out of the hospital in a day or two—"

"Oh." It was the only thing Paul could say.

His brother. His brother, his secret, someone out there—*At least he's still alive…* His thoughts kept spinning, tumbling and couldn't settle.

"I came home and found the lock smashed in," Lorraine said. "And whoever it was had searched the house. *All* of it," and she shivered again.

She was talking faster now, he voice low, but Paul could only stare. *This can't be happening! Whatever it is is going to catch me in the wreckage, worse than her and Greg…*

"Just a few things were stolen," she went on. "That's the worst of it. We can't even know if it was robbery or… something else. So we can't know if they'll come back. Or even if his accident *was* an accident."

"Oh," Paul said again. He glanced back at the path up to the mansion, glad nobody was passing by. Quietly, he said, "And the police say…"

"Didn't you hear me, Paul? A few jewels and things were gone, just like a robbery. We almost didn't report it at all."

"Why not?" The question was out of his mouth before he remembered he wanted her *not* to think of him as someone who spent his days dealing in secrets.

But Lorraine only glared at him. "We wanted to protect Schuman and Son's reputation. You know better than I do how the business always comes first, and Greg and your father wondered if the police would even look that far into a simple robbery."

Her words came faster and faster now, pouring out. "Sure enough, the police only said there was nothing to explain. The same as they did about the crash. So we just put in new alarms and said we'd move on. But I need answers."

"What answers?" Paul asked, then winced inwardly. *I'm just digging myself in deeper.*

Lorraine turned away, looking down the street, as if she'd vented all of her thoughts and needed a moment to gather more. "Answers about… well, whether someone *did* come after us. And *why*, and so, what we could do about it." She turned her gaze back now to search Paul's face. "Greg and his father say it's just a robbery, but I keep worrying there's a reason. And I don't think it's anything I did, I've been racking my brains about it for days… and I haven't really done much that was separate from Greg since we married."

From anyone else, those last words would have been a reflexive denial— or else spoken with a bit of embarrassment. But he remembered how happy she had been to be part of Greg's life.

I can't believe I'm measuring out the amount of devotion in the family I left!

Paul snapped "You really think they'd tell me more than you, after the way I vanished? Or are you asking me to investigate my brother and my father?"

I just had *to say 'investigate'!* Now he'd almost admitted he could—or that he almost could—and how he'd been spending those years since his disappearance; *if she doesn't guess how much I've done, at least she can't let it slip to one of the people I've exposed, or can't force me to keep fixing her problems, or judge me.* But this was still so out of his depth—He watched her eyes, trying to guess what she suspected.

"I'm asking you to protect us," she said. "And I shouldn't have to ask."

Paul held her gaze, but it was all he could manage for one breath, then another. "That's easy to say," he finally muttered. "You're still new to the family. You don't really know how long Dad and Greg and I had been arguing, over everything from baseball to, well, you and your place with them. And now you think some *trick senses* are going let me somehow go all through the city to track down some—"

His eyes went wide. *Track down? What if I'm the one who's been tracked down, by one of my cases, and they're going after my family…*

He shook his head. There was no way, not when he'd rebuilt his whole life to keep himself invisible and leave every tie to his past behind.

"Listen." Lorraine's voice was softer now, and she took a small step toward him. "I'm due to visit Greg now. You can come and see how he is, or… at least use the drive to explain what's happening to me."

"All… right," Paul sighed. *Maybe she's in denial, trying to focus on the other events in her life before she comes to terms with what the power can do to her. At least she's able to* mention *it.*

He went on "But you're just starting to learn about your power, and you don't know how it can sneak up on you sometimes. So I'd better drive, unless you want—"

He bit off the words *another crash,* realizing how cruel they'd be after she'd almost lost her husband in one car wreck. *Or maybe they'd just be cruel to me, the way Mother died.* He braced himself for the explosion.

"Besides," and Lorraine actually smiled, "you're a guy."

Paul had to laugh then, as she dropped the keys in his hand and started down the street with him a step behind. The block felt oddly quiet after their argument, but he knew that could only last for so long.

The night grayed away the colors of the line of parked cars, but Paul Opened his sight a moment, and sure enough, there was the shamrock green of the little Toyota she'd always driven. Then he sighed. *I could have asked her to test her own power looking at it in the night. It could have been her first lesson.*

It had been a while since he'd driven anything, the way his senses just might surge away while he was behind a wheel, but his body settled into the seat naturally enough. As he turned the key, he shot a questioning glance at Lorraine beside him.

"He's at St. Central," she said.

He would be. Hearing the hospital's nickname from a Schuman didn't even sound the same as hearing it on a routine day. The last place where he had seen his family, the place where his power had struck him… but he shook off those thoughts now, not ready to believe fate itself was trying to trap him.

He kept the car at a safe twenty-five miles an hour at first, trying to settle his thoughts as much as control his senses. Whatever else happened, he couldn't let Lorraine go through the horrors of understanding her power all alone. *But this break-in they had… and do I even* want *to see Greg again?* His fingers clenched on the wheel, glad the street was fairly quiet at this hour.

From the corner of his eye, he watched Lorraine, as she sat so still with her hands folded in her lap. *She already knows what no other human being knows about me.*

And now he had to show her how to control a power that was so obviously good at finding secrets, without letting her guess how he'd been using that power himself! *If she connects my being at Animal Alliance with the files that were stolen to start its accusations…*

Paul bit his lip hard, trying to focus on the road ahead. *I thought I'd left all this behind.* But here he was, driving right back to where it had all started. It had been Lorraine's dying mentor that St. Central had juggled insurance rules to raise the bill for. And when Greg's answer to that was to cut a deal with them that covered up what the Schumans knew—and Paul had had to…

The light ahead turned red, and he pulled the car up and took a deep breath.

"About that break-in," he said. "I'm not sure I can be much help."

"What? You've just shown me you have…" Even enclosed in the car, she dropped her voice to a whisper, "…you have this *talent*. And now you say you can't do anything?"

"I'm showing you what I have, what we have. And our '*talent*' can't pull answers out of the air or anything. There's a lot it can't do. Plus, I'm not a trained cop, and I don't have underworld contacts, or any of the things someone would need to play detective about a robbery." He couldn't think which would be worse: getting them killed because simple crime was so much more violent, or letting her or anyone know about how many quieter secrets he *did* work with and what that would lead to.

"But your talent can fix this," she said. "It has to."

"You still don't understand what 'it' is." *Not that I know so much more…*

The light turned green, and he took a breath as he nudged the gas. Maybe that was the key; if he could explain their power to bring down her anxiety about it, and also head off her suspicions about how he was using it.

"Lorraine." He spoke slowly, reasonably, while keeping his eyes on the road. "What we have is the power to increase our five senses by connecting them to whatever we focus our attention on. That's all it is; it doesn't mean we can get easy answers to any question we want."

Lorraine said nothing, and he continued.

"And yes, it does mean it has a danger. The way your senses locked up at the party? That's a risk you have to learn to live with now. But the thing is, you can resist it too, learn to keep it from happening."

He glanced over at her. She was sitting quietly, watching him. He gestured toward the office building sliding past their window.

"Try practicing now. Just focus your mind on something there and then let it go. See if you can let it go before we drive past it. As long as you can learn to recognize when your attention on something is starting to Open your senses, you can keep it from happening when you don't want or from lasting longer than you want. Then you can control it. Try it." He motioned to an approaching streetlight.

"So… that's all it is?" she asked slowly. "And you'll help me with it, and you'll find out who broke into our home."

No I didn't *agree to that!* Paul caught himself before he snapped that at her, and concentrated on keeping the car steady. "Look… if you're thinking this power is going to change your life, you're right—but that means you have to take control of it. And you have to start *now*. For instance, have you thought about what it's going to do to you and Greg? Are you so sure you can stay with him?"

"Don't even joke about that," she said coldly. "And don't try to distract me. We need to figure out who broke into our house."

Who's trying to distract whom? Paul was losing count, but he said "Don't *you* think you can just ignore what's happening to you. Think about this: you got the power when I was focusing mine too closely on you. Don't pretend you forgot what that flood of senses did to you, and it's going to keep happening. And, what if some day you do that to Greg?"

"Oh."

That one dazed sound was all she said, but Paul knew he'd broken a little of her denial. "I'm sorry," he said. "It scared me, too. I don't know what this means yet, but you've got to understand how this works."

"You mean," she said slowly, "you *changed* me? And you've changed other people like this before?"

"I said I don't know what happened to you. If it was me, I'm sorry, and I am trying to help. I don't think I've ever 'changed' anyone else, nobody I've known in the two years I've had… this. But," he had to add, "that may not mean much for you. Not much of those years has been spent around people."

She didn't answer, and he couldn't say more. For a long moment, they sat quietly and Paul watched the street signs, looking for the next turn toward the hospital.

"Paul…" She spoke softly, and he glanced over. She was looking out the window now, but he didn't think she was trying out his exercise for her power. "Paul, do you think the power does come from being touched by someone else's power? Or is it… something else?"

"I never thought so. But I never knew much about that until tonight, Lorraine. I don't even have clear memories of the night the power came to me, only that I was at the hospital. Since then, believe me, I've looked at everything that was in the whole building, and there are no clues."

He stopped a moment. *I'm getting too close to admitting how many nights I've gone spying around the hospital.* Paul didn't like how much that implied about the skills he'd lived by since.

He tried again. "There just wasn't anything unusual in that environment, and there's no sign in my genetics, either. Not from anything I could learn about my family, for generations back. None of us seemed to do anything like this, and I never did before, either. And of course now the other one to get it isn't a Schuman at all," and he gestured to her. "So I don't know."

"You really don't." It seemed to be sinking in to her, a bit of how much he'd been living with.

"I just remember it came to me," he added, not wanting to reveal that he was still struggling to understand what that meant about any kind of purpose for him, even before adding her to the mix.

"There's something else," Lorraine said, almost hesitant now. "That was you who told the media about St. Central's insurance tricks when you left, wasn't it? Did all of this give you some kind of compulsion to…"

"The power never makes me do anything. I told you, what you have to fight is it locking your senses up on something. Or do you really think I'd drag the family through that?" he added, trying to make it sound light, as if there were nothing to worry about. But he felt a tightness in his throat as he said it; he had leaked that information, yes, but he'd picked evidence that would lead the investigation *away* from how Dad and Greg had known. And he still wondered, who had found the rest of the papers…

Fumbling for a joke, he said "I might as well ask if *you* did it. Curtis was your friend, and even though Greg and Dad made that deal to get him the money, they did it by covering up everything they'd found about what St. Central put him through. So, was it you getting revenge?"

"That *is* a joke, isn't it?" and she looked almost hurt. "I'd never turn on the family like that, you *know* that."

"Of course." He tried a different joke. "But only because I know you. We Open our five senses—we don't read minds."

"Oh."

The word seeped out of her, and Paul could hear real relief in it. *If she's fighting to focus on the break-in, what must it be like for her now, hearing the boundaries of her world pulled apart and rearranged with every new sentence we say?* Had she been thinking just seconds ago of what other barriers might have broken, and now she was trusting again that she could think her own thoughts?

He drove on without another word, trying not to imagine how easily Lorraine could destroy everything for him, if word made its way to any of the liars he'd exposed. He didn't even want to see Greg or Dad again after he'd left, but she was so determined.

The vast parking lot was just where he remembered it, not too far from the hospital. The car glided into an empty space all too neatly, no more delays before he had to choose.

They had just gotten out when she stepped suddenly around the car to stand in front of him, eyes locking on his. "Paul. *Please...*"

Meeting her gaze, he braced himself. "What?"

"Paul, I can't let Greg know about this thing. Not yet."

He could only stare. "You can't?"

"Let me figure this out first. Please. He doesn't have to know about you if you don't want."

Trying not to smile too widely, he said, "Deal."

Together they made their way to the front entrance, blending in with the scattered visitors who had night business at St. Central. He and Lorraine weren't standing in lines, but Paul felt as if he were falling into step with something else—his months of discreetly exploring the hospital for answers. The sharp smell was the same, even though he was careful not to Open to it.

After they had passed by the main desk, the crowds grew thinner. The lights seemed a little dimmer, and the orderlies and nurses walked more quietly. Lorraine clipped a "Regular Visitor" pass onto her collar; of course, at this hour, the hospital rules limited who could visit. Paul took a moment to picture them trying to deny his family those special passes, and how his father or Greg would force past their objections, even after the Schumans' harsh history with this place.

Still, he dropped back and stayed a few more steps behind Lorraine. His second-hand wardrobe might stand out if he walked right next to her in her Schuman-quality outfit. He kept his hands "adjusting" his coat and walked confidently, as if there surely had to be a pass clipped on it just under his fingers.

"Lorraine!"

The voice made Paul half turn, and he froze to see the figure advancing behind them. The quiet corridor picked up the echoes of that stride, steady and sweeping along like a force of nature in one compact frame, *my father is walking right toward me…* in the very building where he'd last seen him, the place where Paul had ruined his father's scheme and then left his life. There was not a single person or corner for Paul to step behind now. He was walking right toward them, and Paul couldn't *move…*

And he walked right past Paul and drew Lorraine into step with him, never even noticing his son in his ragged clothes. Paul stared, not knowing what to think.

"I didn't know you were coming by," Lorraine was saying. As if, after two years in the family she still couldn't call him Dad or Ian.

"I wanted to see him. Besides, this gives me a chance to thank you for keeping on top of his accounts while he's in here."

As they spoke, Paul let them pull away, at his father's rapid pace. For the moment, it was just so much easier to stay clear and listen.

"Well, of course," Lorraine answered. "Greg would never forgive me if we started falling behind."

"But then, you'd be more helpful if you'd convince him to put down his phone now and then while he's here. Don't let the nurses keep confiscating it."

Paul winced, as much at the familiar, so-reasonable tone as at the judging edge his father never quite kept out of his voice.

But where Paul or Greg would have protested, Lorraine only laughed. "Convince Greg? You're a stubborn pair, you know."

Before he could answer her, a buzz came from his pocket. He muttered, "Of course, *now*," as he drew out his own phone and told her, "You go on ahead."

When Paul saw his father start to turn back, he ducked behind a corner he'd been keeping near.

"No, we found some new art. You should have a scan of it now. If you give it a look, we can still get the release out tomorrow…"

The rhythm of our lives. Dad, Greg, and he had fought so long to give the firm every advantage, even when Paul had wanted to start journalism school instead. Now, watching his father walk by, Paul thought about how easy it would be to step out and join him. But nothing about his family or his new life was easy.

When his father was gone, Paul moved quickly after Lorraine. Unless St. Central had reshuffled the wards in the last year, she must have headed somewhere up along the next left turn.

The rooms he passed were a mix of silence and quiet voices now. A nurse in the hall gave him an odd look, but he kept walking as if he had no reason to doubt he belonged here, and she turned back to her cart. As he approached each doorway, he Opened his hearing for any familiar sounds.

It was Greg's voice he caught, an amused whisper: "You're an angel."

"You said you wouldn't make calls when they could take the phone away," Lorraine replied. "And I believed you. So if you lose this phone, you're not getting a third one."

"Well, I believe you."

Paul heard a wince in his brother's rich voice, the voice that had taught him to tie his shoes, or taunted him while holding them out of reach.

He shut down the connection and moved around the next corner to sit on a chair near the corridor's snack machine. He pulled out a few pages of newspaper from his coat; the moment they snapped into position to hide his face, he reached his will toward his brother again.

For a moment, he thought he'd lost track of which room it was, but then he caught their faint voices. Two other people were breathing in the room, but those roommates seemed to be sleeping.

"I keep telling you, I'm fine." Greg's voice was a steady whisper, but there was no missing the warmth in it as he spoke to his wife.

"I guess. Oh: your father's on his way in too."

"Huh?"

"He met me on the way in, but he had to take a call."

"Ahhh."

Paul thought he heard another spasm in Greg's breathing. *How hurt is he?* The more Paul could hear, the more maddening it was. Everything he'd learned exploring the hospital and looking after himself were useless when he couldn't *see* Greg.

"How about you?" his brother was saying. "I bet you found time to visit every one of those prospects."

"Almost. Watkins might be interested, and G&B."

"Of course, all Dad will say is that he'll have to close them himself," he muttered. "Is there anything on the break-in?"

"No, nothing… definite."

Paul could hear the awkwardness in her evasion, and his fingers clenched the paper.

But Greg only said, "I hate this. And all this happened when I couldn't be home with you. Or maybe that's *why* they broke in now."

"I know."

"How are you doing?" Dad's voice said, and Paul started where he sat. *I stopped checking for people around me again*; he'd been halfway to being trapped in his senses.

"I'll still be out in two days," Greg answered. More softly he added, "Was your phone call from one of the councilmen again?"

Paul could hear his father moving closer and settling beside them. "He needed reassuring. There was a rumor that you were drunk at the wheel."

Paul's jaw fell open even as Greg snapped, "I was not!"

Dad didn't *say that, he couldn't have just clubbed Greg with how Mom had died*—but, was he just attacking him or was there a kind of real worry in that tone? Paul couldn't tell, couldn't guess from the sharp, low whisper his father had used.

Elsewhere in Greg's room, the two other patients slept on. Their breathing was so steady that Paul wondered if they were sedated. Nobody else spoke for a moment.

"You know, being here…" Lorraine began.

Paul winced. She wasn't a Schuman, and she might not remember what a can of snakes they'd already opened.

"…I was thinking of Curtis again, and how we sat up with him," she went on. "And everything else that happened."

"Do you have to… sorry," Greg stopped himself. "I know he meant a lot to you, and we miss him too. What were you thinking about?"

"Nothing, really. Just remembering."

"That may be the best way," their father said. "Remember the good times and learn what you can from the rest. Let those lessons drive you."

He hadn't mentioned Paul's leaving either, and he sounded so cold. *Is that where this puts us? Is that all I am now? And why am I surprised?*

Paul pressed his focus closer, straining for the next word, but he didn't hear one—only breathing, waiting, nobody breaking the stillness that stretched on…

Some faraway voice said something about "time to." Paul shook his sluggish thoughts to life long enough to catch his father saying, "Of course," to what had to be a nurse in the room.

Trapped again, even now! Paul scrambled to his feet and withdrew up the corridor until he could be sure the nurse wasn't going to keep searching and decide to march him out, side by side with the others.

He still couldn't believe how careless this had been—especially after lecturing Lorraine about what touching people with the power might do to them.

But at least he hadn't ripped Dad's or Greg's senses Open, so maybe it *wasn't* just contact that had given him and Lorraine the power.

The nurse was moving on, and Paul peeped back around the corner to see his father walking out with Lorraine. As they moved along, Lorraine stole glances this way and that, and when she looked back, Paul stepped out and held up a finger, signaling for her to wait for him.

As she hesitated, his father noticed and turned toward her and Paul had to quickly duck back again. But they kept walking.

The corridor was quiet now and the lights were dimmer—including those coming from Greg's room.

Paul stole a glance down that corridor again. His brother was in there, the brother who'd taught him everything and fought with him over all of it. He'd barely ever *seen* Greg hurt before now. He realized his hands were shaking; what could he even say to him?

Lorraine had asked whether the power had *forced* him to betray the family's cover-up. Now he clenched his fists, trying to stop his hands from trembling. He'd exposed the hospital, but he'd tried his best to keep Dad and Greg out of it. And yet the events of that night were still so hazy, he couldn't recall all the things he'd seen. But he did remember having the deep sense that his new power made it harder to let lies like that stand.

I didn't reveal the family's part in it—I didn't. Yet I was so sure *I had to leave them…*

And now his brother was injured and he didn't dare speak to him. He took a few steps to stand at the side of Greg's doorway, enough to see how comfortingly dim it was inside now. Three people lay breathing within, all steady and sleepy. *Too many strangers for any kind of reunion, anyway.*

He leaned into the room just far enough to see the opposite wall, searching for the patient's medical charts. *Or has St. Central stopped using charts since I was here last year, another step in computerizing every-thing?* He leaned a little further.

Now he could see his brother, asleep. His face was so like Paul's except for the short nose, which he used to wish his own resembled. Greg's dark hair was hidden under a bandage—*concussion?* But it couldn't be so serious, not if the hospital was getting ready to discharge him soon.

At last, he spotted his brother's medical chart, and he extended his sight to take in the tiny print in the dimness. Gregory Ian Schuman, it said his condition seemed good after surgery—*surgery!*—to clean up a cracked rib, but everything seemed limited, which fit with him being able to leave soon.

Click… click…

A soft, repeating sound reached Paul's ears. It was so faint that he had to Open his hearing to check as he ducked back, but he already knew. It came from Greg's hand on the control button, calling for a nurse.

Feet marched toward his corridor. Paul darted away, straining to focus his power partly on his legs and his footsteps as he moved, holding the short, rapid stride that let his feet roll along the floor in almost perfect silence. He made it around the corner again and out of sight, where he waited for the nurse to reach Greg.

"Yes, sir?"

"Someone was at the doorway. Watching me," but as Greg said it his voice grew softer, a little hesitant.

"Mr. Schuman, there's nobody there."

"I saw a shadow. Or maybe…" He let it die away.

"It's never easy to sleep here," the nurse said. "You're not the first call I've gotten tonight. But just lie still and try to get some rest." As she walked away, Paul heard her say under her breath, "or at least let the rest of us try."

Paul slipped off before he made it worse. Greg had never been afraid of anything—or even had enough doubts to admit he could be wrong without a fight. But then again, after having his house robbed, it was better he chalk it up to nervousness about that than to think that someone was still stalking him.

Why didn't I just stay away? But the answer was all around him: even in the same building, he couldn't remember, couldn't even be sure why he'd left them at all.

He glared down the corridor, as if the walls themselves were hiding secrets. Yes, it had been a clean break from all his struggles and competition with Greg and his father, and a chance to bring out the truth. But…

As he had so many times, he found himself moving deeper into the hospital, trying to remember something more. For a moment, he Opened to the scent—the hospital's sharp, all-around tangs of disinfectant and sweat, and all the jumbled memories that came with them.

That night had started in the oncology section, he knew. As he remembered, he had moved smoothly through the back corridors, readying his senses to help him stay ahead of the extra staff who would be tending to the cancer patients.

Lorraine's mentor, Curtis, had been dying; she'd learned of it soon after she'd married Greg. And by that night's end, Paul had sent records to the press explaining how St. Central was evading the needs of patients like Curtis.

And then Paul had disappeared from the life he'd lived—

He drew back to let a group of orderlies pass. Being invisible in this hospital was easy, because he'd haunted every corner of the building in search of anything else that could have been the cause of the night that changed his life. All he had ever found were more of the same elusive memories.

Now he started forward, trying to recapture the surprise he'd felt that night. It had been Greg's idea to make the hospital pay for Curtis' treatments by piecing together figures of how many patients they'd manipulated the insurance rules to stint on. And somehow, it had ended with that fax of Greg's that contained all the damning figures— but with the Schuman and Son fax number at the top, which Paul had worked hard to keep out of the news.

Someone else found that, didn't they? I never gave them that. I couldn't have!

Paul hung back short of the central corridor, waiting for a lull in the traffic. He had walked this way that night, to the little meeting room.

He stared at the door far ahead, and could almost hear Dad and Greg in it again, but the hospital staff were still moving in the corridor…

At last, he found his chance and slipped out, retracing his steps. The walls had new paint, too pale, but beyond the door would be the same small room he'd gone to join them in. One step, then another, and he reached it.

He had put his hand on the door that night. He had paused to listen, trying to determine if they were there or if this was the wrong moment to interrupt. His fingers had tightened on the doorknob.

And these other thirty-five rows of figures, the voice had been saying, *if Mr. Thiessen is treated? Will this patient be all?*

It'll be enough, he'd heard Greg answer.

Paul could almost hear the words again, and feel his own rage. And then he'd turned away… or had he gone in? *No, I'm sure I turned away.*

Now he could hear people moving toward him, but it had been quiet then and he had to remember, not listen. He marched off, veering up the corridor to the right, as he had then. With every step, he'd become more certain of the lies. *The hospital had lied, the family had lied. Everyone lied.*

Footsteps moved in behind him, but he kept going, trying to grasp more of his next memories. He remembered what Lorraine had done when she sensed him. *Did I tremble like that, back then? Was this wall something I stumbled against? Was there anyone else there, like I was there for Lorraine, to show me the truth?*

No… He felt as if he were gazing into the sun after a long, sleepless night, a sun that left him exhausted as well as warmed, its brilliance dazzling and dazing the images that came after. During the next hours, he had felt those first desperate surges of his power and he'd begun slipping through the corridors, when he'd gathered Greg's and Dad's notes and separated out that treacherous fax.

Then I hid the fax—didn't I? He still wished he could be more certain; even on *that* night, he couldn't have wanted to ruin his father and brother, he'd only wanted to get some distance from them to cope.

Still, nothing was clear. He drifted to a stop, left with just the ghosts of the same old questions and the footsteps of the nurses and orderlies circulating to his left, behind him, and up ahead.

Sighing, Paul turned and picked his way along to the exit, surprised he had managed to slip away unchallenged. So even now, all he could remember was the sheer truth of how many lies there were in the world. That truth had set him on the path he'd been trying to follow ever since, hoping to make the power make sense.

It had to be easier once he was away from Dad and Greg, but...

Lorraine was waiting at the front entrance, alone.

Before she could speak, he said, "So, have you started testing your power? Are you practicing how to shut it off?"

"Some." She stepped closer, her eyes wide with emotions he couldn't read. "But please, what did Greg say?"

What? Paul stared a moment and then said, "I didn't talk to him."

"You didn't... but, you never told me and, I've been waiting half an..." She stopped and let out a long, slow sigh. "Never mind. But, are you going to help us? Because I need to know."

He closed his eyes, remembering Greg calling the nurse, his own secrets, and all his fights and history with his family. "Of course I'll... do what I can," he said.

It might have been the hospital lights, but her face simply *shone*. "Thank you, Paul. It's the only thing I can say, and it'll never be enough."

How long had it been... since anyone had thanked him for more than some trivial thing he did? He shook his head. "Only if this works.

So, if your break-in *was* about Greg or Dad, I'll need to know what they've been involved with, so I can decide how to look into it. Can you find out?"

"I can get what I have together tonight. I'll meet you tomorrow." She took out her cell. "How do I reach you?"

He sighed, knowing how paranoid it sounded. "Actually, I don't have a phone."

All through the long, rattling subway ride, Paul kept his senses studying the graveyard shift workers, drunks, punks, and other restless souls aboard the train, and testing his knee as he massaged the swelling. When he stepped off the train, he almost turned to slip into the Animal Alliance headquarters, as he'd planned—hours and a lifetime ago. But instead, he unchained his battered bicycle from the back corner tree and pedaled away down the street.

Now even the little breeze on his face was biting cold. *Why did this have to happen in November?*

Not that the problem is when *it happened.* He let the bike hold its own balance and flickered his sight and hearing around the night. He was still worrying about hiding his trail, now when somebody might already know about his family, and when Lorraine knew about the power itself. And he had to show her enough about her new abilities so she could live with them, even though it made her all the more aware how he could be rooting out secrets all over the city…

He made an extra sweep behind the Side Alley, not that he expected anyone to be watching there either, and then pushed the hotel door open.

Bald Mike sat at the stained table that served as a front desk; he was dozing off, as usual. Paul wheeled his bike in and hoisted it up the creaky stairs, probing for any sounds of someone stirring at his arrival. Then, at last, he settled into his tiny room, propped the bike in a corner, and squeezed around it to the bathroom. He soaked a spare shirt in warm water and wrapped it around his throbbing knee, hoping to speed its healing.

Curling up in bed, he picked up a dog-eared John Le Carré novel—but no, tonight he'd had more than enough intrigue. Instead he laid back and tried not to feel the worries pressing down on him. *Just listen to the night breeze over the roof, the distant voices blending together… breath by breath…*

* * *

At least in the morning Paul felt almost rested again. Better yet, he could sense the last twinges in his knee fading nicely.

He left the bike in its place and marched out, still up before most of the hotel's residents. But by the front desk Bald Mike's young son was waiting.

"Hey, Pete!"

"Hi, Edward," Paul said. "Let me guess…"

"Can you look at my homework?" The nine-year-old boy held out his book. Somehow, while his face was the dirtiest thing in the room, the textbook was almost clean.

At the desk, the new day manager—some older man Paul didn't know—smiled as he watched them.

"Isn't the bus coming soon?" Paul asked, realizing it was later than he'd thought. But then he added, "Oh, alright."

Paul had always hated to waste a chance to talk to someone who really wasn't part of all his secrets, but now he felt a moment's urge to tell Edward to try his father again. *And I can't make any sign that I might not be here much longer.* He looked over the math, which was columns of addition exercises, more repetitive drill than anything else.

"There, you missed that one," and he pointed.

Edward stared harder at the page. "But look, eight and five and nine, carry two… it's right, isn't it?"

"Very good," Paul said. He smiled, glad that the boy was learning to stand up for himself. "Now get going."

"Thanks, Pete!" and Edward scampered away. Paul watched him go, trying not to look at the man at the desk. That would be one more person who might noticed him. *No question about it, I've been here too long.*

*   *   *

Greg and Lorraine's new house sat on the edge of uptown, where Paul should have known Greg would go. Blending in here meant Paul kept his battered coat folded on his arm, to show off the cleaner sweater underneath.

The neighborhood didn't leave much room for yards, he noted, but the planners seemed to make a point of having some grass on all four sides of its houses. A taste of the suburbs, right in the city.

He also picked out the buzzing of their security system, which seemed to consist of layers of motion sensors around the property, but no cameras peeping out to record his face. If there had been cameras, Paul knew he'd have had to walk away and meet Lorraine somewhere else.

He rang the doorbell, not sure he could have been heard knocking on the heavy, new door without rousing half the block. And as he heard her approaching inside, he realized that, despite the robbery and all the new defenses, Lorraine was still determined to stay here—even alone.

The door swung wide and she looked out at him, seeming a bit uneasy now. "I almost didn't think you'd come."

Not sure how to answer, Paul only shrugged.

She waved him in. "Come in, sit down. Coffee?"

"Sure," he said as he stepped in. "And yes, we *can* have caffeine without overstimulating senses like ours."

"I see," and she frowned.

The home was a pleasant place, full of bright colors. Greg's books, a film poster, and various trophies stood along the wall, mixed with other items that had to be Lorraine's.

She poured two cups from a waiting coffeepot and led him to the dining room. There on a table waited a stack of what looked like freshly printed computer files.

"Now…" Paul began, "we have two things to work on. So let's start with giving you some practice recognizing the moment you start to trigger your senses." He motioned to the coffee cup in her hand. "You can use anything. So, try to put the cup on the table just far enough from your hand that you can't feel its warmth, and then—"

"Actually, I have a few other things to look at," and she slipped out of her chair almost before she sat in it. "I want to thank you for coming, but I need to stay on the phone. As for the robbery, how long do you think you'll need here?"

"Well, that's hard to say," he evaded, almost by reflex. "Where's your computer?"

He thought he saw her eyebrow twitch in surprise, just for a moment. Then she said, "This way."

She gathered up the files and led him around to a work room, a spot where the mix of her possessions and Greg's yielded to the books and publicity-event photos Paul knew well.

Paul settled at the computer and began flipping through the pages. NatureGrown Foods, Councilman Kowalski, Councilwoman Bennet…

"We don't work with her much," Lorraine said, "but I can't forget that she introduced us to Kowalski. And NatureGrown is the trickiest client, so it's the one Greg is trying hardest to use *his* ideas with, instead of his father's."

"Did he say that?" Paul asked, surprised his brother spoke so candidly. "And does he have some reason to believe they're connected with the break-in here?"

"We tried to think of everyone, right after it happened, but we couldn't get anywhere then. And now I don't want to bother him—"

Her phone chimed from her pocket and she gave Paul a quick look as she pulled it out. Then she was off, arguing with the caller. "Slow down, speedy. I've seen those changes…"

For a moment, Paul considered listening to both sides of the conversation—but random glimpses of their life couldn't be as useful as the lists of people she'd already picked out as possible suspects. And since she'd done so much to start him out, it was only right to leave her alone now.

He opened the web browser and went to work. Business overview, history of known associates, then anything about each company that hinted at risks they took or conflicts that might make trouble. The sites he used were a number of his favorite research sources, clicking his way through the main ones almost in the sequence he'd expected to use. And with Sarah Gomez still sharing the blame for the Animal Alliance's tricks, he couldn't afford to waste time.

As he worked, Lorraine paced back and forth, watching him as she talked, then moreso when the call ended. He clicked faster, from one resource to the next and scribbling notes as he went, hoping to keep her from thinking of the less legal ways he might be gathering information when she wasn't watching. And he felt a certain curiosity as to what a former computer teacher like Lorraine might think of his research techniques… and the old thrill of investigating whether Arthur Quinn had actually done more than glare at Dad since his loans were paid off…

"You're putting Councilwoman Bennet aside?" Lorraine asked as he set that paper down.

"I just don't think there's a motive. And your neighbor Meacham seems to have more of a grievance—"

"Careful there!" she warned. "We have to *live* here, remember?"

Was that real anxiety in her voice? Paul replied, "I just mean, he has more of a reason to make trouble than some of these people."

"But you aren't sure. In fact," and she waved to the main stack of suspects, "you've still put most of them back in there, and it could be any of them!"

"That's true. But I am getting a sense of every conflict with you they could have, short of some petty, personal grudge that would leave no traces."

"And what if it *is* that?" she asked. "What if it's something you can't find on a business report?"

"It's always possible. Someone took the risk of breaking into your home. That might mean it's personal," Paul admitted, wishing he'd never mentioned the limits of these tools. But that was just how he'd missed Koenig and his private grudge against LifeLab, and risked Sarah's career. "But, there's no reason to think…"

Lorraine's phone rang again and she turned away as she answered.

"Hi, Greg… yes, I am… be careful making calls or they'll take your phone away again…"

Paul looked away and got up to stretch. He reached for another page—

As he did, a flash of red caught his eye, a piece of paper that had fallen into the crack between the desk and the wall. But that exact shade of red threaded through the crumpled folds… *like one of the red-bordered memos I liked to use in the firm, that everyone else hated.*

Lorraine hung up and turned back to Paul. "Greg worried that I might have started staying home out of fear today," she sighed. "I hate hiding this from him."

There had to be something he could say. "If it helps, we don't know that what happened here was ever anything more than a robbery. And if that's what it was, it's over."

"So that's it?" The cold eyes she fixed on him actually made him shiver. "You just look at their records and say we'll never know?"

I want to keep this calm. I don't want to show what my powers really let me do. Lorraine seemed too close to asking just that, and he could only think of one way to distract her. "Look… we both need a break," he said. "Do you think you've got the phone settled for a few minutes?"

"Maybe," she said guardedly.

Why does working behind Greg's back bother her so much? But she *couldn't* be that happy working with the man who'd had any part in exposing their games with the hospital, however careful he'd been…

Pushing those thoughts down, he said, "Then let's get back to helping you control your power."

She frowned at the words, but he kept going.

"I know it bothers you. But if you ever want to use it without it using you, you need to practice. Here."

He reached for a page of notes, thinking he might hold it up from across the room in a variant of the familiar vision test. But no, reading far-off pages would only be another hint at all the spying he could do—so instead, he held up his hands in front of him.

"This would be easier with the coffee cup, but this way, it's more of a test. Just close your eyes."

"Why?" Lorraine's anger seemed mostly gone now, but there was still suspicion in her voice.

Soothingly, he said "Close your eyes, and hold up both your hands."

She raised her hands, but shut her eyes only part way, peeking out.

"Now, I'm going to bring one of my hands near yours. Just focus on touch and try to feel the warmth, and tell me which hand I'm near. With your eyes *closed*," he said again, and she shut them at last.

Slowly, he brought his left hand around to the side of hers. It was just two handspans away, then half that…

"Tell me which side," he said as he drew to two fingers' width away. Still she said nothing, and he saw the beginnings of a scowl.

He drew his hand back and said, "Flex your fingers, and think of them. Then think of the air around them."

She twitched her fingers, eyes still closed. As she did, Paul couldn't keep from stealing a glance at the desk the crumpled note lay behind. *Why would one of my old notes still be there?* For a moment, he wondered if it could be the letter he mailed them, just to say he was alive and wouldn't be back. *But after two years?*

"All right, now," he said. "Which hand—"

"This is hopeless!" and Lorraine spun away. "I can't do it!" She stomped a few steps across the room before she turned back, face flushed.

"But… you already have." *She shouldn't even* have *this power, why is it so wrong that she can't work it?* "The moment you sensed me in the dark, at Animal Alliance, you proved you could do this." He sighed, trying to release some of his confusion. "That means you'll be doing it again, it'll all happen to you again if you don't take control. And don't forget, just that one time showed me a lot I didn't know. This gives both of us a chance to learn…"

"This isn't about you!" she snapped, then looked down, not meeting his eyes. "Sorry, Paul. But, it isn't you who's being driven out of your home, or your… while you just keep clicking keys!"

Paul struggled not to flinch back from the burning frustration in her gaze. Now she was almost *expecting* him to go spy out the answers for her instead, as if she'd already all but guessed how he'd been living—no matter how he tried to throw her off. And here he'd been thinking it was safe to help Edward or approach Sarah…

Trying to keep his voice steady, he said "All right. There is one way we can use our senses to help with this." Ignoring how vast an understatement that was, he added, "And maybe you need a stronger reason to try. So, are you up for a drive?"

She looked at him a moment, but where he'd thought he'd see a flicker of hope, she only eyed him warily. "Of course," she answered. "And, are you saying the danger we live with is that we might start amplifying our senses by reflex?"

"That's one way to put it," Paul nodded.

"But I don't have *any* habit of using this power, so I'm not in any danger so far," she said, grinning in triumph. "To start with, this time I'll drive."

*   *   *

The police station was like so many of the city's larger precincts: understaffed and crowded, able to keep its walls clean but with enough people tracking in dirt to make the floor dirtier than Side Alley.

Hanging back in the crowd, Paul watched Lorraine make her way up to the long desk, where she asked for the officer she'd dealt with before. Soon, she moved back and rejoined Paul. The question she'd had since they set out hung in the air between them.

"They'll call me when he comes out," she told Paul, "but it's no use. I've already talked to him about our car, and he won't let me see the wreck. How are we supposed to change his mind?"

"That's not what we need."

"Then how do we get to see the car?"

Paul knew she was thinking of him sneaking around, which was way too close to the truth about him. To distract her, he grinned. "Not that, either. I'd hoped you'd figure it out. It's not the wreck we'll get information from; this is more p-s-i than CSI…"

Lorraine frowned as if she partly appreciated the joke, despite their tension. Paul sighed; it had seemed funny a year ago, though he hadn't thought he'd get to say it to anyone. Then again, *psi power* never quite felt like what he did.

He told her "First, be sure you offer real reasons the crash might not have been an accident. You don't have to convince him, but you have to sound reasonable, not irrational. Which you always do," he added quickly, before she could take that comment the wrong way.

"Thanks," she said, and he didn't think the compliment had helped. "And what happens then?"

"I doubt he'll tell you anything about his findings, if he isn't already about to. But if you raise enough questions, when you leave, you can focus on hearing what he says to the others about it."

Her eyes widened, and she glanced around at all the people in the station. Some were muttering, others were talking, and some seemed on the edge of shouting. "Wait. You want me to use my talent, to listen through *this* many voices?"

"Or I could listen," Paul said with a frown as he wondered, *Why does she avoid accepting her gift and its risks?* He couldn't keep from adding "But you said you wanted to know…"

She glanced around at the people again and then started back to the desk. Just before she turned away from Paul, her lips shaped the word *bastard* as if she didn't think he'd hear it clearly. Or she knew he would.

She moved back up to the side of the desk to wait. Paul saw her looking around again, and knew how nervous he'd been in crowds, back when his power was still new. But this was a chance for her to see that the power could be worth accepting.

There must be a reason she developed this now, and it has to be something besides uncovering the kind of life I live with it.

At last an officer came to meet her, a small man with faint grease stains on the hand he offered her. "Ms. Schuman," he said.

"Thank you for seeing me again," Lorraine replied, following him back behind the desk. She was out of Paul's view now, but it was still easy for him to hear. "When we talked before, you said you were the best at looking at wrecked cars. So, have you had time to look at my husband's?"

"I have, ma'am. But all that means is that we've sent the key parts off for some particular tests—"

"So you need more tests?" she said at once. "I *knew* there was something suspicious."

"There's nothing 'suspicious.' It only means we like to be thorough with our investigation, before—"

"Is he always this stubborn?"

Paul could just imagine how she must be turning to accost another nearby cop with this question, and he smiled at her insight. *I told her we wanted to get them talking after she left, so she's working on priming more than one officer.*

She went on, "I'd bet he already knows, and he's just afraid his boss will hear he bent some tiny regulation by telling me too soon. Listen, I just need to know, now. *Was* there anything wrong?"

"I'm sorry, ma'am, but we *do* have regulations about releasing information. If you'd like to talk to my lieutenant—"

"Oh, never mind," she said with a sigh, and walked away.

A few steps brought her back into Paul's view, and he saw her stop and glance back toward where she'd been talking. He also saw her frown, concentrating.

Then she stopped and shook her head at him—

Paul only had an instant as he shifted from watching her to Opening his own hearing—but in that moment, his hands made a harsh "pushing" gesture asking her to try harder. He heard her start a deep breath.

Then he was following someone else's words: "…was that about?"

Lorraine's cop gave a slow sigh. "The longest river is still De-Nial. Every few years, some driver slips on that Halifax corner—but they have to make it a conspiracy." Paul heard him walking away.

Paul grinned, despite himself, surprised the trick had worked. Sometimes he did get lucky… and Lorraine was luckier yet, if this part of the mystery was as harmless as it sounded.

When he looked over, the grin vanished. Lorraine was shaking as she stood there, shooting wilder and wilder glances left and right at the noisiest corners of the station. *She's being swept under by her power, the way she was when she got it last night.*

Paul quickly stepped forward and around the long desk to make a beeline to her side, trusting the police would let him through to steady her.

As he reached her, she whispered weakly, "I lost it. I heard 'What was that' and a 'river' and then I couldn't… it was so *loud*…"

"It's alright. Come on," he said as he put his hands on her shoulders to lead her out.

Instead, she wrenched out of his grasp and shot him a savage look, then marched away toward the entrance. Paul followed.

She stopped suddenly, in the middle of the crowd, and drew herself up. Then she turned to face him. As he drew close she hissed, softly under the room's noise, "Are you happy now?!"

"I'm sorry, really." He could feel her breath, and for all the anger in her voice, the face so close to him was pale. *She really is scared of the power. But I had to push her.*

Being careful not to touch her, he breathed, "Look, maybe you don't have to do any more of this. Like you said, if you never get in the habit of using the power, it may not start surprising you. I think you're safe. You've got your life with Greg back."

And here I'd been hoping to find an answer for myself, too… but her kind of "key to control" would only help me work safely among real reporters if I could give up *my way of getting to the truth.*

"Besides," he said as he drew back a step and shifted to a more normal whisper, "what he said was that it just seems like an accident. A bad stretch of road. So maybe the break-in is nothing more than that, too."

She only snapped back, "So *you* say."

"What? Why would I lie?" Paul braced for her answer. *Is she going to accuse me of robbing them myself?*

But instead Lorraine looked away, glanced at the people around them, and some of the tension eased from her face. "No, I guess not. And maybe it was just a robbery. But I want to be sure."

He nodded reassuringly. "If there's anything to find, we can keep…"

"No! They could be breaking in again right now! Or they might wait a month and hit us again when we start to relax. I have to know what this is."

Now she took a step closer, and whispered below all the sounds around them. "You have this power. There has to be some way you can make this easier."

"It's never easy," he said, wishing his words could push her back. Her desperate voice, her demanding eyes burned only inches away, and yet she couldn't even say what she thought he could do. She wouldn't be satisfied with anything less than every legal and illegal trick he knew, but she couldn't say the words. *And I can't, mustn't tell her…* Somehow, he managed to hold his silence.

When he didn't answer, she drew back at last. "So, you won't help your brother?"

"I've *been* helping, all morning. And we can keep researching. So," and he took a deep breath, "is that enough, or not?"

A new kind of frown started moving across her face, as if she'd heard the change in his tone. But she said "I told you, I need to be sure."

"Then, I'm sorry." And he turned and walked away.

Behind him he heard her say, "Hold on—" but he kept moving through the crowd as she started after him. He didn't make an obvious dive between people to get away, but from long practice, he angled his movements to slide more smoothly through the human currents, widening his lead with every step.

When he stepped outside the station, out of her view for the moment, he ducked to the side and crouched down behind a heavy trash bin. *It'd be better to just dash around a corner, but I won't simply run from her.*

Opening his hearing, he tracked the steps of a woman's heels running to the entrance and stopping, and heard Lorraine muttering curses. She stayed in place long enough for what had to be glaring around in frustration, before marching off to where they'd left her car.

Paul sighed, feeling some of the weight fall away from him. He'd asked for her patience, she'd refused, and now he could finish investigating on his own terms—and what was more, even now she still hadn't tried some reckless use of her power.

When she drove away, he stood and walked off with his conscience almost clear.

*   *   *

Even under the gray November sky, the crisp air made the softly-lit streets an extra pleasure to walk. Over the next several blocks, Paul practiced a few of his dodges in case anyone was following him, not for fear that anyone was but just for the pleasure of testing himself. Then he stepped into a shop for a couple of rolls and an apple for a late lunch—decent, but not good enough to Open his senses to really savor the taste. Instead, he resumed walking, munching and thinking of his choices.

The notes on Greg and Lorraine's suspects sat waiting in his pocket... but it was too soon to turn back to that problem again. Instead, the Park Branch library was the nearest, and he headed for it.

The afternoon crowd was light, the during-school-hours mix of college students and other ages with at least one homeless man soaking up warmth in a corner. Paul glanced at the New Books shelf, tempted to sample a couple for any authors worth remembering. *But no, not when I have two cases to balance.*

He settled at one of their public computers and logged on to an anonymous remailer website. As he weighed what to say to Sarah Gomez, Paul paused, recognizing the irony: just after breaking his deadlock with Lorraine, here he was making promises to another woman. But at least this time it was his own choice—or at least, it had started as his before Sarah had been caught up in his mistake.

Simplest is best. He typed, "There is more to the LifeLab scandal and the files I left under your car. And now I know who faked them." He sent the message off, the remailer keeping it untraceable, and then logged off.

For the next few minutes, he walked around, browsing the shelves. Changing machines was probably a pointless precaution; if what he would do next actually was traced, the police would search their way along the whole row of computers' records anyway, and either would or wouldn't connect it to her. Nevertheless, he settled back at a different terminal and took a moment to check who might see his screen. Then he logged on to the city DMV.

Paul smiled a moment, thinking of his long night hiding in their office; Motor Vehicles had always been one database worth getting the best remote passwords to. Then he typed "Koenig."

*   *   *

James Koenig's car sat outside the Animal Alliance headquarters, even on a Wednesday afternoon. Paul wasn't too surprised; Koenig's activism had begun by leaving LifeLab, and job-hunting websites showed he hadn't found any other position since.

But the driveway was mostly empty and the voices inside were too few—not enough to cover Paul getting a closer look. He considered looking through Koenig's home while he was away, but first he headed around to the back of the mansion and saw a quiet, unobserved route to within a few paces of the manor's wall. *Leave it to a nature group to let the bushes grow up behind them.*

Paul crouched down behind the brush, pulling his coat tightly around him against the chill that would seep in while he kept still. Opening his hearing, he followed Koenig and some of the group leaders who were arguing about strategies to draw more attention for their cause… nothing dangerous, but he also heard no signs that the others were going to discuss how Koenig had faked the evidence he'd brought them.

Paul had thought not to stay long—not while Koenig's home was empty—but the more he heard Koenig clicking away on what had to be a laptop, the more he thought about just what kind of evidence Koenig had manufactured. As he waited, he took out a sticky-note pad and jotted down a note in case he had a chance to use it. And he remembered the more colorful note he had seen behind Greg's desk… he could just picture Greg crumpling up his last word from Paul and flinging it away, if it could really lie there ever since—if that was what the note truly was.

The activists also talked about a batch of recruits who were expected soon, so Paul was ready at the first sound of cars driving up out front. He slipped around to watch them: there were two dozen believers, mostly young; he recognized some of them from the party the previous night. The way they milled around made it easy for Paul to walk in with them.

Sure enough, James Koenig was with the other Alliance leaders, seated at a table piled with stacks of pages, and in front of him lay an open laptop. The newcomers spread around the room, still so intent on the people up front that they didn't notice a stranger among them.

"Thank you for coming," one of the leaders began. "Too many people wouldn't take the time, even after the media got these pictures." He motioned to the table, and went on "And the net has them, too. They're everywhere—but it's not enough!"

As he went on, Paul edged around at the back of the crowd, and as Koenig drifted farther away from his computer, Paul leaned forward. With two quick motions in half a second, he brought the computer to locked mode, as if it had timed out normally while its owner was away. Then he withdrew to just the right place by the window, off to Koenig's side.

"Tomorrow morning," the speaker was saying, "everyone on the Mile, every door on the Square, is going to show them the face of LifeLab's *experiments*," and he brandished one of the pages.

Its image was one of Koenig's fakes, a photo of a mutilated pig. Paul had brought Sarah other files that seemed to support such practices, but this image might well have been created on Koenig's own laptop...

But Koenig didn't log back in to his machine, and he didn't seem to notice it had locked. *Alright then...*

The recruits began stepping forward to pick up flyers; most of them marched straight out the door once they had an armload. Paul took his place near the end of the line. And as he marched by, he "stumbled" enough to plant a small, goldenrod-yellow sticky note onto Koenig's keyboard.

He faded back again to the window, where he was at just the right angle to catch a faint but unobstructed reflection from the side of the keyboard—enough so he could Open his sight to that spot, the moment Koenig used his password to log back in.

Koenig was moving back toward his laptop again. The room was almost empty now, with only a few of the "troops" staying to talk or look at the flyers they carried, which Paul also pretended to do. He waited. *Once I have the password, I can get the files tonight, or use my Analyzer disk to salvage them if they were deleted.* Or if Koenig used his phone instead, or even went on the run, Paul would still have a story he could be sure Sarah got first, and save her job.

Koenig looked at the keyboard and saw the note with its tiny, discreet writing: "I had to let you know—I'm TELLING the cop everything."

But he didn't reach for the keyboard. Instead he snapped the laptop shut, shoved it under his arm, and his lips were moving. Paul caught "…not that easy" before Koenig walked out the front door.

Paul let him go by, then followed from a distance behind him, keeping him in sight as he took out a cell phone.

Cool and unshaken, Koenig said, "Detective, this is James Koenig. And I don't appreciate your forcing people to harass me." And flipped the phone shut.

Paul watched the suspect head for his car, cursing his luck. If only Koenig had had *anyone* else who shared his secrets, or that he'd been willing to believe had learned them…

Instead I get no password, no phone call to follow up, only an enemy that I've just placed on alert. Paul stared at the flyers in his hands. By dawn, their lies would be splashed all over town to build on his and Sarah's mistake.

"Don't worry so much. Mr. Schuman said he was ready to work with any ads we found."

Paul straightened a little in his chair, but the Nature-Grown executive on the other side of the wall only went on to discuss quarterly earnings projections. And the Schuman name was still the closest Greg's "big client" had come to saying anything relevant to the break-in, after Paul had sat listening in the office suite next to them for what had to be an hour. Paul knew better than to check his watch; the longer the receptionist forgot about him sitting there, the better.

Besides, counting the minutes kills a hunter's patience for whenever the opportunity comes. But then, so does guessing it won't come at all.

He shifted his shoulders and back slightly to keep them from getting stiff. At least he was warmer than he'd been watching James Koenig's apartment the previous night; Paul hated what the colder nights would soon be doing to surveillance. And he hadn't even heard Koenig start up his computer once, but while he watched the man, those recruits had been out spreading their flyers full of lies over half the city.

"Sir, if you'll just tell me who I should call…" the receptionist said now. She stepped around her desk to him, planting her hands on her ample hips.

Paul sighed, checked his watch, and said, "Never mind. I can see he's not coming," and marched out before she could say more. At least she'd let him loiter that long; most receptionists would need a better excuse to ignore a visitor, even one who seemed to *want* to stay out of their way forever.

He'd had slow days before; it couldn't be just the lack of clues that was getting to him. But when he saw the "Working the Works" sandwich wagon pull up in front of the building—carrying some of the freshest food in the city—it felt like the first good news of the day.

"Veggie burger with The Works," he told the tiny, pale man at the window.

"Of course, my friend," the man said, just as he did to everyone. Then he added, "And did you know that Morning Star has moved up its concert to this week?"

"No, I didn't." *And when did we talk about music? I try to never chat with him for long.* Paul kept the smile on his face, trying not to worry. He could at least afford a *few* people who remembered his face.

"Slow down, my friend," the little man said as he handed Paul the sandwich. "Enjoy this fine day."

"I'll try to," Paul lied as he walked away. He Opened his taste as he took the first bite, but even that rush of tomato, mushroom, and nine other tangs and sweetnesses balanced together couldn't change what he knew.

He walked faster, trying not to hear the fierce, petty argument between two teenage brothers to his left. They sounded too much like he and Greg had been once. *I could spend all week looking for Greg's enemies and probably get no more than I already have. And if I find no enemies, Greg will never even know. I'll only end up wasting the time I need to make things right with Sarah—*

Now even the sandwich's taste soured in his mouth. *What's the point of getting to know Sarah or her paper if the first thing I do at any disagreement is disappear again?*

Sarah Gomez wasn't the latest one he'd hurt. His walk was already taking him toward St. Central.

* * *

Maybe he was remembering that the hospital, like most, tended to discharge patients in the afternoon—but he was still surprised when he heard Lorraine's voice in Greg's room.

"Actually, I drove your rental here. I thought you'd like to get used to it, right off."

"Of course you did," Greg said. Paul knew his brother must be grinning. Despite all the years he's spent fighting with Paul, it seemed that with Lorraine, Greg only showed his good side. "Lor, I was thinking, we should try Animal Alliance together. They've already met you. I bet that, between us, we can make them give us a try."

Of course she fights so hard to preserve that life. But all I saw was the pressure she put on me. Paul turned away before he lost his nerve. Lorraine's business card was in his hand as he reached the pay phones out front.

And then he had the phone at his ear, heard it ringing, and had nothing left but to wonder if she would talk to him at all—especially with Greg right there—

"Hello?" She sounded neutral, as if she'd never considered who might be calling her from an unknown number.

"I'd like to apologize," Paul rushed the words out. "I'm out front if you want…"

For one long moment, he heard the deepest silence he could remember. Then the line went dead.

No surprise, really. And it left Paul oddly relieved that he'd made the attempt, and she'd burned the bridge. Now he could finish looking at their suspects between his time helping Sarah, and—

But there she was, marching out from Greg's room and looking around for the bank of phones. She folded her arms as she walked up to him.

"I shouldn't be here," she said slowly. "But Greg trusts me, even when I suddenly have to rush out of his room."

Paul forced himself to meet her gaze steadily, just trying to get the words out again. "It's been a long time since I've had to apologize to anyone… but I shouldn't have just ducked out on you like that. And not just about how I did it."

Lorraine only looked at him, her frown deepening slightly.

"I've had some other work, but I've been checking on your list too. NatureGrown probably doesn't have a reason to make trouble, and… And I had an idea that might tell us more, if you want to try again making people around you nervous so I can see what they do—"

In a cold whisper, she said "When you aren't doing 'other work'? Or did you *steal* enough money to have time for us again?" and she twisted the word like a curse.

It was too much.

"I don't steal!" he snapped, barely keeping his voice low. "Not one thing, not ever!" *Only facts, only the evidence to beat the liars out there.* "How *dare* you judge me like that!"

She flinched, shaken. "Maybe," she said slowly. Her eyes softened a fraction. "Maybe. But you still ran out on me."

"I told you, I kept on checking—" He stopped, resisting the distraction. "But I know I shouldn't have treated you that way."

Lorraine watched him, not speaking, just measuring. This time, Paul glanced away, to look just a little beyond her…

Striding up the corridor, with the nurse and the empty wheelchair…

"There's my father," he said as he sidestepped back around the corner.

Lorraine turned and started toward them, her face unreadable, still not saying a word.

"Look, I said…"

She glanced back. "I know," she said. Then she turned the corner and was gone.

Her voice had been almost warm, Paul thought as he drew back to a second corner, out of their view. After his father and the nurse had passed, he stayed in place a bit longer, letting the tension drain out of him. At least he'd proved he could work with others again. Later, he could contact Lorraine to see if she wanted more help or figure out whether she could accept that the break-in might not have had a reason—

Quinn!

Paul stared around the corner as Arthur Quinn walked by, scarcely believing his eyes. The loan shark had stepped right out of Schuman family history.

He was just an ordinary man in his fifties, wearing a brown suit, strolling along. Paul had only noticed him because he'd taken a moment yesterday with Lorraine's suspects file to memorize the jut of the man's jaw, certain there had to be just one feature in his face that wasn't completely bland…

Paul peered up the corridor, watching Quinn. *The way Dad talks about him—even decades after he got free of his loans. And now here he is.*

Up ahead, Dad, Lorraine, and the nurse were wheeling Greg out in a chair. Quinn headed straight toward them.

Paul knew the moment his father spotted the intruder. He saw him stride forward to cut Quinn off from his family. And Quinn sped up, too, so he was within easy earshot of the rest when he was intercepted.

"I thought that was you, Greg," Quinn said warmly, as if he were some casual friend or neighbor, as if his years as the old family boogieman had never happened. "Congratulations on your discharge."

"Gloating?" Ian Schuman hissed. "I have some bad news for you: we won't need any 'help' paying the bills." He wasn't loud, but the harshness in his voice made one passing nurse turn her head to look.

Quinn sidestepped to get closer to Greg's path, and as Paul's father moved to block him, he continued speaking past him. "I wanted to wish you all the best, Greg. I like to think any of my associates—"

From his wheelchair, Greg snapped, "Why don't you just get out of our way?"

"Your way? There's plenty of room in this corridor, isn't there?" Quinn asked.

"He said, back off!" and with that, Paul's father grabbed Quinn's shoulder and shoved him back… and Quinn went stumbling away to sprawl against the wall. *Dad didn't shove him that hard, he* faked *that!*

"Mr. Schuman!" Greg's nurse gasped, and Paul could hear ripples of surprise up and down the corridor.

Paul Opened his sight to catch Quinn's face as he stood up. He saw the rage in his eyes, the tension quivering in his muscles ready to leap at his enemy.

Still, he stopped to smooth his coat and his features and said "Really, this is a hospital."

"Then show some respect, or you'll *need* a—"

"Is something wrong?" An elegant woman in a fine blue suit stepped up to them, with a big man at her heels and two orderlies following in her wake. *I should know her…*

And instead of playing more games, Quinn only said, "It seems I'm not wanted here," and turned away. He actually seemed to slink off, moving quietly with his head down.

Paul turned back to the others and saw his father extending a hand. "Always a pleasure, Councilwoman."

Erin Bennet? Another of Lorraine's suspects, here? Although Paul had heard only good things about this woman.

"Ian. And your son, I thought that was you, Greg," she said.

Even without a stronger focus, Paul could almost feel the others catch their breaths when they heard her echo Quinn's exact words. But then, it would be the natural thing to say when someone noticed them from across the hall.

Greg laughed, the tension fading from his voice. "I don't suppose you came to talk about the next election."

"Actually," cut in the big aide behind her, "Ms. Bennet is here to meet with the hospital director. And I'm afraid she's running late."

"He's right. Maybe another time, Ian," the councilwoman said as she stepped smoothly away and headed off with her aide, the orderlies dispersing as they did.

"Councilwoman?" Greg's nurse called after her, then added to the Schumans, "Can I leave for just a moment without you folks starting a gunfight?" She rushed after Bennet, gushing apologies for the commotion.

As she left, Paul saw Greg, his father, and Lorraine take a moment to look at each other in the sudden silence.

And in that silence, Paul caught Lorraine taking a long, conscious breath, almost like the one she'd taken when she'd braced herself to overhear the police—but now she only looked at Greg.

She said "So many people interested in us. Are you sure there's nothing you want to tell me, Greg?"

"Not really," was all he said.

But Lorraine *gasped.* With real shock in her voice, she whispered, "Greg? You know you can tell me anything. Why did you look at her like..."

"Lor?" Now there was a tremor in Greg's voice, too, as if he knew she knew—

Paul yanked his senses back to himself and ducked back out of sight. Somehow, somehow she'd done it. He *knew* she had. Lorraine had used their power to read Greg's mind.

Now nothing is safe. Paul stumbled away, fighting the urge to break into a run. All his secrets, the two years of meddling… now she could rip it all from his mind and use it to make him do what she wanted… and see all his own hopes and fears…

As he rushed away, one idea fell into place: *I have to stay out of Lorraine's reach. I have to track down her enemy but stay away from Lorraine herself.*

Starting with, what was that about Councilwoman Bennet?

At the quickest trot he could use without attracting attention, he made his way through the halls, picturing the St. Central layout. He struggled to think about where Bennet would be meeting with the hospital director, instead of remembering what Lorraine had just done.

Three hurried turns later, he caught sight of Bennet's fine suit and tightly-bound, dark hair, all half hidden by the tan-jacketed shoulders of the aide walking beside her. At least they weren't moving too rapidly—"running late" or not—as they made their way toward…

Toward the same conference room section Dad and Greg had used, two years earlier. *Secrets, Lorraine's impossible trick, and now my scrambled memories too?* Bennet seemed to have a small hesitation in her footsteps, and that slowness made every step Paul took felt a little more frustrating as he held himself back well behind them.

Just when Paul was convinced they wouldn't say anything, the aide edged closer and said "What was that about, Ma'am?"

"Vernon, I told you. We ended it."

Paul's eyes went wide. *They "ended it."* Even without Lorraine's shock earlier… Was that what all this came down to? Greg the happy husband was cheating on Lorraine?

Paul's fists clenched; it fit too well. His brother had always wanted things his own way, and he'd treated women like that in his younger days. *But hadn't that caused Greg enough trouble?*

Paul listened for more, but all he heard were their footsteps. And even those… oddly, she seemed to be limping. It was almost as if she had been in a car crash herself, like Greg's.

Suddenly the aide said, "Let me check something, I'll be with you soon," and he quickly stepped away.

Bennet called, "Vernon? What?" But her aide was already rushing along, looking right past Paul and marching on down the corridor. Paul kept his own eyes straight ahead and his pace the same, but he could feel the size and momentum of "Vernon" as he swept by.

The man's urgency made Paul's choice easy; when the Council-woman had turned back and started walking again, he headed after Vernon.

His heavy footfalls also meant the aide was easy to track, and even though Paul made a special effort to keep more corners and people between them, he had to match Vernon's rapid pace. The strain of Opening and then almost releasing his hearing again to keep it from pulling him too far in began to make his head pound.

Once Vernon stopped cold at a nurse's station, and as Paul slowed he heard him say "I'm looking for G. W. Hall, a lab worker."

Paul scowled. Vernon sounded determined, and he already knew about Greg's cheating; how afraid *was* he of it trapping his boss in a scandal?

And Lorraine, it would destroy *her just to know the home life she's been fighting for is a lie… if there's anything about it she doesn't already know. Can she really read minds now?* Paul tried not to think about that, just to concentrate on following the aide.

When Vernon reached the records room and walked in, Paul slowed to stroll on past the entrance, keeping his hearing Opened.

"Can I help you?" a clerk asked.

Vernon might have been asking about sandwich choices. "Is G. W. Hall back there now, with the records? I want to talk to him."

"You'd have to make the request through…" The clerk broke off.

Paul Opened his hearing further, embracing the sudden stillness where the two men had been talking, the babble of other voices pressing against the silence that stretched on and on…

A rustling sound made Paul start, jolting him from losing himself in the sounds. *That's money being handed over.*

"Right this way."

Paul edged back, closer to the room's entrance, to help him maintain his connection as Vernon and his guide moved through the long room, past one worker after another. *Is this the answer? Is this the same man who'd been willing to break into Greg's home? What is he up to now?*

Paul heard Vernon's guide turn away then, and a door swing shut behind Vernon.

An older male voice, a bit impatient, asked, "What is it?"

Then a gasp, three quick steps of Vernon's, and a low thump. Paul could hear 'Hall' wheezing for breath, and panting with fear.

Outside, the rhythm of voices went on unchanged, babbling away just beyond the door.

"Where are the records for Gregory Schuman? He was just released." Vernon's voice was a low growl that could barely have carried beyond arm's reach.

"The—the hard copy's there," Hall managed to say.

Paul felt his blood pounding almost as hard as the victim's gasps. *Am I going to let this happen? Could I stop it?* The office bustle continued outside, while within he could make out each grunt of the manhandled victim, each rustle of paper being turned.

"I knew it!" Vernon hissed. "Look! They pulled Schuman out of a crashed car, but the blood tests said his alcohol level was over the limit. And just like they said, you *were* on lab duty then. Why didn't you report it?"

"I'm… not sure… what shift was—"

"WHY?"

"He was so close! His number, it was just a half a hair's over, he'd just had a brush with death, he shouldn't be arrested too… please-don't-hurt-me…"

For a moment, the only sound was his whimpering. But Paul realized he'd heard no blows or screams either. At last, Vernon said, "This is a start."

"Put that back, it's…" Hall started to say before breaking off.

It's really happening. A man is being brutalized, and someone is using this hospital to attack my family again—

Paul marched into the room at the quick stride that could sometimes rush him past people before they could react. As he passed a table, he snatched up a medical form and held it up close to his face, hoping it looked more like dedicated reading than a makeshift mask. He swept by the front desk and on into the main area beyond, looking for the room Vernon had entered.

"You keep this quiet," Vernon was growling. "You already broke the law, and now that you've let this file get away…"

Paul made a beeline for Hall's door. Voices stirred around him, muted by his hearing's focus on Vernon and Hall, but nobody had started to look at him yet, and the door stood just ahead.

"That is if you ever *get* to jail… don't you faint on me!"

The door swung silently open at a touch. Paul saw Vernon's back, saw him leaning over the limp form of a small man in white he was bending back over a desk. Vernon shook him, blind to the rest of the world.

And on the closer corner of the desk lay a simple manila folder. It was a St. Central medical file, so it would have records of lab results at the back and nothing to fasten the pages…

The thought triggered the action. As Vernon gave the man another shake, Paul Opened so that he could smooth his motions into silence, took the three quick steps forward, and slid a finger between the bottom of the folder and the pages above it. One curl of his finger flicked the bottom page out into his grasp. *That's one thing I can do.*

The next instant, he faded backward to the door again and slipped outside, leaving the door open behind him. *That's the other.*

This time, he walked more slowly, hoping people would notice what was going on in the office instead of noticing him. He held the page from Greg's file and the form he'd grabbed earlier up to his face again—and realized the whole office could see him holding up a page from Greg's private file. Somehow, that thought made his knees go weak, scaring him more than anything Vernon had done.

But as he kept walking, nobody seemed to notice him at all. One easy step and another, and nobody looked up, none of the staff shouted at him—or at Vernon and Hall, either. How far from the door had they been? *How lucky can Vernon be?* The councilwoman's aide obviously knew a few reckless ways to get what he wanted, or even to get Hall's name as the one on Greg's report, but he had to be half crazy to throw people around that way—

A heavy stride sounded behind him. Vernon was less rushed this time, clomping toward him with the footstep of maybe half again Paul's weight and closing behind him.

Why couldn't they have caught him choking Hall? Paul's feet burned to run as Vernon drew up behind him, but he didn't dare. The front desk lay just ahead, with room for only one person to get around the end of it.

Paul stepped aside, and the big man strode past him and on out.

When Paul's legs could work again, with the fastest march he could manage, he moved directly *away* from the turn Vernon had taken. *That's the single stupidest thing I've done since I changed—no, in my whole* life! Yet his fingers could only clutch Greg's blood test results more tightly, desperate to keep hold of it. *And all to hide how drunk my brother was as he drove his mistress around—*

It took a moment to notice the heavy hammering of Vernon's footsteps at a run behind him, scrambling back into the records room. For a moment, Paul couldn't believe what must have happened; who would be so reckless as to take out a stolen file and look through it again, right in the corridor? Or to charge around like that, no matter who noticed?

Paul crumpled Greg's page and the office form and stuffed them into separate pockets. *He can't catch me with this!* The thought made his whole body shake, but he forced himself to walk more slowly now, to seem like just one of the people scattered around the corridor. As he kept to that easier pace, he Opened his hearing to reach back toward the records room again.

"...was back here? *Who?*"

"Will you *please*... Look, there was just you and that blond guy, in the coat..."

Paul dropped the connection and bolted forward. Of course, of course Vernon had walked right past him, might remember him, *and he mustn't see me!*

Mustn't see me...

Mustn't see me...

It whirled in his head, bursting out from where it had been growing in the back of his mind and raging through him, drowning out control and flooding him with the need to flee, even as his body stumbled and he toppled forward. Desperately, he struggled to rise, but the urgency clutched him tighter.

Deception, liars... the first time I was here and again today... schemers hiding what they are, liars that mustn't win...

Sensations rippled around him, every crack of the floor, footsteps and voices spattering sound off the walls, smokepots of their sweat stinking within disinfectant haze. The corridor shook as he struggled to get his feet under him—

Vernon was charging up, *can't let him see me with this!*

Paul flung himself up to dash for a hallway ahead, but he knew in his bones Vernon was already too close and would get to him first.

There's still one way. Paul reached into a pocket, not for Greg's record but for the form he'd grabbed as he walked in; crumpled up, they'd look the same. He cocked his arm back, ready to toss it up the corridor, away from the side branch he'd take.

But his fingers only squeezed tighter, refusing to let it go, gripping the blank form like the last leash on a rabid beast.

Vernon's heavy feet closed faster, almost on him now.

Somehow, Paul managed to fling the paper away and scramble around the turn. As he dashed around two men, he heard Vernon pause at the branch to grunt, "What's *on* that..." as he headed toward Paul's decoy.

Paul ran faster, knowing he'd only bought a few moments to get out of sight before Vernon returned. The thug probably wouldn't have bothered with the paper if he hadn't seen Paul's agony over tossing it—but why *had* it been so hard, just to let some blank form out of his hand?

They can't get the evidence... not like last time.

The new insight made Paul sway on his feet again, but he kept running. He dashed up another hallway, heading for a set of rooms he knew was almost a maze of rooms. Probably a quiet place, at this hour.

This memory, was it just fear, or guilt? *As if I gave out the fax that tied Dad and Greg to their cover-up? But I didn't, I'd never have!*

He slowed his steps, gasping, and Opened a moment to locate Vernon, whose feet were still a turn behind him. All Paul needed was to duck out of sight. He seized a door.

Locked.

Paul looked around. Scaffolds and stepladders lined the walls, electrical panels hung open—how had he not noticed he'd run into a closed-off section? *Are there* any *unlocked doors here? No wonder it sounds so quiet, the whole work team must be away on a break.*

"Hah!" Vernon stood up at the turn, looking right at Paul. Then he charged straight down the abandoned corridor, with nobody to see him.

Paul scrambled away, barely able to keep his hand from clutching fiercely over the pocket with the precious paper. He stumbled around a heavy vacuum unit and nearly tripped over its hose.

With Vernon almost halfway to him, Paul darted toward a bathroom door, hoping to at least flush the paper away. In mid-lunge he realized: *Inside, it's a dead end—*

He bounced off another locked door. He caught a glimpse of a janitor's mop standing in a bucket in front, the one reason to lock a bathroom. Vernon closed in, giving him no time to run.

Paul could only swing a foot out to kick the bucket toward him. The mop fell away and the water spilled out. Vernon pulled up short, not slipping but losing speed, and Paul dashed away again.

Corridors branched off up ahead, still a world away with Vernon so close. But one door stood open, and as he dove through he glimpsed Vernon snatching up the mop with fury in his eyes.

Paul stepped past the long shapes of computer banks, which ran almost from wall to wall. From his months of searching the hospital, he knew there was one door in the back of the room—

And it'll probably be locked, too. Paul stopped to slide in behind one row of machines, out of view of the door. Fighting to keep from gasping, he Opened his hearing. Vernon's heavy feet were just pausing at the entrance.

No time to go for the back door now, too risky. But none of this is safe, even grabbing the page means nothing if Vernon dares to go back to print it again! But even that sickening truth felt almost dreamlike against the crushing need to just keep the thing *away* from him.

Vernon tromped into the room. Paul dropped to a crouch and tracked his footsteps. *Anything to keep away from the liars…*

I'm sure they'll pay it all, the liar's voice had said, the night Greg had blackmailed the hospital. Quinn's voice.

Quinn? Paul crouched lower in the cold room, straining to focus on Vernon's footsteps. But now the more he Opened his sense, the more he heard the memory. Only those words.

Head pounding, Paul tried to think. He glanced left and then right around the computer bank, knowing Vernon might appear around either side at any moment, probably swinging that mop at his head. Left or right, if he knew which way his enemy *wasn't* coming, he might manage to circle around… but he could only guess.

We both came in from the left side. So Vernon must have rushed in partly facing right, just as I did, and maybe he'll keep going and come in behind me, too. It was the only thing Paul could think of, so he scurried forward. Even without Opening his hearing, he could keep more quiet than the humming electronics around him. He rounded the corner.

Right in front of Vernon.

Paul couldn't move. Just a pace away, Vernon froze, too, his heavy, rage-twisted features loosening in shock. The pole he clenched in his hand didn't stir… but Paul could feel his own muscles start to move again…

Paul turned and ducked back behind the computer bank, then started across the room, but something *smashed* into his arm, knocking him to one knee an instant before the white-hot pain flared.

Move, have to move… Paul scrambled up and lurched forward. He could hear Vernon behind him somewhere, through the pain, which made him throw himself forward faster. As the far end of the computer bank loomed, he reached across with his good hand to grab the corner and half swung, half slid his way around it, somehow keeping on his feet. As he did he caught one glimpse of Vernon struggling to manage the mop's length as he charged between the banks.

Paul turned for the entrance, but new waves of pain slashed through him, slowing him down…

He staggered out of the room, right into the midst of several maintenance workers—too many, pressing too close, and all muttering at him in confused outrage. He tried to shoulder past one—but his arm flared pain and crumpled him to the ground.

Choking back tears, he stared up at the ring of angry faces, and at Vernon closing in behind them. The big man had already abandoned the mop and Paul could see him forcing the rage from his face, trying to think of a way to deal with the onlookers.

All he has to say is "stolen records" and then they'll be searching me…

One weapon left. Paul Opened his sense of touch just enough to hold his throat steady enough to calm his voice and draw some of his attention from the pain in his arm, and he looked right at his enemy.

"Vernon? With Councilwoman Erin Bennet?"

Paul tried to sound a little smug, to squeeze something into his tone that hinted he knew Vernon, knew about Bennet's affair, knew a dozen more damaging secrets he could spill in a moment. He tried to keep his face neutral, but he stared straight into Vernon's dark brown eyes. *How much do you want to risk?*

Vernon coughed, then coughed again as if he couldn't breathe. Then he said, "Yes, that's me."

The oldest of the men turned from Paul to Vernon. "And? Why were you guys running through here, you maniac!"

"I… we…" For one long moment, Vernon looked from one worker to another and then back to Paul. Suddenly he said "You, you dropped something."

"What?" Paul said, caught off-guard. He had only spoken out of surprise, but it came out as a question.

"Well… this."

Paul wanted to laugh out loud, realizing that the moment Vernon had let those first words out of his mouth, he'd left himself no choice. The big man slowly reached into his suit coat and brought out the rolled up shape of the rest of Greg's file.

The foreman barely gave it a glance, probably not recognizing it as one of the hospital's own. Instead, he snapped, "You say *you* dropped some paper, and *you* found it, and because of that you had to go tearing right through our repair job—"

"Sorry," Paul said, trying to hide the pain as he pulled himself upright. "Just like the old cliché, I guess. He yelled, I panicked, and we just kept going." With his good arm, he reached out for the folder.

Through gritted teeth, Vernon said, "Sorry," and let the file go.

"It's alright. Really. And I'm so sorry about the trouble, to all of you. Was anything broken?"

"No…" The work crew kept staring, from Paul to Vernon and back again. The story was absurd, and they had to see both Paul's pain and Vernon's frustration… but with both sides insisting on the story, what could they do?

Paul added, "So, I'm guessing Ms. Bennet is waiting for you?"

"Right." Vernon took a long moment, moving his eyes over Paul's face to show he was memorizing every line. "I'm sure we'll talk again, Mr.…"

Several aliases swam in Paul's mind, ranging from ordinary to insulting. But he didn't need to play games now, and his arm *hurt*. "I'm sure we will, Vernon."

orraine had to be warned, before Vernon thought of some new, more dangerous way to strike at Greg. But still, instead of going straight to her, Paul took the subway back toward the Side Alley.

At least the ride gave him time to test his injured left arm, confirming that the bone wasn't broken and the muscles weren't torn, though Opening to the pain to chart the damage almost made him pass out in his seat. And even though his power now worked better than it had in the hospital, he still couldn't Open without hearing some echo of Quinn's *I'm sure they'll pay it all.*

But that wasn't the only thing that haunted him. By the time he reached his room, he wondered: danger or not, could he really walk up to Lorraine again knowing she could see *in his thoughts* how he'd been living? He had two years' worth of petty enemies, any one of which might want his head or worse if there was a single soul who could let them know—

Still, once he actually laid eyes on the growing purple bruising of his arm, he knew he had no choice. She had to be warned about the man who'd done this, and Paul couldn't watch for Vernon while trying to keep out of her sight, too. And in the end, she was still Lorraine. *I have to trust her. She's just struggling to save her home.*

Paul tied one of his shirts into a sling for his arm and headed straight out again, before he lost his nerve or his strength.

The sun had long since set by the time he reached their house. He could see both Lorraine's Toyota and a blue BMW in the driveway now, and pictured himself pounding on the door and confronting both of them about what Greg's affair had gotten them into. But it was Lorraine's marriage, her choice how to deal with it, now that it had turned so dangerous.

Paul watched from up the street, seeing her pass by the windows now and again, cleaning up from their dinner. Did it worry her, knowing he might be watching them this way? Was that a little like his own uneasiness about her new power?

Well, if she could hear thoughts…

He started forward, moving at a slow stroll past the house, and concentrated. *Lorraine, Lorraine, look outside, we need to talk.* He made the thoughts scream in his head and tried to fling them out toward her.

Nothing. He walked on to the end of the block, even lingered there by pretending to tie his shoe, but the door never opened. *Sensing minds seems to have limits, too,* he thought with some relief.

Instead, he waited until she'd put Greg to bed, then moved up to the door when she passed near it to knock softly. And for some reason, while she was undoing the locks, he slid his sling off and hid it in a pocket.

"I could barely get Greg to sleep or even to take his pills," she whispered as she waved him to follow her to the kitchen. "I had to take away the phone I'd smuggled him, and of course, he has to see *all* his clients tomorrow. At least, if we can make time, I'll be able to make him a real dinner."

She turned back to the cookbook she'd set out on the counter. Paul moved next to her, noting that the phone she'd mentioned sat beside the recipe. She began measuring one of a row of spices into a bowl.

Now, while she has her eyes off me—Paul forced out the whisper "So you read Greg's mind."

Her hands froze, but she didn't look up. "What? You knew?"

"You take a kind of deep breath when you focus," he said. As she started to turn, he hissed, "And don't say that's intruding, *I'm* the one standing two feet away from a telepath!"

Stupid, stupid… but at least it's out in the open now.

He saw a mix of expressions flash across her face: shock and what looked like guilt, tangled with frustration. Then she turned away and sighed.

"If it matters, I couldn't even make out much. There was only a sudden nervousness when he saw the Councilwoman. And I *never* want to read him again," she added firmly.

"How did you do it?" Paul had to ask. "I've never been able to Open to thoughts, not in two years."

For a moment, she didn't answer. Then, "I just concentrated. Maybe it helped that I know Greg so well. But it's so wrong that I ever tried it; he's my *husband.* Trust or no trust, to go right into his mind—" She turned back to the spice bowl and started measuring again.

"But—" Paul stopped; this was no time to argue about methods. He took a moment to check Greg's breathing, still sound asleep upstairs, and said "Well, you were right. Bennet's big aide Vernon was probably the one who broke in here, unless this thing goes a lot deeper than most of them do. I caught him trying to steal this." And he pulled out the file from his coat.

"What?" Lorraine took the folder but only stared at it.

"It's all about the last page. Greg's blood work shows he was slightly drunk when he crashed. We can hope Vernon doesn't risk going back for another copy."

Lorraine still stared at it and then looked up at him. "Paul, what did you do? Why are they after us?"

"I'm not sure…" At least, the only clue he really had was how Bennet had pronounced two words. But with Vernon on the rampage now, Lorraine needed the truth, and Paul made himself look right into her blue eyes. "I think Greg was having an affair with her."

"Oh."

"My guess is," Paul rushed on, "Vernon was looking for some kind of leverage to be sure Greg kept it quiet—"

He stopped then as Lorraine turned away, and he caught a glimmer that might have been a tear in her eye.

"So it's true." She sounded almost normal as she started pouring another spice. "My mother would have said it served me right for prying at all. Of course, she'd just mean listening in on the phone—"

Suddenly, she snatched up the spice bowl and smashed it down on the cell phone she'd taken from Greg. The phone squirted across the counter, ricocheting off one wall, another, before spinning away to settle on the floor just beside the fridge.

Lorraine turned back and began brushing spilled herbs into the sink.

Not sure what to say, Paul Opened his hearing and found Greg was still asleep. He looked along the floor for any loose shards of the bowl, then knelt to pick up the cell. As he did, his left arm shifted, and he grunted.

"What was that?" Lorraine was watching him.

Paul rubbed his arm as he stood. "I told you Vernon was dangerous."

"No, you *didn't* tell me. But there's one good thing," she added.

Paul had to smile a little. "Good? What's that?"

"We just got these for pain." And she reached down the counter and picked up a bottle of pills.

Me, lying drugged out for a few hours? "Oh no. Keep them."

Lorraine crossed her arms and gave him a long look. "You're his brother, alright."

Does she have to put it that way? "No, I'm a person who can Open my senses, and tell the damage to my arm isn't that bad, and I can tell what treatments would do the most good. And I can also focus on anything that *isn't* hurt, to help numb the pain." *Or at least numb it a little, if I concentrate every second...* "The danger," he added, "is Vernon and Bennet. We need to watch them."

"'Watch them.' Right, just like that." Lorraine's eyes narrowed. "Paul, you said you don't steal. And I always thought you were part of exposing Greg's cover-up for the hospital—"

"I was just exposing what the hospital did. I don't know who dragged Dad and Greg into it." *But with my new memories, how sure can I be now?*

"Of course you aren't a thief, I should have known a thief could afford better clothes," and she smiled slightly as if his threadbare coat meant something more than that. "You can use your power to overhear secrets, and you've learned other ways, too. And you've been willing to fight for us—"

"You're family," Paul broke in. "I'm not some kind of hero, I can only think I have this power because... well, because I'm meant to have it."

He sighed, looking at the floor.

"I'm trying to undo some of the lies out there—not every injustice in the city, I only take a closer look at the businesses and politicians. I do what I can without taking real risks—and even if I get the story wrong, I walk away and hope I've stirred up enough truth to help expose the liars. I keep telling myself that never doing the same thing twice is better than any chance *at all* that somebody dangerous will figure out that there's someone who can do what I do and... try to control me. Or drag Greg and all of you into danger… but here you are anyway."

Paul stopped, out of breath… almost it seemed like he *couldn't* breathe after saying all that. He kept his eyes on the floor.

"Here we are," Lorraine repeated. "And here you are trying to make it all right. Believe me, I appreciate—"

"One other thing," Paul cut in, looking up. "I remembered something else from the night I found the power: Arthur Quinn was there."

"Quinn?"

"Yeah. I thought he had an old grudge. But he was there, saying something about your mentor—" *and when did I remember it was about Curtis?* "—and he said, 'I'm sure they'll pay it all.' And all this came back to me right while I was almost letting Vernon kill me because… I just couldn't stand having someone embarrass the family again."

He clamped his mouth shut then, not believing he'd blurted the whole thing out. Even when he'd been trying not to give away the wilder details of things, or how reckless it had made him, he hadn't been able to stop.

"Anyway, Vernon is dangerous. He's determined, he can be violent, and I guess he doesn't think before he acts. His boss, Bennet, may be even worse—I'm not sure yet. But Greg has to be warned."

"I know," Lorraine said. "But he cheated on me…"

"So you want…" He didn't know what to say.

Lorraine closed her eyes. "I don't want to think about that now. And if I told him now, I'd probably end up saying that I read it in his mind, and then I can *never* take back how he'll always know I might be looking at his secrets, his fears… No wonder you hide what you do," she added.

Paul frowned, thinking. "So, you don't want to tell him much."

She shook her head.

"Well, there's another way."

* * *

Worn out, Paul was glad to slip unnoticed up to his room again. His arm hurt worse than ever, and he already regretted not getting a few of Greg's pills.

He lay down, starting to focus his hearing around the street and hoping to pull far enough away from himself to sleep. Even that was harder with Quinn's voice still echoing in his memory whenever he Opened.

Still, one thought made him grin coldly. Tomorrow, his cheating brother would go to his new rented car and see the big note on the windshield: *"We will keep Erin Bennet and her aide Vernon from breaking in again, if you don't work for Animal Alliance."*

* * *

Bennet's office was easy. The Councilwoman had managed to get her own little building, so Paul only had to slip in behind it to listen around the whole place. Standing next to the back door helped keep him warmer, too.

He couldn't hear Vernon anywhere, which left him less worried for his own safety but wondering what the aide might be out doing. But Bennet was already in, asking her other staff for some zoning reports.

The longer Paul listened, the more she sounded like the honest official he'd heard about, and her other aides seemed harmless enough. Paul swept his hearing out, but then pulled it back before he could be drawn in, feeling like a fisherman who had to catch his breath between each cast of the line.

And yet Quinn's words—*I'm sure they'll pay it all*—seemed to echo a little more strongly with every new probe. Now he couldn't keep from wondering: *Was the loan shark really involved then, or now? Am I wasting my time just observing Vernon's boss?*

When Vernon's heavy tread marched in, Paul almost missed it, but he crouched back out of sight and listened to the burly aide make his way to Bennet.

"Are the snowplows ready?" she asked.

"You were right, they needed a reminder."

And they moved on through more city work, tracking first energy budgets, then sanitation. Even away from the rest in her office, the most underhanded thing either did was for Bennet to tell Vernon her concerns about union pressure on one hotel and then let him be the one to raise those objections when they spoke with the union leader. *So she lets Vernon be the bad guy when she needs to…*

"Hi, can I help you?" A young woman had stepped around behind the building, one of the aides he'd heard inside.

Careless, careless! What if Vernon had caught me back here? "Just keeping warm," Paul said, rubbing his hands together by the door.

"Sure. Can I get you a cup of coffee? Or a list of shelters—"

"Save your campaigning, lady. I already know I'm voting for the other guy!" and Paul stormed off down the street, just glad to get away before Vernon noticed.

Stupid! I should have found reasons to sit in one of the shops on either side, even with Quinn's echo cutting into my power's range. For now, he waited for the woman to leave and then he headed back to the same spot, determined to be more alert this time. Or was there even any point to staying now? If Vernon wasn't on the move, he might use this time to contact Sarah—

Bennet was saying, "You realize the lab is preparing to sue you."

It's another lab. Probably. He heard Bennet pause in what had to be listening on the phone, but as he strained to hear, the memory of Quinn's *I'm sure they'll pay it all* seemed to swallow most of the other end.

"…no proof. And if…" the other side was saying.

"And what is it they advise?" she said.

"… want… ask him yourself?"

"I think," she said slowly, "that I should talk with you and Mr. Schuman before this gets worse."

As she hung up, Paul could only think, *It can't be! I told Greg* not *to…*

"I'm going out."

"Out where, ma'am?" Vernon's voice cut in.

She hesitated a moment, then said, "I'm trying to talk some sense into Animal Alliance and their new publicist. Greg Schuman."

When Vernon answered, his voice had no expression. "Is that a good idea?"

"Accusations, flyers, lawsuits, and now they've got a publicist egging them on? I think this is our last chance to stop this from getting much worse."

"Then I'd better come with you. After you look at these—"

Paul didn't wait for her answer, just ran for where he'd left his bike, still struggling to believe it. *Because of* course *Greg would take one look at the "no Alliance" note I left for him and do just the opposite.*

*   *   *

How long? How long could Vernon's other business delay him and Bennet, before they drove out? The thought lashed Paul as he pumped the bike pedals, straining to keep his balance without leaning too much weight on his aching arm. The least he could do was get there in time.

This is all my fault, now more than ever, Paul thought every time he squeezed the bike between traffic and parked cars. Greg would have been just looking for clients, he'd barely have glanced much longer at a losing position like Animal Alliance… *but I just* had *to dare him.* And now Paul's own chance to fix his last mistake, to vindicate Sarah, was under attack by the only other people he had to protect. Worse than the hospital cover-up, this time it *would* be Paul linking the Schuman name to the schemers—if he dared expose them at all.

A big, black shape swept by, just one more car to batter Paul with its wash of air—except this time he glimpsed Bennet in the passenger seat. The car never slowed down. *Even Vernon doesn't look at bicyclists' faces as he passes them.* Paul pedaled harder, knowing that it might be the last good luck he'd have.

Finally, gasping and feeling like his arm was on fire, he reached the Animal Alliance mansion. Bennet's car waited in the driveway, alongside one or two others—and the very BMW on which Paul had placed his note to Greg. He stumbled around toward the back of the building, already far too familiar with the hedgerows, and Opened his hearing.

"…aren't supporting you either." That was Erin Bennet's voice, the cool, reasonable tone he'd been hearing all morning. "The Alliance doesn't have many friends left. So I have to ask, do you really think you're helping your cause by making so much out of one incident?"

"In other words, we're doing what nobody else could do," and Greg's smug *we* made Paul's teeth clench, as he heard another voice mutter agreement, then another. Greg went on, "And we're winning. People can see the face of animal experimentation all over the city."

"Whether or not the experiments ever happened," Bennet replied.

"They did. It's there on the flyer, in front of the eyes of everyone who never thought about these things before. There are thousands of flyers, Councilwoman, each seen by dozens of people—no matter how fast you wish they'd been torn down. Imagine us holding a rally right now—or after another action or two that *really* keeps the image in their minds."

One of the real activists added, "Yeah! And how many votes is that?"

Paul could picture his brother waving around their precious fake photo as if he'd shot it himself. *It's just like Greg. My note might have made him suspicious of Bennet, but what really drove him was a chance to make himself right.*

"Votes? That sounded like a threat," Vernon snapped.

Still calm, Bennet said, "Let me ask you, have you really looked at the reports about your 'evidence,' and its authenticity? Are you aware that there's a police detective doing just that?"

And it was James Koenig's voice that replied, "The people seem to think it's good enough. And no, none of us will disclose exactly how we got it."

Koenig had always been quiet. *But now he's pumped up enough to almost brag about his fraud…*

Paul finally reached the back door and dug out his keys. Even with the perfect key for a range of Ames locks, he couldn't seem to focus his touch enough to position it just right. And with his hearing normal, the voices inside were just loud enough to carry the growing tension.

At last the lock turned and Paul peeked into the room they'd used as a kitchen. He Opened his hearing again.

"Greg, what does Ian say about committing the firm to this?"

Wrong thing to ask my brother, Councilor.

With just a hint of frost, Greg replied "The firm depends on proving we can bring clients what they want. This is an opportunity to deliver that."

Like your success in pressuring St. Central? And when this crashes too…

"It's an opportunity to endanger both your reputation and Animal Alliance's cause."

"Not if we win."

He is so, so stubborn—and I'm the one who'd pushed him...

Everyone was clustered in the front room. Paul peeked out the kitchen doorway and across the room between them. Through the opposite doorway, he could see Bennet and the backs of Greg and his supporters.

He heard the councilwoman say, more quietly, "Is this really the kind of gamble the firm wants to take? Against so much opposition? Please, think." Paul heard the smallest catch in her voice, but ordinary ears wouldn't have noticed any sign that these two had been lovers.

Vernon added, "That's good advice, Mr. Schuman."

Paul saw his brother draw himself up straighter. "Councilwoman, you've come in here speaking for the industry side of things, and yet you haven't looked at how hard these people have had to struggle to be heard until now."

"I'm always willing to listen."

One of the activists said, "Just a minute, I've got..." When Paul heard him start toward the room between them, he ducked back behind the kitchen door jamb.

Bennet might have to listen, but Paul knew Greg wouldn't. His brother sounded almost ready to start a riot rather than back down. *But he's family. I can't...*

The footsteps drew away again, and Paul glanced out to the two rooms. In the farther one, Greg's clients were beginning the story of the animal rights movement. In the closer one, he could see papers and maps, as if the activists had been meeting there before Bennet arrived.

Koenig's laptop lay on a chair, closed and alone.

Paul stared at it, and then ducked back. Nobody was looking. Koenig had proven he wouldn't get careless with those files that might be the only evidence of his fraud—but Paul could find people who knew how to unlock the laptop, even without passwords. *Then I'll give the thing back to Koenig.*

But Dad and Greg, they're part of this again and I can't…

"And all that was without a rich supporter," Greg said. "Of course now…"

As Greg spoke, he moved off from the doorway, and while his voice drew their eyes away, Paul slipped into the room between them and sidestepped out of their view. As he grabbed the computer, his eyes fell on something else familiar: a briefcase with the initials GS, a case large enough to…

I can't! I can't shame them again.

But I didn't before—and this is my *choice!* Savagely, he stuffed the laptop into Greg's case, leaving the case just open enough for Koenig to spot the laptop within once he saw it missing, and darted back to the kitchen. *That* should break up their new partnership a lot faster than trying to crack passwords…

"Can I see you for a moment?" Vernon asked just then.

Something cold in his voice made Paul shiver… and remember who the real enemy was. *What am I doing, trying to destroy Greg now? Whoever did it before, I can't want this!*

"What is it?" Greg sounded guarded, but he still stepped into the middle room with Vernon.

Paul crouched behind the kitchen doorway, holding his breath. Whatever Vernon wanted, he couldn't do much right next to witnesses.

But, why didn't he speak? Both of them were silent; they had to be standing still as angry statues.

Then, "Just what do you want with him?" Paul heard Koenig walk in to join the two.

The missing laptop… Koenig, and Vernon, and then Bennet, all there ready to walk further into the room and see Greg "stealing" it…

Paul could only crush himself harder against the wood as his thoughts slowed to a helpless crawl.

But they never moved toward it, never saw it. Vernon simply said, "Just thinking how sneaks look alike."

Greg didn't answer. *He didn't say a thing.*

Then one lighter footstep entered the room, and Councilwoman Bennet said, "Vernon. I have to stay here a little longer, but I need you back at the office."

"Yes, ma'am."

Vernon sounded as close to calm as he had before. *He calls her "ma'am" even though she's barely older than he is.* But Paul could hear a hint of the heavier tromp to his footsteps as he started away, the same angry sound he'd made in the hospital.

Paul let out a slow breath as the others headed back as well, but he had no time to waste. The moment he heard them enter the outer room, he slipped forward and returned the laptop to Koenig's chair, then ducked back before they had time to get comfortable and their heads might turn around again. *At least I can still guess when people aren't looking.*

Then he flung his hearing out past all the rooms, toward the driveway, just in time to hear Vernon's car roar off… up the road to the left.

If that's my only clue… He slipped outside and moved for his bike, breaking into a run as soon as he dared. He pictured the city streets, trying to match Vernon's possible targets with the direction he'd driven off. He was driving away from the hospital, and he'd already searched Greg and Lorraine's house.

I just might have time.

The ache in his lungs didn't matter now, and the pain of keeping his left arm on the handlebar only reminded him of who had caused it and what he might do again. But one thought did break through: *all Vernon saw was Greg, so did "sneaks look alike" mean he'd recognized the resemblance to me?*

Vernon's car stood just a block from the office building, and Paul hoped wildly that it had slowed him down a few minutes to get that parking space right on the Mile. Paul dropped his bike on the pavement and rushed into the building.

He reached for the elevator button but then snatched his hand back. *Getting into a tiny room, when Vernon might be anywhere, near other people who might remember me?* Groaning with what little breath his pedaling had left him, he staggered for the door and hauled himself up the four flights.

At last, he sagged in the stairwell against the fire door and Opened his hearing, straining to hear past his own gasping breath. The Schuman and Son office lay just up the corridor beyond.

Thump, thump... Paul froze as the angry tread stomped by and past his door. Paul had to lean out around the door for a look at Vernon's back to be sure it was him. *Why would he still be outside the office, when he must have gotten here so much sooner?* Paul ducked back behind the door, fearing whatever dirty work Vernon had had in mind was long since completed.

Only when he heard Vernon march up past the bend and then start back did he realize that the man was only pacing back and forth, trying to plan his attack. Paul listened as one woman swerved to give him a wide berth. He wondered how long a floor full of witnesses would hold Vernon back—or if they'd just fuel his rage past caring.

The police. I could call the police and report him for suspicious lurking, to chase him off and get some record of him... but would that make him think twice, or just make him hit back harder? And with Councilwoman Bennet on his side, he could laugh off petty accusations...

"See you later, then," Lorraine said as she stepped into the corridor. For one moment, she and Vernon walked directly toward each other—

Then they passed, neither one reacting and neither admitting they recognized the other. Vernon paced on down to the other end of the hall, and as he turned the corner, Paul stepped out and motioned to Lorraine. She started but smoothly moved to join him in the stairwell.

As the door closed behind them, she said softly, "Listen, if your 'getting the story wrong' meant Sarah Gomez, and you'd like to do more than apologize to her—"

"Shhh," Paul said belatedly. Then he had to add, "And stop reading my mind."

"Don't joke about that!" she snapped.

"Quiet! That's Vernon!"

She made a small gasp but fell silent as he turned back to the closed door and the sounds beyond it. Vernon was still pacing, heading back now, walking away from the office and them again.

Far away, he heard Lorraine whisper, "Anything?"

Paul held up a finger to make her wait a moment, then let his connection fade. "Hasn't made his move yet," he said.

"Paul, I *don't* spy on your thoughts. And I think you deserve something good in your life; I wanted to say that while I had the chance."

He raised his finger again and switched back to Vernon, still pacing…

While she has the chance? He looked back. "What did you say?"

She was breathing slowly, some of the steadying breaths she used to gather her power. "We want to know what he's thinking, don't we?" and she moved for the door.

Paul stepped in front of her. "No! He almost killed me, remember?"

"But I'm the one who's supposed to be here. He won't…"

The fire alarm slashed through her words. Paul clutched his head, more from shock than pain as it shrilled on, and he saw Lorraine looking around, confused.

Then, as he heard the first rumble of people stirring on the floor, his brain remembered where they stood. "Here it comes," he said, and he gave Lorraine a firm nudge toward the stairs downward while he scrambled up and around to the next floor.

For a few seconds more, the people were still out in the halls; he could track Lorraine starting down the stairs, and one trotting sound in the hall that would be Vernon putting some distance between himself and the alarm he'd pulled.

Then the deluge began. Some arguing, a few shouting, almost everyone at least moving a bit faster and louder than a simple crowd, a whole building's worth of people swept toward the stairs with the alarm. Sounds flooded in as doors opened above and below Paul, and he gripped the handrail to let everyone move past. So many sounds, echoing in the concrete walls of the stairwell…

Opening was useless. Paul could only wait until the flow began to thin out and then peek down at the people leaving his floor—including the ones who'd know him—until he could probe again and be sure the Schuman office suite was silent.

Except for one figure, one big man. *How impulsive is Vernon? Is he grabbing an armful of papers he hopes are damaging, or…*

Paul took the steps in a jump and flung open the stairwell door. As he did, he heard feet running up behind him and turned.

"What now?" Lorraine whispered harshly over the alarm.

And on below her, was that someone else coming back? "Stay here!" Paul hissed as he Opened to the sounds beyond the office door.

Metal clanged on metal and squealed. *At least Vernon isn't setting actual fires…*

Paul extended his hearing down then. There was still a floor left before the other person reached them… but that steady, driven pace… *Is that Dad, about to walk in on…*

Lorraine pushed past and dashed for the office.

For an instant Paul could only stare. And she ran full speed, in the moment it took him to head after her she was reaching the door, throwing it wide.

Vernon turned toward her, looking up from the file cabinet he'd sunk the crowbar into. Lorraine raised her arm.

"Gotcha!" And the cell phone in her hand clicked.

Vernon *roared,* not a word but a sound of pure rage, and lunged away from the cabinet, bringing the crowbar up. Lorraine stumbled backward and Paul saw her eyes go wide with fear, with *shock* that their enemy would simply—

Paul dove in front of him, fists up. As Vernon raised the crowbar, Paul yelled, "Two seconds, that's all it takes!"

Somehow, the warning made Vernon freeze. "Huh?"

"That's all it takes to send your picture to the news." *If she has them on speed dial, but I can't hesitate—*

Paul looked right into Vernon's furious eyes and added, "And someone else out there—"

And then, coat collar pulled high up to screen his face, Vernon dashed past them and down the corridor.

Paul let out one long breath of relief. Then he started to bring up his own coat the same way as he turned for the door.

Where his father stood.

6

"**P**aul??"

Ian Schuman barely got the word out. He wheezed it like a choking man, almost lost in the clang of the fire alarm, but his eyes blazed as they flicked over Paul.

Then he got his breath.

"What are you—*you're* the one breaking in, I never thought—why would you—why, even now, wasn't showing how we covered up that hospital *enough* for—"

"I didn't—" Paul clenched his eyes shut for a moment. *I couldn't have, how can he—* "Can't you see *anything*??"

The words came out a yell, and his father flinched back a step. As he did, one clear thought clicked into Paul's mind.

He added, "At least be grateful Lorraine was here."

"Lorraine?" His father blinked in surprise, and then turned to look past him to where she stood.

And now his father's eyes, those *eyes* were off him—in an instant Paul found himself diving forward, with all the strength he had left and no thought except to get away. He ran through the door and bolted down the stairwell…

On a landing, he sagged to the floor, drained. But still, habit or sheer masochism made him Open his hearing for more.

"…was Paul, Greg! I just saw *Paul* breaking into the office!" his father was saying.

Paul strained harder, and this time the voice coming through the phone was all too clear.

"Dammit, I hoped I was wrong. Dad, I got this note. It said Erin Bennet and her aide needed 'stopping' and to avoid Animal Alliance."

Lorraine added, "But that was Bennet's aide breaking in. And Paul stopped him."

"Lor? Are you alright—"

"She's fine," Paul's father cut in. "She saw the man moving in, I saw her going back after him, he ran off, and Paul did, too. Everything's… well, nobody's hurt."

For a long moment, none of them spoke as they savored a few slow, relieved breaths.

Then Paul's father went on "What note? You didn't tell me? And *that's* why you rushed out to sign with Animal Alliance?"

"Dad, I don't know what Bennet's up to. And I *really* don't know what Paul's doing, but if it's the same tricks as before, we can't let him destroy the Alliance."

"I suppose not. Certainly not after you've committed us to winning their fight," he added darkly. "How soon can you get back here?"

I didn't put your damn fax out there! Why don't you ask Quinn? Paul thumped his fist down on the stairwell. The metal echoed hollowly, almost lost under the clamor of the alarm. On the lower floors, he could hear the voices of the authorities finally gathering below.

Finally? It's only been a couple of minutes…

Paul heaved himself upright and started down the steps. Whatever else had happened, the trap around him still had the same three sides:

Vernon and Bennet, driven off for now… Quinn and the hospital and his powers, a haunted memory from years ago… and Koenig's frame plus the family's support, all against…

*   *   *

"Sarah Gomez?" Paul's hand tightened on the phone.

"Yes?"

"Um. Ms. Gomez…" What could he say?

Voices babbled around him, mostly people heading up the street for the concert. He could hear the same sound through the phone, but they were much louder inside the hall.

"You missed my call at the paper," he said at last. "Do you have a second?"

"Not really." She had to raise her voice to be heard over the crowd, but he thought she put a bit of sympathy into her curt words. "Who is this?"

Through the phone, he heard a woman say, "Come *on*, girl! Tick-tock!"

Paul held his hand over the pay phone mouthpiece, to cut off a bit more of the sound of the street. "I'm sorry that I haven't had any news about the fraud within the Alliance."

"Who *is* this?" she asked again, and now he heard a new tone in her voice.

"You're going to be under some new pressure soon. They've got new friends," Paul said.

He knew his father and Greg would figure out her connection to the case and start telling her she'd been used by him, and how could he explain that to her?

He tried again. "Um, I may have another story for you. I'm not sure yet." Except that Vernon hadn't left his home all afternoon since

Lorraine took her picture of him, and Paul could barely Open at all now; how could he tell Lorraine whether to send that picture in or if Vernon was already beaten—

"Hold on!" Sarah said. He heard her friend start to say something and then that voice growing fainter, as if Sarah were stepping away from her. When she continued, her voice was softer. "First, what you already gave me about LifeLab was amazing; half the materials I didn't dare use, so far. No matter what else, I've wanted to thank you for that all week."

"Well, you're welcome," Paul said weakly. Was the low, intense energy in her voice just her trying to whisper over the crowd, or true enthusiasm?

"And then the story went bad and you promised to help me save my job—and then nothing. Now you say you have a whole new story, but you're not sure?"

"There've been… complications. So many. But I'm trying to get you the truth." Paul sagged against the kiosk, suddenly tired of trying to tell her more than he could. "At least, can you believe I've got no reason to lie to you?"

"Please," she laughed, and it sounded almost warm. "Once I stopped swearing, that's what I came to. I'm sure you wouldn't do all this just to hurt my career—but you might be doing it to ruin Animal Alliance, if their claims are discredited. Or maybe it's the lab you want—or both."

This is not *how I pictured our first conversation*— "So then, why do you think I'm still calling?"

"Either you want to dig them in even deeper, or maybe…" She paused. And somewhere up the street, some scalper called out, "Morning Star, two tickets for—"

"I knew it!" Sarah said. "You're here at the concert, aren't you?"

Paul looked up the street toward the concert hall, half a block away. He Opened his hearing to search for her voice, but the more he strained, the louder Quinn's *I'm sure they'll pay* echoed in his mind.

"Do you want to meet?" she was saying.

"I don't… think that's safe." *Especially for me. If she learns one more thing, I'm not sure I can keep from telling her all the rest.*

"It's part of the game, for me," she said. "And there must be some payoff for you, or you wouldn't be here. Or are you just stalking me?"

"No!" Or maybe he was, the way he struggled to track her before she saw him… But either way, his power was scrambled now, and he knew he couldn't meet her like this. "I'll call you when I have something," and he hung up.

As he did, he saw her step out under the marquee. Really, she was just one more shape in bright party clothes, but the way she stood, her dark hair flying as she looked furtively up and down the street… *beautiful.*

Paul turned and started striding away. Of course, Sarah Gomez could think on her feet—he should have guessed that from her work. But he hadn't expected her to sound so impressed. She'd looked almost eager to find him there. And with his father and Greg blaming him, and Lorraine not able to meet him now, just to hear someone agree with him again…

Three nights ago, I wouldn't have known the difference. He paused and took one more look back.

Sarah was just turning away, going back inside. He waited one second, two, three. Gone.

Paul turned away, walking slowly. She was one more thing stuck in limbo now. He'd still had no luck with James Koenig. They had the picture of Vernon, but he wasn't sure how to use it. And he still had no idea why the memory of Arthur Quinn was blotting out his power, only that his family blamed him for exposing them, back then.

Behind him, the first chords of the concert sounded, faint and half swallowed by the rising roar of the audience. Morning Star, in town at last. This should have been another concert he'd savored from a block away, but with his power in this state…

Always at a distance, right. He'd fought to bring a few truths into the light, so sure it was the only reason the power could have come to him… but that only left him living in third-hand clothes, trying to sell a few pieces of the facts for bread. *Would I have been so quick to pass along Koenig's lies a year ago, when I wasn't worn down by the lies and the hiding?*

He shivered, hugging his coat tighter as the night deepened.

No good. It was time, to either steal a million from some deserving criminal and get a quiet place in the wilderness… *somewhere warm…* or take some real steps to come in out of the cold.

* * *

The shop that was Arthur Quinn's office was in what would be a decent area by day—but at night, the streets were all but empty. Here and there throughout the cold blocks, Paul heard a dog's bark, a shout, and sometimes a siren. The city had worse districts, but many better ones.

Paul stood across the street and studied the building, a simple brick shape of three stories, with Quinn's office on the second floor. An ancient-looking iron fire escape stretched down the side.

A faint breeze made him shiver, reminding him what a drawn-out approach in this cold would cost his body. But with his arm stiff and hurting, and his power weak, this was no time for anything like Vernon's reckless moves.

He Opened his sight to study the building, then his hearing, and the maddening *I'm sure they'll pay it all* swelled in his mind. The endless chant was worse than real sounds because he remembered it was vital—somehow. But why had Quinn been there on that awful night? What had he known about the hospital's tricks? And how had Paul's family been exposed, too… *unless it was me who did that…*

Slowly. He stared harder, seeing the simple alarm wires along the window above and then probing the silence beyond it. Something rustled faintly within, or breathed; he struggled to steady his thoughts. The sound was too light for normal breathing.

Then feet shifted a moment, too many feet, and he heard the clatter of hard toenails on wood. A dog.

"Damn, damn, dammit *all!*" He thumped a frustrated fist on his thigh. Leave it to Quinn to find the only thing around with better senses than Paul at his best. Nothing would stop a trained guard dog from giving the alarm, it wouldn't be like distracting or bypassing a person or disarming a machine, and Paul's skin crawled at the thought of trying to fend off those teeth.

As he stood in the growing cold and tried to remember the few times he'd been willing to go near dogs at all, the building's front door swung open.

A uniformed guard glanced up and down the street. Paul froze, hoping his position was shadowed enough to hide him, and focused his sight. The guard looked youngish, his eyes all too steady as they scanned the street, and his hand was never far from the gun at his belt. After a long moment, he stepped back inside again.

Paul let out a slow sigh, watching his breath freeze in the air. The loan shark's office might claim to be just a furniture shop squeezed into a larger building, but Quinn had made sure the place's watchman was all too competent. *And with that dog, he* will *know I'm there.*

Paul moved across the street, slowly slid the fire escape ladder down, and climbed softly toward the window. Even Opening just a little as he did, he could hear the dog moving a few paces inside. The animal was well aware of him.

Pausing on the ladder, Paul threw his full strength into probing the sounds above… or at least trying to. Quinn's words echoed back through his memory, drowning out most of the room's sounds like storm-tossed waves covering all but the loudest bells on the sea. The dog, the wires on the window, the guard pacing in the corridor…

Instead, he had to guess. The room wouldn't have motion sensors armed, since the dog would set them off; the sensors on the window-frame should mean it wasn't nailed shut, especially if some law required the fire escape to be accessible.

Paul pulled himself up the last few rungs to crouch on the metal landing and peeked in the window.

At least I can still Open my sight to cut through a bit of dimness. A large room spread out before him, with desks and tables for sale here and there, the door out and one other—

And the vicious brown-and-black shape already rushing at the window. Paul only pulled back as the first barks split the night, and tried to slide down the fire escape without banging his arm on the metal.

When he'd reached the ground, he raced away around a corner, and the barking ceased. He could hear the guard pounding into the room, searching briefly as he cursed the dog, and then resuming his patrol.

The guard… I could find a place to jump him, and see if I could wrestle him better than I used to wrestle Greg…

No. This was no time to risk new tactics, and especially not with an injured arm, going up against a guard who could probably fight off two of him.

Paul turned back to where he'd left his bike. The only way to get at Quinn's secrets—and maybe his own—would be with the right tools.

* * *

At least the bus terminal was warm; it felt like the warmest Paul had been all day. And the people walking here and there barely looked at him as he opened the locker.

He took a moment to wonder whether he'd still keep these caches around the city, if he could struggle back to a proper job and a safer way of life. *If I can spy my way to normalcy*, he thought with a smile.

Then he took out the tools he needed: Two empty cardboard boxes. Heavier gloves for the cold night. And a light, folded net he'd scavenged the previous year… he knew at a glance that the net would be no help with the dog, but that wasn't his plan.

On the way back, he paused at a pet shop. The place had no alarms, and the lock opened almost as soon as he sharpened his sense of touch. Since Quinn's dog would be trained never to accept food from a stranger, he simply took the bag of birdseed he'd wanted, plus a spray bottle of cleaner he found in the closet. Then he threw some money on the counter and left quickly, with just the act of stealing anything from some random person leaving a bad taste in his mouth.

As he stepped outside again, something touched his face. Snow was falling.

Memories pressed down on him, crushing thoughts of the last two long winters of shivering nights, with fewer crowds outside to hide in, and always dreading the tracks he left in the harmless white stuff drifting down all over the streets. Knowing winter was closing in made everything worse, somehow. *Couldn't it have waited another two weeks? I know I could settle Animal Alliance's frame in one more week…*

And my family's part in it? and Vernon and Bennet, and Quinn's secrets?

Instead of cursing, he only sighed and climbed on his bike. The first dusting of snow made his tires wobble, but he hoped the streets wouldn't actually be blocked so soon. Half the night was gone, and he had one more stop to make.

* * *

The pigeons *moaned.* It was the only word for their frantic cooing from the cardboard box he'd crammed them into. Even winter had its uses, at least it made the birds desperate enough for food that he could net half a dozen within walking distance of Quinn's building. And as that brick shape came in sight, Paul stopped to pour more seed into the box to quiet the birds again.

He left the cooing box halfway up the block, in the alley behind the buildings, and moved forward to Open and study his target again. Same dog, same window and alarm, and he waited until he could just make out the guard still patrolling inside.

Alright then.

First, he walked under the window and along the alley, back and forth, scuffing his feet around until the still-light layer of snow looked as if a whole gang had marched through it; a clumsy camouflage, but he could hope the guard wouldn't look too closely. And with any luck, this would be finished before enough snow fell over those to make his later tracks clear.

Then, he hefted the biggest discarded bottle he'd been able to find, and flung it straight through Quinn's window.

An alarm shrilled and the dog exploded into barking, both sounds ringing down the streets through the window's broken pane. The dog fell silent again, almost at once… too well-trained to keep going when nothing more was happening.

When the alarm cut off and Paul could hear the guard moving inside again, he darted up the block with the box of pigeons. Then he waited in the cold until the guard had made his sweep around the building and settled back inside. *I thought some of those wires were in case someone broke the window. But that's all I need for now.*

He poured another helping of seed into his cardboard pigeon-coop and began easing the four-way overlap of the top flaps open. With all the care he could manage, he parted them just enough to reach both hands in—wishing he could use his thicker winter gloves when they pecked at him—and pulled out one struggling bird before closing the top again. He placed that pigeon in his second, smaller box, and carried it under his arm to the fire escape and up.

The dog stood right under the window, a brown and black brute that looked like a Doberman but seemed a bit heavier than most. It growled but didn't bark yet, and for a moment Paul wondered if his plan would work.

Then he raised the box up to the high window-pane he'd smashed, and popped the pigeon through the hole.

The dog went mad. The bird beat its wings to catch itself in the air and fluttered around the room with the dog chasing it and barking in a frenzy. The animals hopped from one desk to another as the pigeon circled but couldn't turn tightly enough to stay airborne within the walls…

Paul slid back down to the alley and ducked around the corner. He strained his hearing to focus past the barking and the echo of his memory, praying that the trick would work.

Not that he had any trouble hearing the guard's "What in *hell*…?" Paul could imagine him watching as the dog and bird chased around the room. A moment later, the barking ceased and Paul caught one wild flutter of the pigeon. It was outside again, having finally squeezed back out the broken window.

Paul followed the guard's cursing all the way to the window and heard it grow louder still the longer he stood there. When he stomped away again, Paul could only wait in the cold, and found himself envying the other pigeons that could huddle together in his box for warmth. But the guard didn't come back to cover the window; the top pane he'd smashed would be difficult to block, as Paul had hoped.

Carefully, Paul pulled out another bird from the box, trying not to think of the one slip of his hand that might let the struggling flock burst free and ruin his whole night's work. Again, he sent the bird inside and then dropped back out of view as the dog's barking split the night. When he heard the guard enter again, he grinned wickedly; since the window was broken, was it so odd that birds would try to get to the warm room inside?

Then he heard a loud metallic *cough* sound, a "Damn!" and then one more cough, and then the dog hushed. As the footsteps moved away, Paul realized what the guard had done.

He'd shot the pigeon. He'd blown it apart so they could get back to work, and he'd done it using an illegal silencer and an ominously good aim.

Paul crouched down in the dark, chilled through with a cold deeper than the winter. He'd always maneuvered far away from armed guards, targeting secrets or at least strategies that kept him away from real physical danger. He chose his own cases, sometimes selecting unsavory types—but he'd never dared go up against a real criminal like this loan shark. Arthur Quinn seemed more dangerous by the hour.

Quinn's *They'll pay it all* echoed louder than ever in his mind, and Paul wondered how many ways Quinn made his enemies "pay."

Paul shook his head, trying to clear it. Dangerous or not, Quinn's words were all he knew about that night and whatever memory was blocking his power. *And if Quinn was part of that night, maybe I've always had to stop him.*

The next pigeon seemed to tremble a bit more than the others when he pulled it from the box. Paul tried to hold onto his city-bred contempt for the "winged rats," how there were always more of them and more pigeon droppings everywhere they flocked. But the more the bird thrashed in his hands, the harder it was to keep his touch from Opening to feel its panicked heartbeat.

This pigeon was luckier than the last; the guard shot once, then swore and walked away, letting the dog chase it out the window again.

For the pigeon after that, the guard didn't come at all. *Finally.*

Carefully watching the alley's corners and windows for observers, Paul took his last bird and other tools up the fire escape. The dog stood just behind the glass with its teeth bared, waiting.

But this time, Paul peered at the window, looking from the hole at the top on down to the latch and then to the tiny, hidden sensor along the jamb inside. Even while Opening sight, he could barely make out its wires there along the side of the frame, against its mate on the window itself. He unwrapped a sliver of metal from his pocket, his gloved fingers careful of the sharp edge on one side.

He stared harder at the tiny switch, struggling to push back the shadows that pooled around the wires. From the design, they should be about *there* and *there*, and he'd done this many times before. But this time...

He Opened to listen again for the guard, took a deep breath, and strained past the thunder of *I'm sure they'll pay it all.*

They won't pay.

Paul started, looking around the alley below. But nothing had stirred except the drifting snow; the thought was another memory. *They won't pay,* Quinn had said that night. Paul knew it now. *They won't pay.*

But he must have said "They'll pay!" Which one was it?

He gritted his teeth. Gripping the metal piece as firmly as he could through the glove, he Opened to the shape in the shadows along the window, fighting to ignore the two memories so he could just *see* the wires, *know* the distance…

In one move, he reached down through the broken pane to stab the metal's edge into the wood below, pressing its length between the sensors at just the proper angle. Nothing snapped, no alarm blared… and he yanked his hand back up as the dog snapped at him.

The metal stayed in place. He tried to Open his hearing to follow if the electrical path had changed, but all he heard were Quinn's words and the dog's thwarted growls.

Time to find out.

The dog watched his every motion now, so he took the last pigeon from his box and slid it through the hole. The dog barked as the bird fluttered by, but this time, it turned right back to the window as Paul reached in again to flip the latch.

He pulled his hand back in time, but the dog kept barking, and Paul could only hope the guard was still sick of false alarms. *And that the other alarm here…*

The window slid up, just three inches for now. No bells rang, but the dog snarled and snapped just beyond that gap.

And Paul raised the pet store's spray bottle and squirted cleaning fluid into its face.

The dog yelped and pulled back, giving Paul a moment to fling the window up. As the dog started toward him again, he gave it another spray, then caught up the bird net and flung it over the beast.

Paul grabbed the bottle again and leaped through, into the room.

A few desks and cabinets stretched around him in the dim light. He turned back to see the dog already shaking off the thin net, as expected. He stepped back and pumped the spray as the dog charged—but it squirted once and then the trigger clicked in without pumping any liquid. He back-pedaled and pumped more slowly, but now the spray only made the dog flinch back a moment.

The inner door's this way—Paul took a step, and his hip bashed the edge of a desk. The dog lunged.

He spun around the desk and threw himself at the door. For one frozen moment, he wondered if he'd ever heard the guard open it. *What if it's locked?* Then he seized the handle and wrenched it open, which sent a spasm through his injured arm.

As he stepped through, the dog came up behind him. Paul ducked sideways and gave the spray bottle trigger one hard squeeze. The spray drove the dog back only a step, and Paul pumped wildly, felt the trigger catch on nothing—He smashed the bottle into the animal's head, knocked the dog away, then leapt back out through the door and slammed it shut.

Gasping for breath, he listened to the dog's muted barking for a moment. The spray bottle had split open in his hand, and he set the its remains quietly on the floor.

Paul looked past the desks to the office's little file cabinet and then marched back to slide the window shut and gather up the net. That left him in the space between the alarms, with the dog trapped, and the guard tired of checking out all these noises.

"Alright, what *now?*" the guard growled, as the outer door's lock clicked open. Paul dropped flat, behind a desk just as the light came on.

He heard the guard march in as the dog in the side room kept barking and scrabbling at the door. He tried to Open his hearing to track the guard better, but then broke off as the memories of Quinn's voice almost deafened him. Somewhere up near the ceiling, he heard the pigeon still fluttering around.

The guard stomped down to the inner door and paused in front of it, listening to the dog trapped behind it. "How did you pull *that* off, boy?"

Oh God, when he lets the dog out— Paul peeked over the desk at the path around the furniture to the outer door. He'd only have a moment while the guard was distracted—

He heard the pigeon flap toward his hiding place, saw the guard start to turn his way and ducked down again by reflex. The bird landed right on the desk, and Paul held his breath, but he couldn't hear the guard move. *Please, please…*

"Yes, sir?"

A phone call, now? Paul strained to hear the voice on the other end, but heard only *they'll pay it all, they won't pay, they'll pay…*

"Thor got into the back room, sir. Someone broke a window here, and he's been chasing the birds that keep flying in…"

The guard's voice stopped so suddenly that Paul knew his boss had cut him off. Paul tensed, waiting.

At last, he said, "Understood," and walked away from the door. The dog kept growling behind it, but he said, "Sorry, boy, that's enough excitement for you."

Then Paul heard a faint beep and looked out to see the guard pushing a combination on the alarm control panel. Paul *threw* his thoughts toward seeing that keyboard, but the mocking memories choked off his concentration.

The guard turned away and Paul remained crouched down until he heard him finally walk out and shut the door. *Gone. I'm safe.*

Safe? No, Quinn must have told the guard to leave 'Thor' in the back room…

Paul struggled to fit the pieces together. So now Quinn knew about this latest disturbance himself, but the guard hadn't told him about the others? *Of course*, their alarm system must have left the inside of this main room clear for the dog to patrol but kept a silent alarm in the back room. *That* was what Paul had triggered by knocking the dog in there, and what the guard had shut off now… and that alarm was the only one that signaled Quinn personally.

So now Quinn is awake—maybe even on his way here, if he's suspicious enough. And I just shut the dog in with the only things Quinn made sure to monitor himself!

Paul scowled at the net he'd gathered up; it had barely slowed the dog down before. He glanced around, looking for something else to use. Maybe a chair, to fend the beast off or hit it… no, if he missed once, the dog would drag him down. But what if Quinn *was* on his way, and time was running out? This might be his last chance to learn what was haunting his power…

Paul yanked off his coat and moved to the door. He spread the coat out in both hands and crouched down, feeling for a moment like a baseball catcher with some flimsy, two-handed mitt. The dog barked louder, scrabbling right at the door.

Twisting the knob, Paul kicked the door open and turned that step into a crouching lunge forward, springing to meet the dog and wrapping the coat around it. They crashed to the floor together, his arms clutching Thor in a bear hug.

The brute writhed in his grip; he felt its jaws straining to rip free from the few layers of cloth that kept them from his captor's chest and throat. Paul crushed the coat around it, desperate to keep the dog from getting leverage. With all his weight, he pressed the dog to the floor.

His injured arm burned and the dog's nails ripped at his thighs as the jaws fought to get their grip. Paul could only hold on, thinking *Tighter, I'm still twice your size, dog, and I* need *this…*

After an eternity, the dog's thrashing stilled. Paul hung on a little longer, his muscles aching, his heartbeat settling as one fear faded to another.

His hands fumbled around the dog's sides and he Opened to feel for its breathing, but felt only the flood of Quinn memories now. As he let the power fade, he caught a weak stirring within the dog. It was alive.

Relieved, Paul staggered to his feet and dragged the limp body outside the room, then closed the door to leave himself in the dark. For one long moment, he felt every tremble in his gasping body. Sweat soaked through him and his new injuries flared with pain that was almost worse than the throbbing of his abused arm.

He felt weakly along the wall until he could work a light switch and then looked around.

The room was tiny. A few posters lined the walls. Instead of a desk, it had a small, empty table, set between a well-padded chair and a TV set. Nothing else.

aul gazed around the near-empty room, struggling to hold off exhaustion. The place was set aside for resting, not for work and secrets…

But Quinn put the extra alarms here for a reason, he must have! Paul glanced numbly at the table and fumbled his hands up and down the chair, searching for anything hidden in its cushions. He turned to the TV and glanced at the only other objects in the room: four posters of different vacation spots around the world.

He ripped the posters down but saw only simple wood paneling behind them. Unless… he gingerly rapped on the walls where the posters had been, straining to hear any whisper of hollowness. But he couldn't be sure…

His battered left arm could barely move now, could barely pull off the glove from his shaking right hand. But slowly, slowly he laid the backs of his fingernails against the wall, hoping he could keep enough control not to brush the surface with his fingers' pads and leave prints.

Now. Now, or never. He Opened his touch.

I'm sure they'll pay it all… they won't pay… they won't pay… Quinn's words about the hospital boomed through his memory again—both versions—and with them Paul felt the *need* to face down schemers and secrets like Quinn. The need shook him, stronger even than the trembling in his fingers or the agony that tore through the body, the pain he tried to focus away from. *They won't pay, they'll pay…*

He'd fought through to Quinn's own room, and he couldn't get past just the memory of the answers? *No.* Paul gritted his teeth and pressed… not forcing his fingers against the wood but pushing all his focus, all his will, and all his need into his awareness there.

Fingernails glided over wood, but felt only wood. He focused harder and brushed it again. Again, again… he felt the finer shapes of the boards, and brushed again, clutching for more sensation. He shut his eyes, gave up his hearing to feel the wooden lines. Up and down, side to side along the wall…

He felt his eyes open, hearing the catch he'd clicked and watching the soundproofed panel swing back. Within the compartment lay two huge envelopes—and bundles of cash. There were thousands, maybe tens of thousands of dollars.

Paul knew the faint line next to the hinge was one last alarm, already triggered. He snatched up the envelopes—

And stared at the money. How many contacts could that buy? Maybe even a peaceful cabin away from the world. And every dollar taken would weaken Quinn, too…

I didn't get this power to steal! He slammed the panel shut and ran for the door.

The dog stood waiting. But as Paul rushed forward it whined and crouched down low, and Paul snatched up his coat and ran for the window. In a few more motions, he smoothly slid it up, stepped through, and dropped down from the fire escape to the alley below.

His injured arm struggled to clasp the packages, but all he had left to do was trot away through the snow, twisting his way up and down the blocks and trying not to feel the cold as he worked to hide his footprints. At last, he reached his bike and took the time to pull his coat on, but that made little difference with the holes the dog had torn in it, or the shocked exhaustion within his flesh from what he'd forced himself through.

A colder wind began blowing. The snow drifted as high as his bicycle wheel rims, sometimes twice that, and Paul pushed the bike along through it, in no shape to ride it without it slipping out from under him. He could only keep walking, more and more slowly, watching the last of the city night fill up with paler shadows.

They'll pay… they won't pay…

Somewhere on his long trudge, a little more of that memory fell into place. Quinn *had* said both things that night. And since it was in that place, he must have been talking about Lorraine's mentor and trying to offer his "help" with the bills. But… but…

Even with dawn beginning to shimmer in the air, Paul grew colder with every step. By the time he reached the Side Alley, he was shivering wildly and certain that whatever had happened that night was much more than Quinn's schemes or any simple locks and guards.

He threw himself down on his bed, knowing he should sleep. But instead, he could only huddle in his blankets as he began poring over Quinn's envelopes.

Sure enough, he found pages with long, handwritten rows noting loans and the payments made. They had only initials to mark them, but Paul flipped back to the long-ago June 13th that the Schuman boys had been raised to curse, and sure enough, he saw "K.U., $60,000."

K.U., Ian Schuman's initials if they're moved two letters forward on the alphabet—Paul's hazy thoughts dredged that fact up from some of the codes he'd tried to keep his own notes in. And with the code's key, he could check every other entry for anyone interesting… *When I wake up…*

But instead of letting himself drift off, he flipped ahead a number of Septembers, for one glance around the date when he'd heard Quinn at the hospital. Not much stood out, except…

There on the next page, in slightly larger letters: "K.U., 750,000."

It's a different I.S. It has to be. But no other initials were written quite so large. Paul stared at the letters; in among all the other, smaller rows, those initials seemed to crow Quinn's triumph at bringing "the one that got away" into his debt—again.

If that was a new loan, it had been made in the months after the hospital cover-up had failed, after discovering the firm's fax that branded Schuman and Son a family of backstabbers. The exposure must have hurt the business far worse than anyone had known…

No wonder Dad hates whoever handed over that fax. And if he thought it was Paul instead of Quinn…

Not Quinn.

Wrapped tightly in his blankets, Paul felt a new kind of cold wave sweep out of his memory. Whoever had added the Schuman name to Paul's exposé, he somehow *knew* it wasn't Arthur Quinn. And whatever had really happened, why it wasn't Quinn… *that* was the real memory he was letting Quinn's voice block out, even now.

Was it something he'd tried to stop… something worth risking *everything* to stop, even his family? Or something someone had done. Something just too *wrong*…

When Paul slept, none of his dreams were pleasant.

*   *   *

Still tired, Paul stumbled down the stairs to head out, moving on past the two other seedy residents of the Alley who were talking in a corner.

"What did you *do?*"

Paul kept walking for a moment before he realized those words had been from the day manager, and they were aimed at him. He turned, trying to think. The skinny man at the table hadn't tried to speak to him since he'd started work last week, but wasn't this the first time he'd seen Paul come down this late?

And it was Saturday, he remembered.

"I saw those marks!" the manager said angrily. "Did you pedal that bike all over town just to track the snow in here?"

"Sorry," Paul said. He should have taken a moment to knock the snow off the tires and frame before bringing it in… but he'd been so rundown, he was forgetting common sense.

"Don't talk about 'sorry'! Who's going to pay for us mopping it all up before everyone here noticed?"

Noticed? Noticed the same as most of the grime at a place called the Side Alley! Nobody pays, and nobody cares. Especially about two wet tires when everyone's shoes were tracking it in anyway.

But the little day manager was noticing *him* now, and so were the two other men. "Look, I pay on time," Paul said. "I don't start fights. And it won't happen again. I mean, who'd want to take a bike out now?"

"No fighting, sure. But," and the manager lowered his voice to draw Paul a step closer to his table, "I've seen the hours you come in and out. You think I don't know what you are?"

Paul felt a faint urge to laugh, thinking of this little man with his nervous eyes realizing how much he'd been freezing… or wrestling Dobermans and his own mind. *He doesn't even have a guess what I am, that's why he's keeping his threat so vague.*

The manager leaned closer. "I've got half a mind to take the cost out of your rent…"

"*What* mind? And what cost?" Paul snapped, and the manager jerked back. "I told you I don't make trouble. And all of you always find someone here to clean this or that for a break on rent. But if you think you can squeeze an extra quarter from me… now *that's* trashy."

He turned away before the manager could answer and marched out into the grayed-over street. Just before the door closed behind him, he heard a "Hell, yeah!" from the others.

Careless, drawing attention. But the manager had probably just been testing to see if Paul could be bullied. He probably would have found it even more suspicious if Paul had paid up. *And he deserved it anyway.*

Paul waited a moment by the door to be sure the manager wasn't calling the police or raising any other ominous questions. *Good enough.* And the snow was really only a layer of well-trampled slush on the sidewalk now, with no more drifting down. For now, anyway.

*   *   *

"I told you it was a joke…"

"If you'd like to be spanked, press 4…"

"Just don't forget the cat food…"

On the subway, Paul found he could sustain his power better just by concentrating to reach past the memory of Quinn's words. He was able to pick out both sides of the passengers' cell conversations again, and he found he could glance into their books from the far end of the car, despite the train's clatter.

The last of his plan fell into place. Whatever Bennet and Vernon might do—and whatever evidence Koenig might have about the LifeLab frame—he couldn't keep ignoring his own part. Somehow, Arthur Quinn was tied to his powers. He'd been there that night at the hospital. All Paul had to do was get his father alone.

Well, maybe I'll start with their Animal Alliance plans, as an icebreaker, and build up to Dad taking Quinn's money. The weight of the envelopes in Paul's coat steadied him. They were the weapon that just might break their enemy's grip.

He felt his hands trembling, but that had to be fatigue from the long night. *I have everything I need. Why should I be nervous?*

That tiredness was still with him when he reached the office building, dragging himself up all four flights of stairs and one landing above to keep clear of anyone from the Schumans' floor who might try to pass by. He kept probing as he climbed, but neither Greg nor Vernon was waiting to ambush him.

Paul sat down on the cold metal step to rest and Opened to listen around the office. Hopefully, his father was still there, keeping his usual Saturday hours. A glance at his watch showed it was almost one in the afternoon.

For a moment, Paul pictured himself walking right in, simply demanding to see his father alone, and asking him about Arthur Quinn. Then he wondered why he wasn't doing just that… although they would probably talk more freely away from the others—

"Just handle those calls," he heard his father say. The older man was at the elevator almost before Paul got to his feet. Paul lurched down the steps, racing down the floors as best he could. At least he knew which side of the parking structure he'd use to head him off.

He caught up just as the BMW came around the structure's corner and planted himself in the car's path. It screeched to a stop, and as he moved around to its door, he realized it had never crossed his mind that it might not stop in time.

"Have you lost your mind?" his father yelled, leaning out the door.

"I *didn't* give the media that fax of yours, no matter what you think. And I'm the one who found out it was Vernon who broke into Greg's house. I think you owe me!" he added as the car lurched forward.

But instead of driving away, his father only pulled over a few feet to the side of the lot and rolled the window down.

Paul closed the distance and leaned over to say, more quietly, "And I know why you can't keep Animal Alliance as a client."

"You're making demands?" his father asked quietly. Paul thought he saw the older man's lip curl just a hint, as it did when he didn't bother hiding his distaste.

"I'm trying to keep you from making a mistake. All their precious 'evidence' about LifeLab's experiments? It's under investigation, and more and more signs are turning up that it's all wrong. Or didn't Greg tell you that?"

Ian didn't answer. His face didn't move at all.

"Well, it's fake, and the truth is already coming out… so do you want to jump on a sinking ship or not?" Paul rushed the last words out and stopped, surprised he could cover it all so quickly.

The pause lasted only a moment before the low, steady answer came. "We're already *on* that ship. The question is, if we don't cancel our commitments on your word, will you start looking for ways to make us look like worse frauds than you say the Alliance is?"

"I never did that!" Paul's fist banged on the car door. "I keep trying to tell you, I gave them the hospital's same patterns of neglect that you found, but not the fax that linked you to the secret."

"So you only *mostly* betrayed us?" His father shook his head. "Even if that were acceptable… if you didn't do it, who did? Just who was this so-convenient 'real enemy' of ours?"

Why don't you ask Quinn, the next time you're paying him off? But Paul didn't say it. That was the one thing he knew Quinn hadn't done. *And I can't remember why I know… and I can't even try to justify that haze in my mind without explaining all about my power!*

He looked into his father's cold face and couldn't guess which would be worse—hearing him tear apart a story like that, or starting to believe how he could exploit a son with those powers.

But Quinn was still the real reason Paul had come, and he knew he needed to get back on track. He reached inside his coat for Quinn's papers.

"Hey, get away from… *Paul?*"

Greg's voice spun him around. Paul saw Greg running toward them with Lorraine following. Greg pulled up short, an arm across the hurt ribs his run must have aggravated, but his face was a tangle of other emotions.

What, you thought I was a carjacker? Are you wishing I was now?

Meanwhile, Lorraine kept a few steps back, as quiet as he'd ever seen her.

Behind him, the car door opened and shut, and his father moved in. "Greg, Lorraine, I thought you were running late. But you're just in time to hear Paul tell us who *really* accused us of blackmail."

"I don't know!" was all Paul could say, and he heard it echo around the parking structure.

The others moved closer, close enough to speak more quietly, but he could only look back and forth at them, trying not to think of the sheer bad luck. *Greg must have been planning to meet our father at the car just when I made my move.*

Looking at both Schumans, almost in arms' reach now, he hissed, "But it *was* blackmail. Don't talk like you weren't doing just that!"

"Whatever we did, we did for Lorraine's sake, and her friend's," Greg shot back. He motioned back to his silent wife. Paul fought the urge to look at her for help; even when he'd been part of the family, she'd known she couldn't stop one of their fights.

"So," his father snapped at Paul, "now you're the judge and jury for who's allowed to keep their secrets?"

Paul looked straight at him. "When you tried to help Curtis, how many other patients did you sell out as the price? And now you're helping someone blame LifeLab for something they never did."

"Maybe," Greg said. "Or maybe they're one more of the hundreds of cases where labs abuse their animals, legally or not, and they just got caught. Are you so sure?"

"Yes I am!" *God, I just confessed! Is there* anyone *in town who didn't hear that shout?*

But instead, his father said, "So we should take the word of whatever you've become… what, some petty crook with a few connections? I'm sure you're not *CIA*. And whatever resources you have, you're throwing your weight around now after staying hidden from us for two years?"

You mean, not letting you use it to drum up business? Or would you just sell me to Quinn? Paul opened his mouth to spit the last accusation at his father, but stopped, glancing at Greg. Quinn's name was one bomb he couldn't throw—not with Greg there to stop their father from admitting it.

Breathing deeply and trying to think, Paul said, "This isn't just about how we left things then. I've been trying to keep you safe from what I've done. And now, I'm the one who found out your enemies were Bennet and Vernon—"

"So?" Greg cut in. "Lorraine was the one who took that picture, and that's kept them from bothering us since then. We may not even have to use it—"

"Maybe not," Paul snapped back, turning to him. "A shot of her aide prying your files open probably worries her more than your affair with her!"

"Paul!" His father stepped in front of him, eyes blazing. "Is that what you've become, someone who flails around trying to hurt your family?" He lowered his voice to a fierce whisper and added, "Even Lorraine? How could you say that in front of her?"

As he motioned to her, Paul looked over. Of course she wasn't shocked, but she wasn't pretending to be, either. Her face was just the same, silent wall now.

"But as it happens, you've failed in that, too. Because Greg told us how his indiscretion had put us in danger last night. Families tell each other what they need. But then, how did *you* know? How did you even know *anyone* had broken into their home? Have you been spying on us, too?"

Carefully not looking at Lorraine, Paul tried again. "I'm just trying to stop someone from using the Alliance to frame people. Everyone already knows Koenig's photos don't fit the facts, and I'm trying to save you—"

"You're *saving* us?" his father laughed.

"We don't need your help," Greg said. "You're just so sure this 'frame' of yours is going to turn and destroy the Alliance and everyone who helps them. You think five pictures matter, against all the support we can help them raise? We're giving them the respect they never had, faster than you can take it away. It might even do some good for all the dedicated people in their ranks that you don't care about."

"And you care?" Paul took a step toward his brother, fists clenched, but what he threw at him was, "*Try* and tell me you knew a thing about animal issues before yesterday, when I told you to stay away from them! Go on, tell me!"

"Uh…" Finally, Greg had no answer.

And they say I'm *playing God!* With a grim smile at that victory, Paul turned and headed off as fast as he could walk.

"Don't you—" he heard Greg say, and his father's "Don't bother," and then he reached the street and let the noise of the people swallow him up.

His shoes slid in the snow, but he only cut his pace a little, just enough so he could keep moving without thrashing for balance. To throttle back any more would probably...

Next time. Next time, when Dad and I can talk about Quinn, I'll make them listen.

*   *   *

At least the Animal Alliance rally wasn't hard to find, even with just the first people gathering at the corner of the park. Whenever some of the dogs inside their two vans started barking, anyone could hear them from halfway down the street.

Apart from those vans, Paul saw fewer than a dozen of their members out, just milling about at the edge of the first trees and huddling in little knots, whispering together. That and the barking was enough to draw some attention from the other people who were at the park for their diverse Saturday interests. It was enough to slow but not stop some of them passing on the street. Inside the park, more and more people began to look.

What Paul couldn't see was his father, or even Greg. Instead he listened to a few of the would-be protesters.

"Why'd the snow have to hit *today*? Will any of us even get here?"

"Never mind that—will the news get here?"

Paul looked around again. Maybe, maybe those two at the picnic table were reporters, judging from the way they were watching the crowd, but he couldn't see anything like the city news vans. He moved back behind a big rest facility, not used to having to watch for people who could recognize him on sight. Not to dodging family.

Still, there was no sign of his father or anyone from Schuman and Son—only the protesters' vans and the corner space the group was holding.

"It's just too fast!" one older man was saying. "Do those PR boys think we can pull this out of nothing? Hell, what if we need some kind of permit?"

"You mean you don't *want* to get arrested?" a younger woman asked, sounding dead serious.

Another woman added, "Well, I don't think it's fair we brought our animal friends. They don't represent the lab's victims or the ones in all the other labs…"

Now Paul saw it: a few cars parked here and there with the owners still sitting inside, but each with a dog, cat, or other pet beside them. Were they waiting there, trying to keep the animals warm inside?

"…or how we have to pay double for any food that wasn't raised in a straitjacket. How do we cover that?"

Koenig! Paul saw him marching up the sidewalk toward the group at a quick stride with a knot of others barely a step behind him. Among them was the Alliance leader—what was his name?—and others Paul had seen at their different gatherings. Even if half of them hadn't carried long bundles or other shapes, their pace alone would have shouted to Paul that they were moments from making their move.

And like generals directing from a hillside, his father, Greg, and Lorraine stepped out from the crowd across the street.

"…wish we could bring some wild horses here, too. 'Course, I wish there were enough left that we dared to bring any! How is one, last-minute gather going to make any…"

"It's a cold day," crackled the Animal Alliance leader's voice through the megaphone he'd kept behind his back until the moment he reached

the group. "The first cold day of a long winter. And in every corner of our concrete jungle, cats and dogs are struggling to keep the snow off them while they root for scraps or fight to hold off disease…"

He gestured, and two of his people pulled on ropes they'd tossed over a branch, and hoisted up a huge poster of a half-hairless waif of a cat. Gasps and yells burst out around the street. Paul saw two photographers snap the moment as if they'd been waiting for it.

The leader shouted down the street, "And how many of these did you buy for your children, and then send away when they weren't cute any more?"

Now the audience was gathering, people from the sidewalk and families from the park. Paul moved into the flow, trying to edge toward his father. Yes, there he was, waving some of the protesters toward the vans.

The leader went on. "*These* are some of the animals that have been left in the pound or dragged off the streets. Just look at them as we bring them by, and ask yourselves why they needed 'rescue.'"

Protesters filed out from the vans and moved in from the cars, each carrying an animal in their arms. On cue, another two pictures rose up under the trees and a loudspeaker boomed out recordings, from one ordinary voice after another:

"Taking Jenny in was the first thing I was ever really proud of."

"Sometimes I think about whoever put the scars on Nibbles' legs…"

Two of the protesters passed near Paul, each holding a small dog. They held their pets close and away from any strange hands that tried to touch them, but the animals still seemed almost calm amid the people and noises. Paul wondered how many of them were really as traumatized as the speaker said.

Looking up, Paul saw the leader pulling a sheaf of papers from a cardboard box, and thought he saw him steal a glance at the inside of the lid. *Notes? And did he script this, or did Dad and Greg?*

Just then, James Koenig hollered out, "These are the lucky ones! All the animals you can see!" His unamplified voice carried nearly as well as the leader's, with a harshness that roused some angry mutters in the crowd.

"He's right!" the leader said. "Some animals suffer because they're forgotten, but other animals get all too much attention from humans."

And the next image they rolled down…

Always that damned pig! Was it even in pain before Koenig started juggling pixels?

Koenig shouted, "We asked the lab director to come here and explain himself! One guess what he said?"

The angry parts of the crowd did more than mutter now. They shouted back, their ugly voices here and there like spreading sparks.

"Actually," the Alliance leader said as he stepped in, "he was out of town. But while we're waiting for him to come back, I hope you'll take a look at the pictures we're passing out."

Someone shoved a flyer in Paul's hand, and he realized he hadn't noticed their next action was already underway.

"Our website's listed on these—of course," and the leader got a bit of a laugh for that, "or you can just call the local number and leave a few words about an animal you know. Just think: five seconds to dial and five more to say whatever you want. That might be all it takes for you to make someone else take another look."

And the loudspeaker came in again with more recordings:

"They say they kill whales for scientific research. And then they sell the meat."

"How can we keep cowboy movies longer than we protect wild horse herds?"

Then the orator added, "While you're looking at those, we have some friends from the press here…"

Sure enough, Paul saw his father sending a group of reporters forward, wrangling them with perfect ease.

All the Schuman and Son tricks, but Paul had never seen them used with such rapid-fire effect, or pulled off with a client they'd only taken on the previous day. *Oh God, I see why Dad said they were already on the sinking ship. If I prove the whole LifeLab campaign was a fraud, after the hospital blackmail, will the firm* ever *recover?*

Or could he stop it at all, with all this momentum against him? So many animals, so many people who cared… *What did Dad call me? Judge and jury about which truths mattered?*

From the front, one reporter called out, "So is the LifeLab director really out of town?"

Koenig replied, "Maybe he wishes he was!"

Paul shook his head. James Koenig had been so quiet and unreadable, but now that he had his chance, he seethed with his grudge against the lab. Was that what Paul had sounded like, talking about Koenig's fraud?

"Is it true," a woman's voice rang out, "that LifeLab is planning to sue your group for fraudulent accusations?"

Sarah! Paul searched frantically but couldn't see her through the ranks. He knew where she was, just from the wave of angry heads turning toward her.

His father stepped to the front, just a pace or two to put him with the group's leaders, and smoothly said, "There's been no official word of anything, and the noises they make could go either way. We only hope this can be worked out peacefully."

Another reporter called, "So Greg, if they do, will you countersue?"

They know Greg's behind it, even with Dad at the mic? He really has *been sticking his neck out.*

"We hope it doesn't come to that," answered Greg, and he stepped over the same way his father had. "Especially since neither lawsuit is going to help any of the animals that need it. And today shouldn't be about just *one* lab, or how angry people get over that. We mean to make sure it's about more than that."

"Yeah!" someone shouted.

No.

Family or not, Sarah was right; LifeLab never *did* hurt those pigs, no matter how loudly people here yelled. And this "Alliance" needed to remember who they were hurting when they tried to make the facts more convenient.

More questions were flying around now. Paul's father stayed in his place fielding them, with Greg at his side. But Lorraine was still off talking with some of the protesters. Paul began working his way around toward her, keeping the thick of the crowd between himself and his father and brother.

Maybe she can help me get my father alone—if she dares look at me with the family so against me. But no, as she finished one protester's question and waved him on, he saw her stealing a long look around the crowd, searching. Another protester grabbed her attention before she looked toward Paul, but if he just stepped a little further to the front…

Then he saw them, standing off beyond her and watching the rally. Councilwoman Bennet and Vernon.

Paul edged back into the ranks, wondering what they were up to. He Opened his hearing, but they weren't speaking, only watching. Paul leaned against a tree to wait, but as he did, Bennet spoke.

"Still think they're going to riot?" Then she sighed. "I just don't understand why Greg would be helping them. It doesn't seem like Ian's idea."

"I said he was trouble," Vernon muttered. "Why you let them get the permits…"

"Enough. I know Greg was a mistake. But the permits weren't; these people can make all the trouble they want, but with the Schumans in charge they won't be breaking any laws or windows to make their case—they won't have to. And I think we have real work to do."

"Right. If you head to the office, I'll check up on the snowplows…"

"Both of us," she said, with just a hint of warning. Vernon followed her away.

Is she suspicious about why Vernon goes off on his own, and she doesn't like it? Or is she as dangerous as Vernon, but more careful? Paul didn't think she sounded too menacing, even in private with Vernon. And everything he'd heard and then observed of Erin Bennet painted her as a genuine public servant—whoever she slept with.

Paul looked back to Lorraine, but the protesters at the side of the rally had moved on, and she was gone. He edged along the side of the crowd, keeping several onlookers between him and the open as he searched past the trees and outer knots of people for where she might be standing, directing more of the rally.

Instead, he saw Sarah Gomez making her way out of the crowd. A graying, older man walked with her, a man with the look of a fellow journalist.

He was saying "You had to mention the lawsuit, didn't you?"

"If it's a fight, that makes two sides to watch." Sarah's voice didn't waver, even when a couple of the people nearby gave her cold looks.

"Fight? Were we at the same movement today, Gomez? Nobody's going to remember what the lab did or not."

"If what the lab did is worth remembering, who else is going to remind people?"

"Tell them that at the next rally—if Greene lets you anywhere near it."

They separated, her colleague heading down the street while Sarah moved back into the thick of things. But she walked more slowly now, turning her head one way and another to watch the rally. She seemed slower too, dispirited.

It was too much.

He moved around behind her as she headed deeper into the flow of people, and leaned forward, just at her back. "Don't you give up!" he whispered.

Sarah froze. Paul shifted to look mostly away from her, able to watch her start to turn but only needing an instant to angle away and become just one of the people behind her.

But she didn't turn.

"Who's there?" she said. She didn't move her head at all; even the long, simple earrings never stirred where they dangled.

With all the reassurance he could put in a low voice, he said, "I told you, it's all a fraud."

"James Koenig, right?"

She knows? I never gave her that name, but she must have dug it up.

"I thought the files were too good for anyone but an ex-LifeLab employee," she whispered.

"Right. And I'll get you more soon. But don't give up."

"Um…" she said slowly. "It's not that simple. Can we just talk?"

Paul took a step away. She didn't look around, and he turned and slipped away.

After a few steps, when his Opened hearing told him she wasn't following, he risked a sideways look around. Back through the people, he could just make her out, still standing there, not looking.

Up ahead of him, standing on the center of a play area's see-saw and looking down from the edge of the crowd, was Lorraine. Watching him.

Paul looked on past her and moved clear of the people, and she didn't look at him as he walked by her and knelt to "tie his shoe" just behind her.

As he did, she said, "Reading minds isn't the only stunt that can scare people."

"You're getting better at picking out someone in hiding."

"Actually, I was watching her—"

"You there!" As Paul spun, he saw the detective who'd discovered Koenig closing in. "I have some questions for you, about that office break-in—"

Paul bolted out of his reach and straight into the crowd. He heard a "Stop there!" from behind him, but he kept moving, weaving around one person after another after another. In moments, he'd pulled ahead, and a glance back showed him out of view of the cop as well. *Easy.*

He yanked off his coat to change his look… and as he did, Quinn's envelopes spilled out at people's feet.

No time! Bundling the coat tightly under his arm, he sidled off to the right, following the crowd's currents. He moved as little as he could, focusing his hearing to pick out the detective's half-running pace and frustrated false starts one way and another. Soon enough, those feet slowed and headed away, leaving Paul safe in the thick of the crowd.

The cop's footsteps almost melted away, becoming harder to distinguish from so many people as his pace slowed. But Paul kept still and tracked him all the way back to Lorraine.

"Detective Reid, Ms. Schuman. Who was that?"

She only said, "What do you mean?"

The detective didn't answer. Paul remembered his silent-treatment questioning of James Koenig. *He always starts these informal interviews by saying his name. It figures that a cop named "read" might want people to think they couldn't hide anything from him.* Except Reid had shown it was only a name for him, unlike Lorraine…

"Just what are you implying?" she added.

And she waited. Paul didn't hear one of her focusing breaths, but no doubt she was trying to sense just how much Reid suspected.

A few moments later, she said, "You spoke to someone behind me, and he ran off. That's all I know."

Reid said nothing, as if waiting for her to make herself nervous. At last he asked, "Do you know what these are?"

Quinn's papers, he did find them! But Lorraine only said, "No."

"Your husband was just telling me about the man who burglarized your office, and he said that was him there with you. He said the man is dangerous."

"Was that him? I didn't think so."

This time, Reid didn't bother trying to scare any more out of her. He only said, "If you see him again, I'll expect you to call me." Then he walked away.

Paul kept tracking Reid to be sure he had left the rally. But still, he couldn't miss when Greg and his father called Lorraine over to them, acting as if it were just business as usual.

T he rally broke up soon after, sending people on their different ways while they were still buzzing about it. Paul knew that by evening, people all over the city would start claiming they'd been at… whatever the public decided to name this event.

Sorting out the name was probably the only reason he couldn't already see T-shirt stalls.

Greg and Dad wanted to build up public sympathy faster than the facts could come out, and they sure succeeded. Paul knew better than to bother chasing Koenig or any other clues about the frame—at least until he could have a real talk alone with his father, to *stop* this lie.

But all through the rally's teardown, the three Schumans had kept close together. Paul watched them through the trees of the park, staying alert in case Reid circled back. His father seemed to be keeping a closer eye than usual on Greg and Lorraine. *He's probably still uneasy at being dragged into this venture.*

Not that either of them was holding back. Paul kept imagining the next steps the firm would take. They'd probably arrange for more quiet events to build some deeper public support under this surge. Then they'd place ads, arrange debates, recruit the right celebrities…

When the Schumans left, still together, Paul had to run down the street, wishing he had his bike. At least from what they'd said, it wasn't hard to predict where they were going.

*   *   *

Sure enough, both his father's car and Greg's rental sat in the long valet parking section beside the 'Hat. Still gasping for breath, Paul moved across the busy street; it would be safer to loiter in the mix of cigar stores, exercise studios, and bookshops along that side than in front of the grand restaurant.

Pretending to search through the bookshop display from inside gave him all the view he needed of the famous 'Hat windows, fifty almost-continuous feet of smoked glass along the restaurant's front. Paul couldn't extend his hearing through both places' windows with the cars purring by between them; instead, he Opened his sight to peer through the dark glass to where Greg, Lorraine, and his father sat.

Their meals were already out when Paul arrived, and he waited for his breath to steady and hoped they finished soon. *Or I could rush past the waiters, ruined coat and all, just long enough to demand Dad talk to me about Quinn…* He smiled at the image, but knew he'd only wait and intercept his father in the parking lot. If that failed, he'd catch up to him at his home.

As the cars sped by between them and the night deepened, Paul began trying to fill in in in his imagination what he couldn't hear. The three didn't look as if they were talking much together, as if they still had tension between them. His father had what must be his usual ribeye steak, but Greg wasn't drinking, a silent reminder of how he'd crashed one car.

A graying man in a tux walked up to their table with a hostile crease on his brow. Paul tried to imagine their words.

—Why did you put on that spectacle downtown, Schuman? You might have hurt my LifeLab stock, and that's all that matters.

—Oh, we were just arguing what a big risk it was, but to you we'll only say we did it to prove we can make anyone famous.

—Really? Then I need you to help me make my company look greener, too. And richer.

—Of course. That's why we took all your calls in the middle of the rally…

When the new client shook their hands and went on his way, the three seemed a bit more comfortable, eating more slowly and talking as they did. Maybe it was that new success, or just being reminded that it was always them against the world.

But beyond that, when Paul looked around the restaurant, he couldn't see many tables where people seemed to be having as good a time as those three. The family always went from work to play and back in a minute, always quick to smile even after outdoing each other in some petty competition. *No wonder Lorraine can't go against the family to speak up for me.*

Another visitor came to the table, a younger man who offered them his hand at once.

—Of course, we've always wanted to support animal rights, it has nothing to do with stopping whatever my crazy son is up to.

Then Paul's eyes went wide, and he shifted his Opened sight beyond the Schuman table. Councilwoman Bennet, and Vernon, walked in.

They settled in the back, and they and the Schumans didn't seem to notice each other. Paul felt his first surprise fading; everyone who wanted to be seen came to the 'Hat sooner or later anyway. He let his vision blur away and strained to Open his hearing, but all his effort couldn't reach much past the jumble of echoes against the glass.

He started again when Vernon stood up, and his lungs ached at the thought of racing to catch Vernon again without even his bike… but the big man only moved off to another table, chatting up the older couple there.

Paul looked back to the family and saw his father was standing up now, too. But he took their meal check as he did and moved toward the exit, turning even farther away from Bennet and Vernon. Behind him, Greg and Lorraine leaned a bit closer together.

Paul stepped back from the store window and moved quickly out to the street, hoping he could catch the cross-light in time. But another look across showed his father pausing at another table, too, still networking. Paul moved to the corner light and then paused to look in again.

From the corner, he couldn't see his father now, only the other side of the restaurant. Greg and Lorraine sat there, talking closely—

Just then, Lorraine shook her head sharply as if spitting out some curse. She jumped up from her chair and stormed off, and Greg looked after her for a moment and then scowled and turned back to his plate.

But Lorraine didn't move out toward the exit, but back deeper inside. Paul shifted his focus back up the street to keep her in view, as he realized she was making her way straight toward Greg's mistress. Paul couldn't see her face now and could only guess at her plans from her firm, purposeful walk.

Five tables short of Bennet, Paul saw Vernon catch Lorraine's arm. He whispered something in her ear. And then he led Lorraine away, pulling her along, and she didn't resist.

They walked not back to her table, but out toward the rear of the building.

Damn her, what's she doing? Paul took a step onto the street, but as he did, the traffic streamed across to block him.

He mashed the WALK button and searched up and down the street for any break in the traffic flow. The lights for that direction glowed the same unflinching green, with no sign of yellow.

Beyond the street, the door opened. Vernon led Lorraine out, waved his ticket at the attendants, and marched her straight into the parking lot. Paul risked a step into the street but had to jump back as cars sped by.

He drew in a breath, wanting to yell something to Lorraine, but let it puff out as useless. He did manage to hear that the two weren't speaking, and take a good long look at the big black Cadillac Vernon pushed her into, license number and all.

At last the light changed and Paul scrambled across… just as Vernon drove into the street and away.

Paul raced after them, unable to think past catching them at the corner—but instead of stopping the car turned right and swung around the block. Paul stopped, sagging where he stood. *I need a cab… no, I need to get to Bennet…*

"Get in!" Greg yelled as his car screeched to the curb.

Paul stared at the open door and his brother's furious face. He stepped forward to lean inside: "Look, we can just talk to Bennet…"

"Get… *in!*" Greg caught his arm and yanked, sending a blast of pain through the arm Vernon had injured even as he sprawled on the seat. The car leaped forward under them.

Paul yanked his feet inside and curled himself up to pull the door shut, then clung to the handle as they roared around the turn Vernon had taken. *Greg crashed his last car, even before the snow hit…*

But Greg kept them steady, bearing down on one black shape and then pulling on past it as he saw the car was far too small. Paul struggled into his seat belt, his left arm still hurting too much to help him click the buckle together, and stared up the street's rivers of light into the dark.

They swept past one block, another, weaving around traffic to close on every black car from a Corvette to a minivan and moving on again. At the next turn, they lurched to the right again, making Paul glance at his brother's iron grip on the wheel and wonder if he'd made the turn just from a need to try different tactics. Where *was* Vernon anyway?

When they pulled up at a light and Greg spun his head savagely left and right, Paul took the moment to say, "Just call Bennet! Vernon will listen to her…"

"Here!" Greg tossed him a cell phone.

Paul caught it clumsily, wondering for a moment how fast they'd replaced the last phone, the one Lorraine had tried to smash.

Still searching the streets, Greg said, "It's 7… 8…"

Paul punched buttons and then listened as the phone only rang and rang. *Even if she answers, would Vernon take her call now?* When the recording came on for the second time, he hung up, not bothering to leave a message.

"Nothing?" Greg said.

"She probably won't take calls from the guy she had the affair with," Paul snapped, then added, "And you just had to have one, didn't you?"

"*Shut up!* This is all your fault!" And Greg stomped down and lurched them forward again.

"Careful—" Paul started, then caught himself. Greg was keeping the car under control, and they didn't have time to argue. Not when Greg was still deluding himself that he could really tell black cars apart at night.

Instead Paul Opened his sight to survey the street ahead, then snatched side glances as they rushed through an intersection chasing another wild black goose. As they swung past that car for the next one, he braced himself and stared hard up the cross-streets—

"There!" and he pointed at the back of a Cadillac just turning out of view from the side street.

Greg wrenched the steering wheel, slamming Paul up against his seat belt but somehow bringing them safely around the turn. They sped up the block and twisted around the corner, but then Paul's fist thumped the seat in rage: the car was too big. Greg brought them up beside it and then roared past at the sight of only women inside.

Where would he take her? As Paul tried to think, he saw tiny, bright spots dotting here and there across the windshield. The night air shimmered with the first teasing threat of more snow.

Think, think! But he didn't really know Vernon White; he only knew that the man was impulsive and dangerous. Still, he wouldn't take Lorraine to his boss's office if he wanted to protect Bennet.

"Turn left," Paul sighed. "We'll work our way east."

"Wha-at?" Greg growled, as if startled out to have his angry thoughts broken in on.

"Vernon's listed as having a home in the Hills, and it's all I can think of. I don't think he'd keep a regular place set aside for…" *Whatever he's about to do.*

"But if he takes her home…" Greg's voice broke for a moment. "That sounds like he's given up on letting her go."

A lie would be easy, and Greg's frightened eyes begged him for one. But all Paul could say was, "We just don't know."

The car settled into the next left, at a pace only a little faster than the shapes it weaved between. A grim pace.

Greg would know, as well as Paul did, how every moment made Vernon more likely to have pulled off the streets or left them too far behind. And unless the snow flurried out, they'd skid more and more on every turn.

Still… Paul clenched his fists and kept searching the night, but the thoughts kept lashing at him. He just *couldn't guess* what Vernon would do. Even the threat of Lorraine's picture of him hadn't stopped him now—not when the betrayed wife could have been about to call Bennet a homewrecker in public.

But why had Lorraine gone with him so willingly? She'd just let him pull her out of the safety of that public place. *Does she really think a few days of her new power will let her outwit someone as volatile as Vernon?* Or was it like when she'd taken the picture, her own impulsive act followed by freezing up when danger rushed right at her? Paul knew how long it had taken him to learn to react—

Except, he'd learned those street smarts knowing any mistake could be the end of him, he hadn't had someone else with the power stepping in and out of his life and making tricks look easy. *God, maybe this really is my fault—*

"Up there!" and he stabbed a finger up to the left, just before the street slid away behind them.

Greg swung the wheel—the car skidded a moment, then curved around to turn back and twist up the side street. As he drove, Greg said, "You're crazy! There's nothing here!"

Not in the first block, no. "Two blocks up," Paul said. Then he added "About two. But I know it's there—I bugged their car."

"*What?*" Greg gasped.

"It wasn't working before," Paul added quickly, and he cupped his coat collar up to his ear as if concentrating on a tiny receiver. It was an excuse he'd thought of two years ago, that he'd never had to use. "Line of sight helped, but I'm not sure how much—*not so fast!*" he yelled as Greg brought the car surging forward.

"Now *you're* giving orders? Stay out of my way!" Greg shouted, straining forward over the wheel in search of his target.

"He'll hurt her!"

The engine slackened.

"As long as he's driving, he's too busy to touch her," Paul went on, knowing it was almost true. "As long as he thinks they're alone. But the one thing he has to notice at night is a car rushing up at him."

Greg didn't answer, but with his knuckles white on the wheel, he let the car drop to a modest speed, just edging up to five car lengths behind the Cadillac. Paul took a long, Opened look to the back of the passengers' heads and felt something unknot in him: the blonde wave of Lorraine's head, turned a little toward Vernon, alive. And him… talking?

I've got to hear! Paul squinted at the glass and then let his eyes relax, and his muscles, as he tried to focus on sound… but he reached only to the Caddy's window, that layer of vibration muffling it, and Quinn's echoes about pay…

No. Paul closed his eyes, threw off the doubts, and flung his power forward.

"…about, can't you understand? You just *can't* drag Ms. Bennet down in this! Not after everything she's done for us! She's halfway to rebuilding the whole city tax structure, too. You can't! She can't have all the people who need her just seeing her as a woman who got seduced by some married man!"

As Vernon paused for breath, Lorraine said "You realize, you're talking about my husband?" She said it softly, as if testing if he'd even hear it.

But Vernon only went on. "It can't happen, it can't! I'll do whatever I can to stop you. I can't live with that picture hanging over me anymore. Why couldn't you just leave us alone?"

Paul pulled back, eyes still closed, enough to say "She's alright so far. She's listening to him rant."

"What's the bastard *doing?*" Greg said. "Just driving around trying to think?"

Of course, probably just that—

Growling engines smashed through his focus. Paul wrenched his eyes open to see traffic in double lines pouring between them and the departing Cadillac, as it drove away beyond the red light.

"That bug *better* find her!" Greg snarled. "It had better. You and your secret deal with her, you're what pushed Lor to fight with me and go after her, so *you find them!*"

Paul had no answer. He could only sit, watching the cars that blocked his senses, trying not to think. The snow, the damnable snow kept drifting down.

At long last, the light changed and Paul stabbed his sight through the dark, past one truck and around another car as his eyes swung to the side, searching.

"There, just keep going," he sighed. He kept his focus on the distant car as they worked away at the remaining gap.

As if from far away, he heard Greg mutter, "Is this how you always drag people down now?"

It's how I save them! The way you're begging me to, between one curse and the next! But Paul knew Lorraine's danger *was* his fault, so he only sighed. "If you mean Animal Alliance, I'm trying to protect the lab from an ex-employee with a grudge. Or if you're talking about St. Central again, I never told the news you knew about their tricks. Why can't you believe that?"

"Who else could have?" Greg snapped.

Back to that again. Paul couldn't remember, and he couldn't explain why without talking about his power, or starting the world thinking how many ways someone they could use his "bugs" for their own ends—

Greg went on "You know Dad went back to Arthur Quinn after you made us look like blackmailers? He doesn't think I know, but I do. I can't even blame the old shark. He never knew about it. But Dad had to go to him for more money, after all these years—because of you."

Vernon's car edged out of the shadows, at about the distance Paul had been able to listen across before. But instead of listening, he said "You see these rips in my coat? They're from Quinn's guard dog—but you're right, Quinn didn't do it." And at that, he pressed the collar to his ear, as a reminder for Greg to be quiet and let him "listen to the bug."

Still, as his eyes closed, he heard a far-off, almost impressed, "You robbed *Quinn*?"

Then even that fell away as he reached for the voices up ahead. Lorraine was speaking.

"I tell you I just want my husband back, and no more broken locks on our doors, isn't that what everyone wants? I didn't ask for any of this, but you turned it into a war! Just tell me, when did we give you one sign we wanted to use any of this against the Councilwoman?"

"Um…" Vernon said slowly. Then he added, "Who's back there? Him again?"

Paul's heart almost stopped.

Somehow, he still heard Lorraine's, "Who? You *must* be nervous. But you've got a right to be, because we both know this has to end."

Paul screamed, *"Turn away!"*

"What?" Greg's shout seemed almost louder than Paul's.

"Now! And nothing sudden, for God's sake!"

Greg's face went as white as his knuckles, but he brought the car into a perfect, ordinary turn up a side street.

They slowed then and, more to break the stillness pressing on them than to really explain, Paul added, "He was starting to think he was being followed, and he got nervous."

"How nervous?" Greg breathed. "If we don't find them again…"

"We'll find them. And then we'll stay well back, and we'll move when he pulls over."

All Greg's bluster was gone now as he brought their speed slowly up again. "Do you think he really might…?"

"It's Vernon," Paul said. "We don't know yet."

They paralleled Vernon's street for a block, as fast as they dared in the snow, then swung back toward where they'd left him.

As they closed on that street, Greg gasped "Got you!" and spun them around to a side street. Paul Opened his sight and then his mouth to tell Greg the Rolls was a false alarm, but Greg had already cursed and shoved the pedal down to arrow past that car. Paul heard him gasp for calming breaths and didn't warn him about his conspicuous turn.

Instead, they settled into a rhythm, gaining speed during each block and slowing at each cross-street as Paul flung his senses left and right. Wrong, wrong, wrong… He realized they were moving eastward, with the unspoken understanding that Vernon might have nothing left but to take her to his home. Paul tried not to think what that might mean.

At last, "There!" and Greg glided up to a distance almost half a block behind Vernon's tail-lights on the quiet street.

Too far, too far with all the glass between us— Paul brought the window down, ignoring Greg's surprised look, and leaned out, hooking his arm tight over the metal to keep his head still, straining to wall out everything but the sounds ahead… And yet, he couldn't reach past the churning of the Cadillac's engine.

He pulled back inside, brushing snow out of his hair. At least he could see Lorraine's head, still conscious. He glanced toward Greg, tempted to ask him to edge them slowly closer.

But Greg was staring ahead at the car, muttering, "Please be alright, please! She's always there, she makes everything better for us, but she's so helpless alone, it's just not fair…"

Paul looked away. He could feel some of the same fears crawling through him, but one thought stuck with him: *helpless?* Lorraine didn't have his years of hard practice, and she'd made it clear she wanted just the opposite. But with her quick wit and her powers…

Paul had to know. He leaned back, relaxed his breath, his muscles, his eyes and touch and all the rest. *If this power ever did anything, let it hear them now…*

Only the engine, the crunch of tires in the night air.

A sudden thought jolted him out of his trance. All this time, he'd never thought of calling the police!

His eyes went wide and he looked away to keep Greg from seeing his shock. His brother seemed too trapped in blaming them both to think beyond saving her himself—*but have I lived in hiding so long that it* can't *occur to me? And yet, by now…*

Vernon was desperate to protect Bennet, but was he really ready to kill, or just not seeing a way out? And how long had Lorraine been listening to him, trying to guide him to a better answer? Greg's phone still lay in Paul's lap; he could raise an army with three digits and the word *kidnapped.*

Or he could let Lorraine work.

I have to… I have to believe in something.

"Paulie…" Greg whispered. "When you left, that letter you sent, the one that said not to look for you? You should know, I thought I could keep it. But one night I balled it up and threw it…"

"Look, there." The words left Paul's lips before he knew it as Vernon's lights began to slow in mid-block. "Remember, let's just see what he does."

As Greg eased their speed back, the Cadillac turned into a small apartment lot. They drew closer, and Paul Opened to listen, but heard only the quieting engine and two people breathing.

As they drove slowly past the driveway, Vernon stepped from the car. And walked off, alone, up the apartments' walkway.

"Where's Lor?" Greg gasped.

"She's fine." Inside the Cadillac, she was breathing clearly. He heard her gasp and then break into sobs.

The moment Vernon disappeared behind his door, Greg swung open his own, jumping out of his car in the street to scramble toward the lot. Paul snatched up Greg's phone—just in case—and ran just behind him, almost slipping on the snow.

As they closed on the long, black shape, its door swung open. Then Lorraine and Greg were in each others' arms.

Paul saw them cling together for a long moment, clutching and whispering. Until—and he couldn't tell who moved first—they began walking, still wrapped around each other, back toward their escape.

Paul returned to the car first, opening the door and looking back to wave them in. Just then, he saw Vernon stepping back outside.

Greg saw him too.

"You!" Greg spun to face him as Vernon trotted slowly toward them. And instead of yelling, Greg kept one arm around his wife and hissed, "If you *ever* look at her again, I'll send that picture straight to *Dina's Dirt* with the whole story! And *then* I'll kill you."

Vernon's fists came up and he snarled, "Don't you ever threaten her..." Paul knew he didn't mean Lorraine.

But then Vernon let his hands drop, and looked at his shoes. "Just... just let it end, alright? She liked you once, and I have to trust you sometime."

He reached into a pocket. Paul took a step forward, and heard Greg move, too.

What Vernon drew out was a small, cloth-wrapped bundle. "Here's the jewelry and the rest I took from your house. I just wanted it not to be too obvious that I was looking for leverage on you. Just… leave us alone."

"Leave *you*…" Greg began, but caught himself.

Softly, Lorraine answered, "That's all we wanted."

Paul watched them look at each other, Greg and Lorraine watching Vernon and his extended hand as he studied them and then Paul, too. No doubt Lorraine was reading the big man's thoughts, but everyone's gaze was sharp, heavy with evaluation.

None of them broke the silence. Vernon simply handed Greg the bundle and turned away, his footsteps muffled in the snow.

Greg and Lorraine moved for their car, arms still around each other. Paul watched them together and then placed the phone on the seat.

As he walked away, the soft, steady snowfall never slowed.

Paul woke early, lying on the lumpy bed and trying to doze off again. *Ah, Sunday. Nobody at their work for me to watch, a whole day both urging me to relax and pushing me to search every room people have left empty.*

He shifted under the covers, trying to steal another hour of recovery from his injuries, his worries, and his long night at Quinn's. Had that really been just one night before Vernon's drive?

It was useless trying to sleep, of course. Too many new changes and old questions kept chasing through his head. And he knew what he still had to do.

My father wouldn't even be up yet. Paul trudged out into the dawn, finding still not much more than an inch of snow to shuffle through— *thank God!*—as he took the subway to the locker that held his rarest possession.

It had been three months since he'd risked taking out the battered old laptop he'd scavenged, even to copy his journals to it. But now he tucked the computer into his backpack and made his way to Lou's Lunches for a cheap breakfast and a good download speed. *Maybe there'll be something in my past cases that will inspire me—or help me stall.*

He took his time eating and delayed running the letter-replacement tool to decipher his journals, first checking the email accounts he'd used in the past when one-way remailer messages would have been ignored.

And there it was. It had been sent to an email he'd used months ago, when he'd needed a brief dialog with one reporter about a bribery case he was giving him. *A reporter at Sarah Gomez's paper.* And now that long-cold trail had a new message, as untraceable as some of his own, but all too clear:

"Are you standing behind me or standing behind me? I have facts on *him* but not much time."

Sarah figured it out, that her colleague's story was my tip, too—or else she was sending testing emails like that to every anonymous source she heard about. Paul grimaced at the screen, wishing he'd just given her a real email account to answer instead of goading her with one-way messages.

Worst of all, she was right. Just as at the rally, he'd been staying "behind her" more to evade her than to really help her recover from his mistake. And what did her having "not much time" mean?

He opened a reply but then closed it again and tried typing the facts he had about Koenig's frame. Which bits could he tell her, or promise her, or…

He clicked the laptop shut. No point, there was no point in making any more promises until he stopped his family from drowning out the truth.

* * *

Don't accuse them, don't fight with them, somehow I've got to get through! He kept telling himself that all the way to Greg's house. Chasing Vernon at Paul's side might have made Greg more grateful than their father was, but Paul had no illusions about how long every-one's tempers would hold.

Still, he walked boldly up to the house, delaying only long enough to be sure nobody was watching. This was no time to bring trouble on any of them.

He could hear both Greg and Lorraine moving around inside, so he rang the bell.

Long seconds later, Greg's footsteps reached the door and it swung open.

Before Paul could open his mouth, his brother said, "Whatever it is, don't say it yet. We're heading to Dad now, so why argue it all out twice?"

Because you might listen, and then he might even listen to you. But Paul swallowed and nodded, not trusting his voice.

Greg leaned back inside. He'd sounded a bit cold to Paul, but his voice warmed as he called, "It's him alright. How soon can you be ready?"

"Right now," he heard Lorraine say. And only seconds later, she stepped into view, carrying coats and a sheaf of papers.

She didn't look at him.

As Paul followed them to the car, he saw how the couple twice found reasons to touch each other, and yet they also seemed to hold themselves a bit stiff, farther apart than usual. He settled in the BMW's back seat, not sure what to make of it.

He tried focusing his thoughts as a message for Lorraine: *Am I still the enemy?* and sometimes, *How much did you tell him?* But if she sensed anything, she gave no sign. And Greg only seemed awkward with her, not shocked enough for him to have just heard he was married to someone with impossible powers, let alone *that* frightening talent.

Paul could only worry about his own case now. *Will any of them really listen to me?*

The drive took forever.

They headed to the Schuman office, never doubting their father would be in the middle of his usual Sunday visit to evaluate the week's business. It was only in the elevator that Paul asked "Does he know about last night?"

"Of course we told him." Greg still sounded a bit cold, but still unreadable.

Then Greg was unlocking the door and Paul found himself following them past the empty desks and silent phones to the one room someone moved within. When they neared the door, Paul pulled ahead of the others and opened it himself.

Ian Schuman was standing, hands behind his back, surveying some of the pictures and mementoes on his wall—unlike Greg, he hung up no inspirational signs or charts of the firm's profits, only tokens of the actual events they'd run.

Is that one yesterday's rally, already framed?

"Just let me say, I'm sorry," Paul said as his father turned toward him. "I'm sorry we keep fighting about… well, everything. But if my helping Lorraine last night means anything, please, just let me say this without going over what you think happened in the past."

He paused for breath, and his father stepped around and sat behind the desk. No answer yet. Greg and Lorraine moved around beside that desk.

"I want your help undoing the Animal Alliance frame," Paul said softly.

"Just like that." His father didn't rush the words, but the tone was as cold as the slam of a steel door. "You want us to tear down something we've put all our resources behind. And you think you can just ask us to forget that you stabbed us in the back."

But I didn't! No, don't fight! Paul kept his fists from clenching, leaving them limp at his sides. Arguing about that night would just lead straight back to his hazy memory, and then the power itself, the secret everyone was safer not knowing.

He said "I'm sorry you had to take Quinn's money again," and when his father's eyes widened a fraction, he said, "I know, and Greg already knew. I'm not sure how involved Quinn is in anything, but believe me: I'd never have done anything if I'd guessed it would push you toward him again."

Maybe if I help Dad break free—but I don't dare *suggest that when I have no idea if it could work.* Trying to settle the break-in had made Lorraine demanding, but to dangle *that* hope…

"But, about the Alliance," he went on, taking a deeper breath. "The truth is already coming out—you know that—about their precious pictures and accusations about LifeLab. It's going to happen. Do you really want to be linked to those liars?"

Greg snapped, "You forget, we already are!" and the blank face he'd carefully kept all morning dissolved to a scowl. "The lab isn't our client, while the whole city knows we're the ones putting the Alliance in the spotlight."

And if I had begged you to stay clear of the lab instead of the activists, you'd have rushed to save them *from me?* The taunt burned on Paul's tongue but he bit it back.

Instead, he took a step toward them, looking from where Greg stood to his father at the desk, and then back. More softly, he said, "Look… this is more important than clients or the firm. Maybe you can save this group from the backlash that's coming, but you can't publicize away how many people still need this lie settled cleanly and completely." *Sarah's career, LifeLab's reputation. Me, after I failed.*

His father leaned back, just a fraction, in his chair. "So, we should change sides because you say the other people are more innocent? You *are* wasting our time."

"But…" Paul looked at his father's features set so rigidly, with no hint of the pride or passion they could display when a goal connected with him. *He has no idea what it means for me to have a purpose—but maybe if he knew about me, or Sarah…*

"Look, I… I screwed up," he began. His father's eyes flickered, colder than ever. "I guess, by coming here at all," he finished.

"Stop saying that!"

"Lor?" Greg turned to his wife, but not so quickly, as if he'd half expected her to speak.

"Paul, we *do* owe you." She put a hand on Greg's shoulder, but her blue eyes looked straight at Paul. "I asked you to figure out a break-in, and you found it was Vernon, trying to protect Bennet."

"I keep saying I'm sorry—" Greg said.

"I know," she said, glancing toward him now. "But you've only said it to me."

Greg looked at her, his expression spinning between guilt, anger, other things.

"And Paul risked his life to find out. You don't even know how desperate Vernon was!"

Paul's father said soothingly "We're all glad you're alright, but—"

"No!"

Paul saw both Schumans stare, from the corner of his eye as he did too. *Tactful, helpful Lorraine* interrupted *Dad? We don't do that even half the times we're dying to!*

She went on, "I mean, after that long drive with Vernon and his babbling—after that, I spent the morning online, and I—"

"Good morning! Is anyone in?"

Everyone whirled to look at the closed door and the voice from beyond it.

The voice added, "It's Detective Reid."

"Yes," Paul's father called, and Paul saw his startled face begin smoothing away its shock as he stood up from the desk. "Give me a moment."

"I heard you were at work on Sundays." And Reid walked closer with quick steps that Paul's Opened hearing tracked as he strode deeper into the main room. "I wanted to check on something."

Like if I was here? Paul stole an anxious glance around the room, already knowing there were no other ways out. He took a step toward his father, who paused at the desk, eyeing him curiously.

Then Lorraine moved to the office door and slipped out, opening it only wide enough to pass and shutting it smoothly behind her. "How can I help you?" they heard her say.

"Ms. Schuman." And Reid's footsteps kept coming, moving past her.

No more time! Paul dove past his father and down behind the desk, pulling his feet in just before he heard the door handle turn.

"And Mr. Schuman, and Mr. Schuman," Reid went on. "You shouldn't leave your door unlocked, not so soon after someone tried to rob the office."

"I know." That voice was Greg, sounding a little embarrassed.

Paul tucked himself in tighter as his father's leather shoes shifted their angle, almost in Paul's face. His father turned toward where Reid's voice came from and said calmly, "So how can we help you? Do you have news about the robbery?"

"That would be my question. This isn't the first time a Schuman's place has been broken into."

"If you've seen those reports, you know that was simple theft," Greg sighed.

He left it at that, even after the pause that would be Reid giving him a long look.

Then the detective said "That was how it looked then. But this is the second incident. Followed by the third, if you say you saw the thief near your wife. But you," and Paul knew he was turning to her now, "say it wasn't him."

"I'm sorry, I didn't get a good look at him." Lorraine's voice was the most natural in the room, uneasy with the subject but unafraid, and Paul realized she was the one who could probe whether Reid really suspected anything. "But why would it be him anyway?"

"Do you think there's a danger?" Paul's father broke in.

"There could be, from the thief," Reid said. "*You're* not in danger from the law for hiding anything. Not yet."

"Then let's hope that it is over." And right as he said it, the tip of his shoe *nudged* Paul in the shoulder.

Paul barely kept from gasping aloud. *Dammit, Dad! You* had *to, didn't you?*

"Of course," Reid was saying. "People always tell me they hope a thing blows over, before it does. Sometimes they're saying it through all the time that the one thing they *didn't* say could have ended the problem before someone got hurt, and badly. Think of just how deeply the crowbar dented your cabinet out there…"

Reid paused again and Paul Opened his hearing and flicked a probe from one of the Schumans to the next, testing if any of them were holding or struggling with their breath. All three sounded close to calm.

The detective went on, "Anyway, what brings all three of you into the office on a Sunday?"

"Business. As you said you knew, at least about my own work habits."

This time Reid only paused a moment. "Then I'll let you get back to it. Thank you for your time. I'm sure I'll see you again." He walked out and the door shut behind him.

At once, Paul Opened his hearing again—and sure enough, Reid took only two steps from the door before he paused, stopping to listen. The others let out a collective sigh.

Paul leaped up, spun around his father, and flung up a hand to keep them silent. The next instant he shut his eyes and threw a probe toward Reid again, afraid he'd find him just opening the door...

But the detective waited only a few heartbeats more and then started out again. Paul kept his hand up and crept to the door, pressing his ear against it for the others to see, until he heard Reid pass by and close the outer door. Then he let his hand drop.

Greg hissed, "*Police* now? Whose side are you *on*, Paul?"

"You're forgetting," Lorraine said, "Vernon came here because of you... you and the Councilwoman."

"Right." Greg looked down, just for a moment. "But..."

"Just listen." She stepped away from him, toward the center of the room, where she could face them all... almost where Paul had stood, he realized. "None of us knew how dangerous this was. Or what Paul was taking the brunt of."

"Alright, Lorraine." Paul's father spoke slowly, settling back in his chair. "What is this we've been missing?"

She turned away from the others to face him. "What I think Vernon was really afraid would come out. Not just that Bennet had the affair, but that she had once embezzled some of the city funds."

"*Erin?*" Ian almost laughed aloud. "Impossible."

Lorraine stepped right up to him, across the desk. "Were *you* trapped in Vernon's car all night? Every time I thought he'd run out of reasons to worship her, he'd find more. And I read between those lines, and today I looked up some hints about what happened in her first year in office. I think she repaid all the money later—but she still took it. And Vernon would do anything if he thought someone was about to reveal *that*."

Paul shook his head, watching her in amazement. She'd not only picked the secret out of Vernon's mind, but she'd managed to explain that away while still standing up to both Schumans. *For me.*

Greg moved to her side. "So that's what you were researching—and it's why we've been—Lor, I'm so sorry. Again," he added with a faint, sad laugh.

He reached a hand toward her, and she took it. As if everything Greg had done wrong had just melted away.

Paul scowled. *How can she just…*

"And thanks to you," Paul's father added, "that problem seems to be done with. For as long as we want," and he smiled slightly. "That is, if we ever do need something badly enough from our Councilwoman…"

"No!"

The word burst out of Paul before he knew it, ringing through the room.

"I fought Vernon and searched the city to save you, *not* to give you a new bargaining chip!" Paul found himself at the desk, with Greg and Lorraine shouldered aside behind him as he glared down right at his father's face. Getting close kept him from screaming, but he felt the muscles clench in his neck, his hands, all through him. "Don't you *ever* use that against her, or anyone! Because if you do, believe me, I'll know."

Inches away, those eyes narrowed and blazed back at him. His father didn't rise, didn't move, only growled "Are you threatening me?"

"One threat, yes," Paul spat back. "One line you don't cross."

"I see."

His eyes flicked over Paul, no doubt taking in every smudge and rip in his clothes, looking for weakness. Paul kept his own gaze straight on his father's eyes, his will hammering at him. *Show me, show me your thoughts, however she does it I have to KNOW—*

Nothing.

But his father didn't say more. *Good enough.*

Paul straightened up and stepped back to take in all three of them again. "Just don't. Any of you." He looked from his silent father to his open-mouthed brother to Lorraine, who stood back behind Greg. *She'll be the one facing the real pressure, if she ever lets them know.*

He kept turning, letting his head's motion draw his body around to face the door. A few steps brought him to it, and he looked back.

"I guess I've wasted enough time. Good luck with your truce with Vernon. And," he added when they didn't stir, "when I settle the Animal Alliance fraud, be careful where that leaves you."

The door swung open in his hand and shut behind him, covering him as he marched away.

His steps came quickly, firmly, like the steps of someone ready to win his battle on his own. *Which I'll have to.* Even though his hands shook, and the shock of cold through his veins now was worse than a dozen winters.

My God, where did that come from? No wonder they flinched, I almost bragged *about exposing my family as blackmailers the last time. Do I hate the idea that much?* Paul shook his head, hard, trying to clear it. Did that mean he *could* have done it then? *But I was so careful not to send anything that pointed to them…*

Not that it mattered now. Now he had to undo Koenig's frame, and he had to do it alone.

"So you're still going after the Alliance?"

It was Greg, behind him. Paul froze with his hand on the outer door. Greg was half running after him, and Paul hadn't noticed a sound.

When Greg closed in, Paul sighed. "Their lies are destroying the lab." It was the only thing he could think to say. "Let's just say I have to." He felt numb, emptied out by the last clash. *Why couldn't they let me just walk out?*

Instead, Greg caught at his arm, making Paul jerk back out of reach, as he said, "You mean *you* choose who to stop, and we just back away and let you? Why you?"

Because maybe I was chosen? Because I made it worse? "Because I know. I know about that lie, so I either choose to help the people at the lab or I choose to let it destroy them." Paul felt his gaze dip to the floor, then found it harder to look back up.

"Help them, and cripple the Alliance—just like that? There are a lot of good people with that group, you know. And those animals and their pain are *real*—well, all the other ones."

"I know they care. I've seen them." Paul remembered his rage with his father and how much he'd hated lies and blackmailers. *Does all this just make me crazy? Now or two years ago…*

"So they care, and you don't?" Greg spat as he caught Paul's shoulder again.

At the touch, Paul yanked his head up and snapped, "Neither do you! Just *try* to tell me that they're anything more than a way to get back at me!"

Greg didn't move. Paul saw the angry clenching in his features freeze and then saw his lip tremble, faintly.

Behind him, the office door opened, and they both glanced over to see their father and Lorraine looking at them. Silent.

Then Greg pushed Paul back and tightened his scowl, and said "It's not about you, or them. I'll take whatever helps us build the firm… period."

He's lying, Paul realized. Greg *did* want to help the Alliance, and probably not just them. He wasn't the same driven climber who'd tried to blackmail the hospital… but he'd never admit that where their father could hear.

Whichever way I go, someone good gets hurt. But the truth was already winning out.

"I can't stop," Paul said, raising his voice to reach all three of them. "Koenig's still a fraud. All you can do is insist his lies aren't the whole truth, if you want to still have an Animal Alliance left to work with."

Greg's face didn't change. It was the same hard mask, but after a moment, the lines softened a little. "Uh-huh," he said. "Maybe… maybe you don't have a choice after all."

He turned away then, and Paul thought he heard him mutter something. His hearing Opened almost by reflex and he caught:

"So *that's* who you are, Paulie."

Paul watched him. Somehow, from the fumbling sound in Greg's voice and the way it settled after that, he knew Greg had no idea Paul could hear him. *He isn't thinking about what I've become, he doesn't care about "what" or "how," but now he understands a little of my Why.*

The Alliance, that Greg had rushed to defend from Paul. Paul's old letter, that Greg had tossed away but never cleaned up, and tried to confess about last night. *However much Greg has started to care about the Alliance now, it was my warning that made him go to them… and all because he wanted to find his brother and see if I was really his enemy.*

As he stared, he heard another voice, calmer, steadier:

"No, you have no choice at all," his father said. "But I expect the firm can survive re-inventing one client's image, if we move quickly. You do have a plan, don't you?"

Paul watched his father standing there by the office door, waiting. He didn't smile, but he didn't have to.

"Uh… of course. Just let me check some things."

"Of course. Don't take too long."

Then his father stepped back into the office and shut the door before Paul could find any more words to say. Before he could quite believe it.

*   *   *

Twice, Paul slipped and almost fell down in the slush—his feet couldn't seem to remember where he was. But still, he made it to the library intact, just in time for its Sunday afternoon opening.

The first of the Sunday patrons were already lined up outside. Paul had to walk quickly to get a first turn on one of the computers, and he promised himself he'd make full use of the time he was taking away from all the busy students behind him. He already knew four different searches that he meant to make, searches he couldn't risk doing on the laptop in his bag.

Then he checked the email Sarah had contacted before, and froze.

"I'm sorry, but I can't stay on this. I'm being sent out of town tomorrow. It's a small story, but a chance to save my job."

No!

Paul re-read the words. *Just when I was so close! If only I had answered her this morning—* Then his eyes moved upward to the message's time, and down to the computer's clock. *Two minutes ago.*

Could she still be online? He pounded out an email of nothing but the header "IT'S HAPPENING TOMORROW!", and reached to send it—then caught himself and changed it to a less spam-like "We save LifeLab TOMORROW!" before firing it off. It wouldn't work if she thought his plea was just another desperate ad to delete.

More slowly, fingers trembling, he started tapping out the details in a second message. "We're about to expose Koenig," yes, he had to confirm that, first thing off. "Be at the Alliance press conference tomorrow morning," no doubt Schuman and Son could push them to hold one. As long as—"That is, if you can risk staying in town a little longer. We can talk after"—

A new email appeared, straight from Sarah's address and shorter than his: "I'm in."

Paul sagged back in the chair, with a sigh that made the boy at the next terminal turn and give him an odd look. Paul gave him a grin and then looked back and reread his own message. Everything he needed was already there, especially that last promise to meet her. He added that and sent it off.

Over the next hour, while he twice had to leave and wait for a new terminal, Sarah sent him her research about James Koenig and LifeLab. Much of it matched what Paul had found, but her details—everything from an interview with Koenig's former boss, a study of his past, to information from the friends he'd drifted away from—added new depth to Paul's sense of their target. Koenig was a longtime lab technician who had been slowly drawn into crushing regret over the animals suffering down the hall.

It started with Koenig's guilt. And today was about Greg's guilt over driving me away. And now, my guilt about helping this fraud get started. Everyone's got regrets.

Time to do something about it.

*   *   *

"Remember, our strategy is to keep the pressure on," Greg said. "A press conference tomorrow morning gives the city just long enough to wonder what you'll do next."

"I see," came the voice of the Alliance leader—Wilson, Paul finally remembered his name. "Sounds good, if we can keep them satisfied."

Paul heard a grunt of agreement, probably Koenig. He smiled and shifted in his place beside the mansion's back wall. The plan *had* made perfect sense when Greg and Lorraine told it, and on a Sunday meeting, it was easy for Wilson to make it with so little warning. More importantly, Koenig was there too.

"Now here's the question," Greg went on. "The LifeLab pictures gave you the shock value to get this far. But is that what this has to be?"

"What are you saying?" Koenig asked. Paul thought he detected just a hint of a growl.

More carefully, Wilson said, "Please, don't say the lab was why we've gotten attention. We got that because we have dedicated people and dozens of very real problems we take on, including LifeLab—this is an Animal *Alliance*, remember. Of course, having all your help…"

"…didn't hurt?" Lorraine filled in, and Paul heard several laughs.

"Thanks," Greg said. "We've talked about what you can say next, but the question is, where should LifeLab be in your story when… frankly, when your accusations stop holding up."

"*When?*" Wilson asked, incredulous.

"We've been following the investigation, and I'm sure you have, too," Greg said. "And, there have been some new signs," and Greg paused just long enough to make someone swallow nervously—though Paul doubted Koenig did. "But the real story here is the hundreds of *other* labs and institutions that are almost as bad as you've said LifeLab was, or worse. And when people start disbelieving that one claim, will they ever listen to the others?"

For just a moment, Paul couldn't hear a single sound within.

Then Wilson sighed. "There are always people that don't listen. Our job is to spread the message without them."

"Alright. Just, think about it," and Greg went on discussing talking points and later events to follow the conference. Wilson's broad knowledge and passion helped him build the plan step by step. None of them mentioned the LifeLab charges again, even when Greg hinted at them. And Koenig kept quiet.

Soon, Lorraine said her goodbyes and headed out to her car, leaving Greg behind. Paul met her at the other side of the block.

"I watched Koenig's mind," she said. "I can tell that he's worried and he does really care about animals, as well as hating LifeLab. Oh, and it *was* him that made the fake photos," she added with a smile.

"Ah." Paul felt himself flush; it was one thing they'd never actually confirmed, in all his explorations. "Well, thanks."

"And I think he did it alone. Also, your father says Bennet was glad to help at the press conference, even before he hinted it might help reduce the tension over the Alliance's accusations. Even after Greg's… mistake, those two are still friends." She shook her head, marveling.

When Dad's not thinking of blackmailing her. But Paul smiled back, nodding slowly. "Then everyone's all set. Except James Koenig himself."

*   *   *

Well into the night, the apartment complex was quiet. Trimmed trees and brush lined the paths around the buildings, and Paul could hear a baby crying, probably part of one of the families he'd seen walking when the sun had been out. A nice enough place, cleaner than Vernon's, too simple for Greg.

Too late to back out now. It was ten hours to the announcement— and only three of those would be daylight. *One chance, to stop Koenig from fighting back when we make our move.*

Paul steeled himself and began the careful move to the back door, turning around each of the few cameras and probing for anyone out late. Not a soul stirred, even when he reached Koenig's apartment and his gloved hands slid just the right key into the lock.

Koenig's breathing, deep asleep, gave Paul his direction. Gliding through the dimness of the outer room, Paul tried not to think about what had to come next. *Had to.*

Koenig didn't stir. He only lay huddled in his bed beneath a bookshelf on the wall—a shelf he'd hung a cloth over to cover the books. *Probably related to the career he once had,* Paul mused, *and he's ashamed to see them but he's left them in place as some kind of reminder.*

No more stalling.

Paul crept up, and Koenig's breathing didn't change, as Paul felt along the wall and unplugged the bedside lamp. On a hunch, he slid the nightstand drawer open a fraction; sure enough, the former tech had a flashlight there, prepared for any emergency. Paul carefully removed it, glad there hadn't been a gun, too.

Then he leaned right over the thinning red hair, summoned the coldest and cruelest voice he could shape his throat around, and said it.

"Well done, James."

"Wha… who…" Koenig mumbled as he lurched up and swung a fist around. But Paul had already pulled back, two steps out of reach.

"A successful research firm, a comfortable Alliance… you were the only one unhappy. But you found a way to make your scam just believable enough."

Pudgy hands flailed in the dark, perfectly clear to Paul as they struggled to find the lamp. The switch clicked, useless.

"Who are you?" Koenig gasped as he groped for the drawer.

"Curious," Paul said with the faintest laugh as Koenig found the flashlight missing. "Did you really think LifeLab kept so few records that your one trick would outweigh them all?"

Koenig flung off his blankets and charged at Paul, night-blind and clumsy—giving Paul more than enough time to step aside and then shove his victim against the wall with an unpracticed arm-lock anyone could have dodged in daylight.

He leaned closer to the face he held pinned to the wall and hissed: "Did you even look at how much dirt the newspaper really got? Did you think it was all *yours*?" And Paul felt the shock all the way through Koenig's well-padded frame.

"Who... who *are* you?" The voice was barely a squeak.

"Nobody you'd remember. You only remember your Animal Alliance, and you might remember other anti-science groups who'll never recover from having your lies exposed. You remember LifeLab, and how some people will always blame it for you. But you do not remember the other labs."

"The other... you... you're with the competition?"

"I am now. And thank you for the chance—we'll save a fortune in bribes now that this is ending. Will you keep your pricey PR firm when the contributions dry up?"

Koenig trembled but didn't reply.

"But most of all I came to ask you something. Did you really think you made this near-perfect frame all by yourself? Can anyone fool himself so completely?"

Paul gritted his teeth as he finished. The poison he was whispering was now stinging himself more with every word. He *had* been the first one to fall for the fraud.

But Koenig's struggles stilled from weak to limp. "I just... just wanted to hurt the Lab," he moaned.

"And you did, you hurt one lab. But you didn't answer me: did you think you did it alone?"

"Let me *GO!*" and Koenig lurched back against Paul and wrenched free. Paul stumbled away, his back slammed into another wall and he slid down it.

But Koenig stared around, slowed by pain and the dim light. Before he could charge again, Paul drew the flashlight from his pocket and, closing his own eyes, he switched it on and shone the beam straight into Koenig's.

In the moment Koenig froze, Paul stood and clicked the light off. In the dimness he rushed away, needing only a few steps to reach the door. There he paused a moment to toss the flashlight onto a couch. *I don't steal. I can shatter a man's soul with his own fears, but I can't steal his flashlight—*

Then he was rushing away down the hall, quick and silent. Alone.

Paul didn't stop, didn't even slow down to hear what Koenig said or did in his wake. Not when he feared he could have heard every tear fall.

*   *   *

A few uneasy hours of sleep did nothing to refresh him. A long, hard scrubbing in the tub, twice over, couldn't make Paul feel clean. Even when he joined the first visitors walking into City Hall, well before the Alliance press conference, he could only keep telling himself there'd been no way to guarantee the plan would work except to completely shock Koenig himself… and he still half hoped the stricken man never joined them.

But it was Koenig's fault. His lies started all this.

Or had something older than that been driving Paul? Was it his own hatred for liars—and for being fooled—that drove him to brutalize someone that way? He could only sag against the wall, waiting, waiting.

And in Koenig shuffled, barely keeping up with Wilson and other Animal Alliance members, his father and Greg and Lorraine there beside them. Paul kept his head down as they passed by, not sure whose gaze he most wanted to avoid. He heard them turn the corner to the place they'd chosen to speak, and he waited as more and more reporters trickled in with their pads and cameras—

Sarah.

Black hair shining, fearless step echoing along the corridor, tinkering with the recorder in her hands…

And I want to meet her now, *after doing that?* But he found himself stepping right toward her, too suddenly to hesitate, as another thought crossed his mind: *At least I had those baths.*

He moved up beside her, gesturing on past the corner. "The Alliance is right up there," he said. His voice was perfect.

She nodded and walked right past him, barely looking.

Paul froze, watching her. Every step, every moment, the click of her heels drew her farther away, it was already too awkward to call after her—

Scowling, he watched her turn the corner and then counted twenty more seconds before he let himself follow. Of course, he'd forgotten that not everyone would recognize someone just from a voice.

Around the corner, the sides were gathering. Reporters were joined by more and more people with only an onlooker's attitude, stood in a shifting half-circle around the activists. Or rather, standing around the three or four activists and their banners, that were holding the spot they'd chosen, under tall portraits of several of the city's founders. Paul couldn't remember which founder was supposed to be the early voice for the wilds that made him the perfect backdrop.

Not that it mattered, when the real action would be in the meeting room behind them, where Councilwoman Bennet had arranged for the Alliance to make its final preparations.

Paul eased over to the far edge of the onlookers. Bennet stood near the center front with Vernon beside her; he saw Sarah with other journalists, turned half toward the Councilwoman but really watching the spot where the speech would be.

And all he could do now was listen. *Please, let this work. Let this sick feeling I have be wrong.* He shut his eyes, and Opened his hearing to the room beyond.

Not a sound.

For an instant, Paul thought everyone was gone—then he heard the rustle of pages being turned—turned loudly, faster and faster.

"Where did you *get* this?" Wilson said, and Paul knew why he'd been reading so fast. They'd chosen the papers that would unsettle him most, but he was truly furious.

"Anonymously," Paul's father said without a quaver. "But you see my point."

Koenig began, "Just what is…"

"You tell me!" Wilson snapped, almost shouting. A moment later he went on, his voice low and fierce. "These are LifeLab records. Your pictures, plus theirs… no, *don't bother.* But see these stories? Time after time after *time,* every time an activist group got caught in a fraud… the public faith is lost, reform laws are shelved, there's new suffering—everything is set back *years!"*

"What?" Koenig's voice made Paul cringe. He sounded not just devastated now but completely crumbling.

Lorraine added, "Just why did you join them, anyway?"

"Yeah, why?" someone else asked, and another activist rumbled angrily.

"But…" In a ragged whisper, Koenig managed "But, if we keep pushing them—"

"So it's *true?"* Wilson hissed.

Just then the door creaked open and closed quickly, and another voice said "They're getting restless out—um, I can come back—"

Greg's voice said "Just let us settle a few—"

"We'll be right out," Wilson answered.

Paul heard one startled yelp from where Koenig stood, and then he saw the door fly open and Wilson march out, his hand all but dragging Koenig along behind him.

A barrage of shouts burst from the reporters. Some were just reacting to the speakers' entrance while others had real questions they were trying to shout out a half-second before the rest. Paul stumbled as bodies slammed into him—but he'd been prepared for that moment.

Wilson let Koenig go and stepped up to the front. Even as dozens of voices shouted at him, he kept his head down, flipping through the folder he carried. Paul Opened his sight for a moment, long enough to look closer and see stark fear on the Alliance leader's face. He didn't even stand near the microphone they'd set up.

The other activists moved up around him, carrying signs or plac-ards nearly as large as they were, but showing only the signs' heavy card backs to the audience now as they waited for their leader's direction. Koenig drifted around in their midst, awkward and empty-handed. As more questions flew, Paul saw his father and Greg moving around to the front.

"What's next for Animal Alliance?"

"Was someone shouting in there?"

"What's your reply to LifeLab's lawsuit—"

"We're sorry," Wilson gasped out, flinging up his hand, "about the suit. So sorry. But it's... not what's most important here."

"Jill Marx, *WebNow*!" one reporter hollered, pouncing on his fumbling answer. "So what *is* more important, Mr. Wilson?"

"The other labs!" and Wilson looked straight at the reporters, his words ringing loudly enough to silence them for a moment.

"There's a list," he went on, digging in the folder again. "I know I have it, a list of labs and their medical experiments on animals—or what they always call 'medical,'" he added, and his words began to come faster now. "Labs accused of doing about the same thing as LifeLab, labs that sometimes get sued and sometimes sue the other side first—but how does that matter to the animals? Look!"

He flung up a picture, a rat with a hideous set of straps and wires binding it in some tortuous position. As the crowd gasped, he passed the picture to one of his friends to hold up. He spoke more steadily now, hammering out his words one after the other and not letting himself stop.

"That's from a lab in Portland. And here," he said, brandishing another of a monkey, "is from one in Orange County! Baton Rouge! Denver! Charleston…"

He broke off then, and added "But then, in the time it would take to read all these, whole species will go extinct."

And he spilled the whole file down at their feet, papers flying in all directions.

When Paul and the crowd looked up again, Wilson was staring right at them, spreading his arms in a plea. "I always hear how groups like ours keep begging people to stop their lives because of one single case or another, instead of talking about 'the big picture.' But what I want to ask is, will you… the city… the country… care about what that big picture *really* is, no matter how those few cases turn out?"

"And how," Sarah Gomez called, "are they turning out?"

Her clear shout echoed perfectly after Wilson's question, seizing a pause in the speech that even the other reporters hadn't noticed, and stretching it out, making the whole crowd hold its breath.

"They say," Wilson began again, "that we will do anything to create a moment people will remember. Well, I say there are some things we don't need to do, because the evidence is all around us. We don't need to lie."

"Or, protect someone else who does lie?" she asked.

This time, nobody waited. Shouts and sheer buzzes of excitement surged up, almost as loud as when Wilson had stepped out. Paul saw Sarah shouting her next question and Opened just enough to hear her words: "So who's lying?" But he doubted another soul could make out that much.

Long moments later, the worst of the thunder had passed. Paul saw Councilwoman Bennet stepping forward just beyond the line of reporters. Vernon moved in behind her.

And as he looked around, his eyes somehow fell on Paul, and his gaze turned to pure hatred.

What the—

"It's… true," James Koenig's voice began. Haltingly, a ruined voice with a metal echo from leaning right into the mic. It was a strange sound after Wilson's passionate, unamplified speech. "I used to work for LifeLab, that's on the record. I… just wanted justice for the animals there, and—"

"And you are the obvious scapegoat," Erin Bennet shouted, "for the Alliance to try to back away from the vital truths they have uncovered about this 'medical' lab. And I assure you, I will see LifeLab fully prosecuted, and I will ensure that these poor creatures have not suffered in vain!"

"You—"

Koenig couldn't seem to breathe. Somewhere, Paul heard a car horn honk, far away on the street. But the shock, the shock slowly faded from the liar's face.

"Well," and he shook Bennet's hand, "it's about time!"

Behind them, Paul could see Wilson staring, his face as gray as the snow in the gutters. To the side, his father, Greg, and Lorraine had only begun to whisper together in confusion.

A moment later, Bennet turned back toward the crowd and began answering the questions the astonished reporters shouted. But the more they yelled, the more they pushed and jostled Paul and each other.

He couldn't see Sarah at all now.

Numbly, Paul let the reporters shove forward, edging him back as they shouted their questions at Bennet, echoing louder and more mixed together under the city hall roof. He could see Vernon with the Councilwoman, trying to keep some space clear around her. Koenig seemed almost lost at Bennet's side as she fielded question after question.

"Why your sudden support for the Alliance?"

"I've always supported animal rights. We can't allow…"

It's all wrong. Everything Bennet said, in public or private, has been about calming down this furor, not… Paul drifted to the rear of the crowd, and noticed his father and Greg whispering together. They'd been left behind too, with Bennet and Koenig drawing the attention away from them.

"…and he'll probably tell us to keep pushing, even now," Greg was muttering.

"It doesn't matter. With all the mud slung around…"

Paul wrenched his attention back to Bennet and the questions.

"But we keep hearing their evidence against LifeLab might have gaps. Are you saying that's no longer true?"

"It's always easy to doubt…"

She was moving, he realized, working her way slowly toward the building's entrance even as she gave her answers. Whatever her real motives were, they would never peek out in this storm of attention, and the crowd would keep her too busy to even whisper something useful to Vernon.

Have to think, find my next move.

"Councilwoman!" Wilson called belatedly as he stepped over to take part of the spotlight again. "This is the first time you've given our cause real support. I have to say, I'm surprised."

She simply countered, "You were just saying your work was done by many people, not just the ones who gave their whole lives to it. Don't tell me you're surprised someone agrees?"

On they moved, along the hall. The questions began repeating themselves more and more, and Bennet began walking more openly as she answered, making a smooth withdrawal. Wilson didn't say much more and Koenig stopped trying to keep up as they neared the entrance.

Paul saw his father seize a moment to step up to Bennet's side, and heard him whisper, "Erin, you could have warned us."

"No," she sighed. And then she stepped outside, gone.

Paul looked after her, at the pool of remaining journalists already breaking up or trailing out after her. He needed a plan, or he could just stay with Bennet… *and what, sit around all day hoping she'd mention what she was after?* He'd already tried pushing harder with Koenig, and even recruiting his family. *It's all going wrong! I need to think…*

As he made his way back toward where the conference had started, a movement of Greg's caught his eye, some sweep of Greg's hand that turned his conversation with Lorraine into an argument.

"Didn't you hear her? 'Scapegoat'! As if the Alliance had turned against Koenig to back out of chasing the lab. And the media's going to love hinting this big PR firm pushed them into *that* move! All because you had to help Paulie…"

Paul turned away, not wanting to hear more. It wasn't her fault, or even Greg's. *I'm the one who'd dragged them into my own mission.*

Then he saw her through the scattered people—Sarah, leaning all alone against the wall. She couldn't seem to raise her head, and as he watched, she banged a fist back against the wall.

Let it go, don't… But eight quick steps brought Paul right to her.

"Sarah? I'm sorry. I never planned on this."

Her head shot up. Her dark eyes went from wide to wider—too wide, as if she had been too confused even before she looked at him. Her gaze moved up and down to take in his battered look, which she'd never really seen before.

"Why apologize?" and her voice was ice. "The story just got even better. Except now I look worse for doubting them, and I just defied my editor to be here when Bill's covering it anyway. Already sending the story in, by now."

"But, they're lying." Paul couldn't seem to breathe but he wouldn't let himself look away. "Now Bennet's with them, but—"

"Maybe," Sarah said, nodding slowly. "I bet there's even more under it all, if you're right. Once it all comes out."

"Right—"

"And that leaves me as what?" She stepped toward him then, her hands planted on her hips. "Am I the front for your tips, just the girl who kept quiet about where it all came from? I *told* you, they were asking more about where I got all this than about the story. And what do I do now? Should I still try to get to that damn festival, or stay here chasing what everyone else is after?" She shook her head. "It's all too crazy for me."

"You're right."

The words slipped out before he thought, his tone cold and clipped. But he knew it was the truth.

"You're right, it's too much," he added. "But you'll figure out what to do. Just do whatever's better for your career. Since that's what really matters." And as she gaped, he turned and marched away.

Should have done that a week ago, he thought as the dead feeling settled in his chest. He should never have stayed in contact with her; just her being a smart reporter didn't mean she knew a thing about really fighting for the truth.

Don't kid yourself, and he sighed, hissing through his teeth. Of course he'd wanted to "pay his debt" to a beautiful woman he'd thought could accept a little of his life. Even after his own rage over his father, over just the hint of someone using the power's secrets for their own gain. *How weak can I be?*

He turned to the entrance, determined to hunt down Bennet. As he walked, he felt his laptop's weight in his pack, a reminder he'd use all his resources to follow up whatever he found. *I'll just get Sarah what she needs to take the story back, and let that be that the end of it. And I can still remind Vernon about that picture, or…*

A sharp *click-click* rang out behind him. His hearing Opened to confirm the heeled boots and the rapid pace, heading straight toward him. *Sarah? What do I say?*

He glanced back. Lorraine.

She was still fifteen feet back, but walking directly toward him. Beyond her, Sarah wasn't looking—but any moment, she could notice, or anyone else could. Paul's eyes darted to the entrance and he walked a bit faster, his hand behind his back making a small *Back off!* wave. It was just a flick of the fingers that nobody would spot unless they were looking directly at his back.

Lorraine's heels stopped, but a moment later, he thought he heard them move forward again, a softer step merged in the echoes around him. He Opened his hearing to be sure.

"Talk to me," she was whispering as she walked, "or you won't know what I read from Bennet."

Paul stopped dead, just close enough to the entrance to feel its cold draft. *She would, she just* would *keep the answers to get her way.*

As Lorraine drew closer, he started up again, slowing to let her catch up. As they stepped out into the sun, she drew up beside him, and he muttered, "Farther out." He slowed again to let her to move on away from him. Nothing to see but two people walking past each other.

She headed down the street and he moved slowly after her, falling farther behind along the pavement's well-salted snow. He strolled slowly, Opening his hearing and then his sight, searching around and using the mirrors of the parked cars to check behind him. Nobody sitting too still, nobody really following, no sign of Detective Reid or Vernon or anyone else. At last, he sped up again, to where she stood waiting.

Her first words, instead of any comments about their dance, were simply, "Bennet was being pressured to support the charges against the lab. That and her resentment were all I could sense."

"Thanks." It was the first thing he could think to say, but then he hesitated, just standing on the sidewalk next to her. Of *course* Bennet hadn't wanted to change sides, but to have someone just pull that answer out of the air... *no, no more letting anyone get involved.* "Um..."

"I couldn't tell Greg, of course." She looked past his shoulder, back at the building they'd left. "Not that he'd let me try. He kept saying this was crazy, and..."

Suddenly she looked back, right at Paul, and he saw fear in her blue eyes. "And when I tried to talk to him, he thought *I thought* he was defending his mistress, and he… I almost tried to read him again. I don't know *what* he'll do."

Oh God— "Bennet's long gone from here," Paul said, trying to make the words steady, as if it could fool either of them. "Where's Greg?"

"I'm not sure."

"Ask Dad," and Paul trotted back toward City Hall, struggling to picture its layout from his past cases there. *Where else could Greg go within it? Or, where could he have parked?*

Paul dashed inside, dodged around people, and ran up one corridor far enough to let him look up each branch, then Open his hearing in the hopeless hope of finding his brother's voice still somewhere inside. He ran back out, panting for breath, dashing right past his father before he realized it. The older Schuman had been on his phone, too intent to look around.

Out in the cold again, Paul searched up and down the street's row of cars, looking for the right shade of blue BMW. As he did, Lorraine rushed up beside him, pocketing her cell.

"He hasn't seen him. And Greg's not answering."

"Was your car…"

"It was right there. He's gone," she said as she waved up along the street at the vehicles quick to take Greg's parking space.

Then she stepped past them, out into the street. Just a step into it, but she flung up her arm so urgently she might have been standing in front of a bulldozer, not beside a passing taxi. She didn't have to say a word, the cab simply slowed and pulled over.

Paul bundled in behind her, fumbling when she turned to him for the directions to Bennet's office—which was as far from City Hall as Bennet could put it, he realized. *Some kind of political statement.*

Lorraine sat beside him, quieter than he and pulled into a tighter space, her eyes straight ahead.

Paul forced his panting breath to slow; this was going to be a long ride. And from the twinkle in the young Asian cabbie's eye when he saw the stylish woman with the ragged man, he knew neither of them would dare talk about much on the way.

We shouldn't talk at all. Not with all the danger and confusion he'd dragged them into, starting with her "catching" his power—or years earlier, at the hospital, when he couldn't just walk away from Greg's scheme cleanly. Lorraine's power and wit always made it so easy… *but no, I've cost them all enough.*

He glanced over at her again. Lorraine's hands were folded in her lap and her face looked calm, but he saw the tightness around her mouth. *She's trying to hide her worries—and she probably thinks her fight with Greg drove him to this.*

Paul's fist tightened. She had to know better, but part of her would still be blaming herself. *Why can't she see that she's not responsible for what drives Greg?* Paul knew how his brother could be fun or protective one minute, but then turn angry or work-obsessed.

It isn't right *that she stakes her confidence, her whole life, on someone who can't even be faithful to her.* But she always had, and even now, he had no way to tell her. Instead, he slowly forced his fingers to unclench and lifted his hand an inch. He was tempted to just reach over and take hers, to just—

A flush of warmth broke through him and his hand tingled even as he shoved it back down to the backpack in his lap. He locked his eyes on the windshield ahead, but he could almost feel the softness her hand would have had under his, the surprised sound she would have made at his touch. But he didn't know whether her eyes would have looked up in betrayal or—

Don't look, don't look, this is crazy! At least he couldn't see the cabbie's eyes on them in the mirror. Lorraine made no sound, just sat close beside him as his imagination stretched wider, hotter.

Crazy! And right after seeing how little chance he had with Sarah—that was it! It had to be his reaction to giving up his fantasy about Sarah. But this wave of attraction clutched too tightly to be some newborn feeling—and the reporter had never been so determined, so smart, so loyal as Lorraine—*Loyal, she's loyal to Greg, and this whole thing is insane!*

Paul fought the urge to draw his hands in tighter. *No, mustn't move a muscle, just get through each moment without drawing her eye.* A bead of sweat started inching, trickling, down his brow.

He turned away then, looking out the window and forward, as if probing the blocks ahead… and his eyes flew wide. What if her power itself was opening his thoughts to her?

Don't, don't think about that! He stared harder, Opening to fling his sight across the blocks to the traffic ahead, a little faster than around them—but not nearly fast enough. A red light waiting, street signs still too close to City Hall. Cars and trucks bulking up around them, cutting off his view of all but the tallest buildings. And snow began drifting down in bright daylight.

Helpless. This was worse than any chase, any tight corner he'd been trapped in. And it was so easy with his senses keyed up. Just a thought could shift them around and trace Lorraine's breathing, her perfume… He squinted his eyes, then forced them to relax, and let his eyes drift over the shapes ahead.

Along the windows of the buildings ahead, he rode reflections, following what they showed of the distant blocks. Arthur Quinn's voice whispered to him, the memory of *I'm sure they'll pay* that Paul had to push past.

I'm not afraid, someone had said. A softer voice, farther back in the room, Quinn speaking to… a woman?

The car jolted to a stop—no, it only halted, but Paul's memory lurched, sending a shock through his soul. He gasped and turned toward Lorraine, saw her stare at him like she didn't know.

The cab started again, but Paul yelled, "Here! Let us out here!"

"Okay then," and they slowed again and Paul dove out. Lorraine paid the cabbie herself and Paul saw him give a masculine smirk before he pulled away, gone.

"What was *that?*" she asked. "I thought we were going to Bennet's office."

"It's just a couple blocks ahead, I think. We shouldn't get out together anyway." *And why am I stalling?* He took a step toward her, knees shaking. "The night I left… were you talking with Quinn?"

Yes. Shocked confession flashed through her eyes, just for a moment.

"You were! I knew it!"

"Is that an accusation?" And Lorraine stepped in, drawing right up inches from him, her breath in his face as her eyes flashed. "Yes, Quinn came to tempt Curtis and me with his money, to 'help' with the bills. We didn't take it, and I knew it would make your whole family crazy if I mentioned that name. And—"

As her face moved nearer to his, she drew herself up an inch higher. She held a finger up, just between their faces, stabbing it at him with each syllable.

"It… doesn't… matter! Come *on!*"

She began marching up the street, off to help Greg.

For a moment, Paul couldn't move, paralyzed by the whirl of shock, rage, guilt.

Guilt, he thought as he started after her. For attacking her? For letting his attraction to her twist him around more than ever? *But doesn't she know, that anything tied to Quinn and that night might be a key to our power—and maybe even to the fax that had betrayed them—*

No. No more letting her work with me, especially now! He slowed his pace, letting her draw farther away from him, keeping them separate. Not that there was much he could do anyway, if Greg needed someone to talk him out of his rage.

Lorraine marched on ahead, not slowing as her head turned to search the row of shops she passed. Paul felt himself grin; mind-reader or not, she just didn't know Bennet's office would be on the other side of the street—

With the two police cars out front. A new shiver swept through him as he saw their spinning lights flashing. He saw Lorraine look over, stare, and run for the crossing light… but where traffic had been glacial before, now it flowed all too quickly, blocking her.

Two officers hauled Greg out of the office, Detective Reid with them. Paul saw Vernon's grin and Bennet's expressionless face—and then Sarah emerged behind them. And cars still rushed by to fence Paul off.

Sarah was asking, "Just how much of that do you expect to stick?"

"No comment," Reid replied. "But then, what brought you out here just now?"

"After the Councilwoman's announcement, you have to ask?" she shot back. "But was that what brought *you* here, Mr. Schuman?"

Greg gave no answer; Paul only saw the far-off figure turn back to her a little, and the uniforms pause from marching him to the car.

Instead Vernon said "I don't know what. But I caught him myself, miss—right after he pulled the fire alarm and tried to creep around to Ms. Bennet's office. We found him hiding under her desk."

So smug—as if Greg didn't steal that alarm trick right from you! And hiding under the desk had been Paul's own move, back in their father's office. *My God, first Lorraine chasing Vernon—and now it's* Greg *trying to do what I do?*

Greg didn't answer, and the cops pushed him down into their car—

"What are you *doing?*" and Lorraine rushed up. Paul could hear her shout even as he released his senses to cross the street himself, half a block behind her. He saw Greg trying to shout from within the car, and Reid and the others turn to face her.

"…nothing you can do," Vernon was saying when Paul Opened again. "He almost attacked Ms. Bennet."

"Liar!" Lorraine snapped, as firmly if she could more than guess he was exaggerating.

As they spoke, Paul worked his way along the block, listening but edging forward as well, just one of several people watching on the pavement from a safe distance, four or five shops down.

Detective Reid said, "The charges are breaking and entering… and assault." Then he stepped forward, close enough to whisper to her. "If you want to help him, talk to me. We're already looking into other break-ins, and records of some kind of payoffs that his associate dropped—his associate or his enemy. And after two break-ins of your property—"

"You're *blaming* him for being robbed?" Lorraine asked. "Our lawyers will…"

"Something drove someone to attack his home and office. It may be you don't know your husband at all. Or maybe he has an enemy you don't want to make. I need to know how deep he's involved in this. And in the murder."

Paul could hear her tiny gasp as if he stood right behind her. "Murder?"

"His brother. He disappeared, you all screamed for a manhunt, and then you say you got one letter that said nothing except to stop looking. But," and Reid's whisper softened even further, "we couldn't trace that letter to anything, and we never found the brother."

And the deep breath Paul had been drawing burst from his lungs as a yell: "Try looking over here!"

The shouts, the stares, the pointing—the cops turned to look, unsure what to do, while on several sides of him, Paul heard people backing away and muttering, trying to understand what had happened. He saw Sarah looking at him as if she was fitting the pieces into God knew what kind of picture, and Vernon take a quick step but stop short of rushing at him.

"Is that why you want Greg—to see if I'm alive?" Paul tried to follow up his first words with the same confidence, and to advance on the people to keep the initiative as boldly as Lorraine or Bennet would. His voice sounded strong enough, but his knees wobbled and wouldn't move quickly. "As for the rest, I think Councilwoman Bennet wants a word with me before you go filing charges."

"So it *is* you." Reid folded his arms and looked at Paul, as if the forty feet of pavement between them were nothing. "And what would you like to say about your brother's attack?"

Paul didn't answer, only closed in. If he could just get to Bennet, to use the threat of her embezzling…

Reid added, "Or about your breaking into your family's office?"

"Not him," Lorraine said. "I was there, and the thief wasn't him." She didn't glance toward Vernon or Bennet, but Paul saw Bennet flinch at where that accusation might go.

Then Bennet said, "I'm afraid that doesn't change the facts. Your husband broke into my office, and—"

Vernon leaned down and whispered to the Councilwoman. Paul Opened to hear "…what if he's got more, if he means…"

Something slammed into Paul, smashing him sideways, and kept shoving. Too-ready hands caught him as he tried to twist away and forced him with an iron grip against the wall, pinning him against the bricks.

Only when his thrashing head glimpsed another cop closing in did he have time to think. *Dammit! I tried to stare down the leaders and didn't watch the troopers at the sides, I walked right in among them—*

Clutching hands wrenched his arms around—*God!*—making his injured arm burn. The pain and shock left him hanging limp in the cops' grasp. He barely felt them strip his pack from his back.

"*Do* you have anything to say?" he heard Reid ask at his elbow. "Of course you have the right to remain silent…"

As Reid spoke, the cops yanked him around. Inside the police car, Greg was yelling something at them, his rage muffled by the window. Lorraine watched, frozen.

"Nothing about the stolen LifeLab files?" Reid asked, and this time the detective actually smiled. "Or breaking into the Schuman office, or their home… or how many before that?"

Paul could just manage to hold his face still, a silent scowl. The detective had to be guessing, he couldn't trace Paul to the lab.

Then Reid took the backpack from the uniforms, and pulled out…

No! Why'd I keep carrying that laptop around? Once they crack the codes—

They wrenched his arms together, and even through the pain, he felt the cold click of the handcuffs going on.

He saw Lorraine move then, determination in her face as she reached for Reid's arm.

Not her, too! Desperately, fumbling for words, Paul bellowed out, "It's never enough! Even if you pay them back, do you still have to pay?" and he looked at Councilwoman Bennet.

"Wait!" In an instant, she started forward. Reid's smile tightened as he glanced toward her. The grips on Paul slackened, for a moment.

And Paul flung himself away from one cop and into the other's shoulder, one move kept smooth and perfect by Opened touch as he sent the cop sprawling, and he ricocheted away to dash up between the buildings.

Snow slid under his feet, and his arms behind his back hobbled his motion. Somewhere behind him someone, Reid, yelled "Grab him!" but Paul's focus swung to his legs. Step, *step*, for perfect Opened balance and every twitch of muscles forcing more speed into the shortened stride, *don't* start to slip on the snow—

How far back were the others—still ten steps, five? Soundless, only muscle and snow were real, and the distant dream of the brick corner he ran toward—

His feet skidded a moment as he turned, but he rounded the corner and kept going. *For how long?* some thought flared in the back of his mind. Pieces, building blocks of outmaneuvering the enemy, clicked in his memory. *Can't run back here where the snow's untrampled, can't blend in out front wearing the cuffs—*

That door, back when he'd been watching Bennet here, wasn't it—

He turned as he ran, Opening to his touch as never before. He twisted to catch the door handle with the hand behind his back, braking and pulling and spinning himself around, flailing to stay on his feet, taking the *wrench* on his fingers and arm as he flipped around to slip inside as the door swung shut again.

And he collapsed on the floor, waves of pain from his arm almost drowning out the bustle of voices, the clattering trays and hisses of steam. A bakery, he remembered. He opened his eyes enough to curl up a bit behind a rack of plates, flimsy cover if one of the cooks happened to glance toward the back.

Snow crunched outside; he heard the cop stumbling and skidding on past the door. *He's already faster than I can run… Opened touch can smooth out a motion to make the most of surprise, but it's no match for trained moves or just having his arms free!*

Paul stared up, past the cooks and on toward the front. How could he slip past them? His arm burned away his strength. *Don't try to stand yet…*

No, he didn't have time to stand up. He rolled to his side, his unhurt right side, and tried to slide his cuffed wrists down along his back. The folds of his coat caught, then his arms met his hips, his upper arms tried to slide along the back of his ribs, and *stuck*. His arm, the pain…

No time. Paul Opened to lock his gaze on the gray door looming over him, to forget touch and pain to see only the door that could open at any instant unless he could just *PUSH*—

Somewhere, he felt something slide free, motion swimming in pain. He clung to his sight, just the plastic grayness of the door, as his arms kept moving, trying to fit the cuffs around his heels, as the door moved its first inch.

No-no-no… As the trance shattered, he rolled to the side and yanked his arms free as the agony swept back through him. *Don't scream, don't!*

Through the tears, he stared up at the half-open door, at the lean black face and uniformed body leaning in—not looking around, not behind the door where Paul crouched. Not yet. "Where'd he go?" the officer demanded.

"Who?" a cook shouted back, and Paul curled himself in tighter. Of course, the cop would look back and see his tracks, and now he'd look—

Paul slid along the floor, reaching up his cuffed hands to another rack. Somehow, somehow with his cuffed arms moving together, he sent a plate flying like a china Frisbee, just below eye level, to crash into a column of pastry displays.

"What—" "Who's—" "Got you!"

For one moment the cop lunged forward past Paul, and the cooks' eyes looked to him and back ahead, away from the door. Paul surged up, caught the door handle and spun himself around behind it, letting it shut on the noise inside.

Just cold air and the snowy alley, dazzling in the sun. He ran back along his trail, hopping within his footprints and fighting the urge to leap past them now that his arms could almost move. *Faster, all they have to do is look back out before I—*

For one wild moment he darted between the bakery and Bennet's little building, in full view of the street, where people were still milling about. Then he flew past it and to Bennet's back door, the door he *knew* was unlocked.

Unless they'd changed that after Greg—

It swung open at his touch and he ducked inside, trying not to think how easy it would have been for the cop to come out and spot him, or for other cops to be in the alley. In fact, the whole building seemed empty, with everyone out front for the excitement. Until they came back or looked at his tracks again, he might almost be safe.

A corner near the front seemed to have space, between a desk and the wall. Paul curled up below its window, his abused arm burning so savagely he doubted it could lift a pencil now. His other muscles throbbed, clenching with adrenaline as he tried to lie still.

At least his hearing could still Open. He probed the alley and the street for searchers, picking out the cop he'd dodged, who was still shuffling around, and he heard a second cop in the other direction, up the alley—plus however many cops might be among the footsteps out on the pavement.

Paul stole a look out the window, to glimpse Reid listening to his men on a pocket radio. Around him stood Bennet and Vernon and their office staff, and Paul saw Lorraine and Sarah still among them.

Only one uniform was with them. Did Reid have only those three or so cops, for what had started as picking up an already-thwarted assaulter? But every second, more would be driving closer… there wasn't even enough traffic to slow them down, not the way that street hustled along. And while the cars had all the speed to cut him off, the sidewalk sounded more empty and exposed than not, as far as his hearing could stretch.

Useless. Paul crouched lower, feeling the net spreading around him. Not enough people, not nearly enough to blend in with while he still had handcuffed wrists to hide. Too open a space, with only so many turns and options to lose himself among. And no way out—if the cops didn't see him, they'd make out his tracks sooner or later. Or they'd look back in the office, or Bennet's staff would get back to work…

Why does it have to be broad daylight, and open, and even snow?! My power's almost useless, except for a few balance tricks and tracking the cops—and they wouldn't leave real holes in their net anyway, not enough for this. He could hear the cop starting up past the bakery, then turning back, as if he were already taking a second look at the tracks behind him.

Paul's arm contracted in a spasm, but as he reached his other hand to clutch at it, the handcuffs caught him, starting to twist the damaged arm further.

Stupid! He stared across at the door to Bennet's office. It was a better place to hide, and maybe he could talk to her there and use the only real leverage he had. He pulled his legs under him, tried to stand, and gasped at the wave of dizziness—

The door opened, the front door. Paul dropped back down behind the desk as two young men walked in.

"I've got to call my brother!"

"What, the one who said city politics was dull? Can I listen?"

Ten more seconds! Paul winced; just a little later and he'd have been safe in Bennet's room, ready to use her embezzling to get the answers Greg hadn't been able to get. God, how had he come so far from warning them against blackmail…

At least the two staffers settled at the far end of the office, not right next to him. Paul listened to them, plotted their movements to find the moment they'd be looking away, and leaned up to steal another peek out the window. Bennet wasn't even coming inside; she and Vernon still stood by Reid as he listened for signs of his men spotting Paul. He saw Sarah close to them—probably waiting to tell him all about her secret source. And Reid still held Paul's laptop in his hands!

Dropping back, Paul stifled a curse. With all Paul's journals… how long would the cipher even hold? It was just an alphabet-swap, any letter-frequency table might crack the code in minutes, and just hand them two years of his spying history.

Opening his hearing, he focused on Bennet and her aide, hoping, praying that they'd say something. But his will slipped and weakened, and he couldn't even pull his hearing away from the two men inside:

"What, you want to get back to work?"

"I'll tell her you said that."

How long before they walk down here? I've got *to find a way out!* Staring up at the window, he clenched his fist and his concentration. Opening his sight, he looked into the reflections in the glass, fighting to keep the view of the street from blurring. Just Reid with Paul's life in his hands, Bennet out of reach, the near-empty pavement and busy street hemming them in. Was that Lorraine, up near Greg's blue car? Just standing there, waiting?

Paul couldn't spare the strength. But still, he shifted to Opening his hearing, to hear her whispering.

"Just get to me, Paul, just get out here. Just get out to me. Just…"

Unbelievable. Paul shook his dazed head—he couldn't risk involving her any more, and he *couldn't* get out anyway.

He stared up into the reflections, clawing through his mind and the images he saw. Something to hide him, or move him past them, or stop people from looking… there was just no way, and that laptop would soon have the whole city hunting for him anyway.

He almost missed when the office's back door opened.

"Officer?"

"Sorry, I need to look in here again."

Paul didn't bother tracking them, just stared at the window's glaze, straining his imagination as he gathered what strength he had left.

Maybe there. Desperate, crazy… and too far away, but…

"Do I need to look in the boss's office again?" the cop said.

"No, we were…"

Now!

Paul lurched up and dashed for the front door. A "Hey!" burst out behind him, too far back, and he hit the door and scrambled into the open. With his will locked within his balance, he barely saw the people until he neared them.

One frozen moment. Bennet and Vernon off to the side, not seeing. Sarah, turning toward him. Reid beyond her, just looking up as Paul knocked the laptop from his grasp to send it under the wheels of the blurring traffic. The shape to his left, still too slow—

The detective caught his balance, reached for him. Paul lashed out in a desperate two-armed punch. With a glorious *crunch*, Reid staggered back—

And Paul leaped away, past the parked cars, and jumped straight into the flow of traffic, just as the big SUV finally swept by. Paul reached, grabbed—

lurched—

but clung on to the tailgate even as its momentum tore at his arms. *At least both hurt now,* he thought numbly, but he wouldn't have to move again.

Behind him, Reid ran a few steps before pulling up, shouting around. But they couldn't touch him, no power could slow moving traffic until they could get someone up ahead of it, and sure enough, no shouting or waving made the SUV driver look up from his cell phone. If only the lights stayed green a few more blocks, to get Paul out of sight…

If I can hold on…

At last, after blocks of trotting dazedly through side streets, stumbling in the snow with the effort of watching for the police… at last Paul fumbled the door locked behind him and sagged down in the sanctuary of a bathroom stall.

God, the pure *luxury* of sagging over in a tiny, locked space, a hidden world in the midst of five other stalls that people could walk past, never wondering how long this one had stayed sealed. *Maybe I can stay long enough for the worst of the pain to fade,* he thought as he sank down on the plastic lid. If he could just keep from thinking of Greg waiting for his bail, or everything they had all lost—*I'm in no shape to fight back now.*

His mind drifted in and out for hours of fitful rest as he twisted on the hard seat. Between dozes, he had more than enough time to explore the tiny works of the handcuffs with the scraps of metal he carried—at least, to free his *left* wrist; he didn't dare heighten touch in his doubly-battered left arm to keep the cuffs from dangling from his right. And with his arms free, he could slide down his coat and shirt enough to see the battered, purpling injuries he could sense so well. Muscles weren't torn or dislocated, but many had been badly weakened.

Greg needed him, but he could barely move, and he couldn't go back to his room at the Side Alley when the police might already be taking his picture around every flophouse in the city. He couldn't move, not yet…

* * *

The November sun hung near the horizon when Paul stepped outside again. His stomach growled and the snow on the streets reminded him he'd need a warmer place when the night came. At least he could walk the back streets without wobbling much, and nobody seemed to notice how he crooked his right arm to keep the handcuff from dangling out of his sleeve.

His first stop was the nearest of his three lockers around the city, this one at the bus station. Keeping a careful eye for police surveillance, he pocketed the cache's full set of keys and other small tools. *No reason not to carry them all the time now; if I'm searched it'll be because they're already arresting me.* And sure enough, one of the keys needed only a little guidance and his Opened touch to release the other handcuff.

As the last of the metal came away, he remembered the bus station phones. Lorraine needed to know he'd escaped—

No, he'd endangered her too much already. Calling her was simply weakness, trying to hear a friendly voice. *Besides, what if that secret conversation with Quinn…* no, she was right, worrying over that was just the family paranoia over everyone Quinn met. And in the end, she'd probably trust that he could stay ahead of a few cops.

But with the city libraries closed—*and what genius thought of closing them on Mondays?*—there was no way he could check the net about Greg's arrest or Bennet's secrets. Not that he should risk making a move tonight anyway.

Instead he bought a bargain bag of multi-grain rolls and a mix of fruit and vegetables chosen to help him heal, enough for a few days.

Chewing away as he walked, he counted up his resources. He had to stay away from his room and what things he'd left there—although he might slip back there in a few days, to see if anything was left. At least, with his laptop smashed all over the street, Reid couldn't *know* how many burglaries belonged in Paul's case file.

I still punched a cop and made fools of them all. They'll never *stop looking for me.* But it was better than letting them know how many secrets he'd exposed over the years, better than giving them any hint that he had better tools than the lock picks and the bugs they'd assume explained his best tricks.

But while they were searching, he needed to disappear. And he hadn't even scrounged up the trickier gear on this year's winter preparation list—it took him most of his dwindling funds to buy a second-hand black jacket that looked different enough from his too-familiar brown coat.

Still, the jacket blended in well with the deepening night. Just what he needed now.

* * *

First, the snow. To separate his tracks from his search, Paul left the road a half mile before he reached the first estates in the Glen district, closing the rest of the distance through the woods—this once, he wished more snow would fall, to cover where his trail left the road.

Peering out from the trees, he examined the rear of each great house. He started by checking where he could approach without leaving too long a line of footprints from the woods. Those within decent reach, whether they had walls or not, he searched for alarms—hoping to find a strong system, the best sign of owners who felt free to head south during the gray Novembers.

He hadn't even hoped to find a rock garden. But once he'd plotted the alarm system and the route through it, he had only to step along the tops of the larger rocks, balancing to compress the powder but not knock much off the stone and draw attention to his passage for any caretaker who came by. It was a modest challenge while holding the bag of food, and it left his feet cold; he had to remove his shoes to avoid leaving obvious tread marks.

But then the glass patio door slid open, and he could towel his frozen feet dry with his old coat. As he did, he looked around at his new home. *So I'm back to this trick again, and after all my pride that I didn't have to use it last winter… again I'm one step further from being a public service for truth and a little closer to being a parasite.* He wondered what Lorraine would say if she saw where following their power could really lead—or if Sarah or the other reporters could see their miraculous informant now.

Sarah and the Animal Alliance and the rest could write what they wanted now. All that mattered was his brother, and finding the strength to help him—and what was left of his own code.

The house had a coolness to it. Not only the turned-down heat and the lack of living things, but the way the furniture only partly filled the open spaces of the rooms, and the amount of pale plastic and metal Paul saw among the wood. He moved slowly through the dim rooms, resisting the urge to raise the heat; it would only be another sign that he was here. And, it would have been another thing he was stealing. His rule had always been to use up little more than water and the space itself, and to try to repay them by making some hard-to-notice repairs. After all, he hardly needed the lights on.

Still, he did tuck his bag of food back in the near-empty fridge, and use up a bit of their bathroom's antiseptic on his cuts. He passed a room full of gleaming exercise machines and another with a small village of electronic modules hooked up to its computer and a vast TV screen. Even some of the pictures—man, woman, two boys—had cold metal frames around them. No library, a pity. But he tried not to look in what rooms he could leave untouched, especially once he climbed the hanging staircase and passed by what would be the bedrooms.

Instead, he found the steps to the attic, where he curled up in a mass of their linen closet's blankets at the foot of a tall, metal wardrobe. From the amount of dust, he knew no visiting housekeeper would walk in on him there.

Still, lying on the cold boards of his refuge, Paul couldn't seem to sleep. The thought wouldn't let go: *Power or not, I'm just a squatter again, and a fugitive, too. Is there anything* left *of my purpose, or my secret?* Once he'd cleared Greg, he couldn't even stay in the city—and there would go his last chance of learning how he'd gotten the power, or of being with Lorraine. *Like I ever could.*

*   *   *

Doors, door after door that rattled in place, and tried to swing open before he could shut them. As he paced he heard beyond the doors, each time, and knew he didn't want to. Sarah, a happy laugh from one. Another door a fine-tuned car engine just throbbing to life. As he shut one door he glimpsed another behind it, a grand old door set in a huge house.

He looked around as he walked, searching for something, something, but only the doors stretched around him. He brushed against one as he passed, and heard a friendly dog bark and toss its chains.

The chains clanked louder as he pushed the door closed and still louder while he turned away, looking around for… what was it? He began to run past the doors, past rows upon rows of them. Laughter whispered in the air, Greg's and Lorraine's.

A door ahead of him swung wide, and he stopped short ahead of it. Chains clattered again, somewhere behind it. He turned away and ran, past doors pressing closer and closer, harder to keep from touching. Lorraine's laughter filled his ears.

*   *   *

The dream left Paul soaked in sweat, he and the dusty blankets he crawled out of the next day. At least he always allowed himself his showers, and borrowed scissors to cut his unkempt hair short; it was the best disguise he could manage. Finally, he took out his supplies for a slow meal in the glittering metal kitchen.

If only… if only the food were good… but the cheap package he'd bought was already less than fresh, and it was soaked in preservatives. The last thing he wanted was to Open to that taste for even a moment's escape.

Still, the nearer he came to his last bites of roll, the slower he chewed, knowing that when he finished he'd have to bend his rules another way. With the better part of a day gone since Greg's arrest— even though, by now, he would surely be out on bail—Paul couldn't wait any longer to start clearing his brother's name.

And with the morning sun and the gleaming snow waiting just beyond the curtains, he couldn't risk going out—not when he already had a computer within reach.

Sighing, he moved to the big entertainment room, settled at the overpadded chair in front of the computer, and clicked on the power. ENTER PASSWORD.

"What the *hell*—" Paul flinched at his own outburst, as it echoed through the empty house. He stared at the screen again, not believing his eyes. Who kept total password protection on in the family room of their own home?

His fingers clenched over the keyboard as he wished, once again, that he'd made a real study of hacking tricks. Then he shut down the computer and headed for the stairs.

A house like this would have *other* computers, other chances to run some basic searches on Greg's case and find leverage against Bennet. Any dens or workrooms downstairs would probably have machines just as stubborn, but upstairs, maybe, in the boys' rooms…

He jerked his hand away from the doorknob as if it would bite him. The dream full of doors, and everything he'd done—*I don't want to know what's on the mother's nightstand, or if the kids like superhero or monster movies, I just want to keep my brother out of prison and my powers out of the CIA! If I can just get through it all without losing too much more…*

Shoulders slumped, he made his way back down the steps. Maybe, just maybe, a local news channel would have something about Greg. At least he could do *something* besides fumbling for strategies and wondering if he dared go out in the day.

* * *

By mid-afternoon, he had worked his way clear of the Glen woods, certain now that he could enter and leave unnoticed. Carefully, straining his senses to listen for any chance patrol cars, he returned to the city streets.

The library computers first. But he found himself taking a different route. *Just call her and make it quick…*

He kept closing in on the little tower where the Schuman offices lay. His family deserved a proper apology—but he knew he couldn't risk showing himself. He just needed to see that Greg was out safe. *Sure, keep telling yourself this won't be to say goodbye…*

All too soon, he reached the fire stairs, and began climbing, each step slower than the last. The first floor loomed almost at once, and then…

A door creaked open below him, at the ground floor level, a faint sound that Paul almost missed. But an instant later, he Opened his hearing to listen, and he heard the secretive step of a man leaning in to peer up between the stairs. *Someone's trying to get a glimpse of me!*

Reflex made him clamp his stride down into the same steady pace, not trying to run or freeze, and he didn't bother trying to soften his footsteps' light echoes in the metal-and-concrete column of the stairwell. At least he could edge nearer the wall, out of view. As long as the watcher didn't know Paul had spotted him…

Feet rang on the stairs now, running hard. Paul threw himself forward, fighting to keep his footsteps soft enough for the cop to lose them in his own echoes. *Just stay a few turns ahead of him, then duck out a floor before the office! Faster!* He flew around the turns, then yanked the door open and darted out.

Right in front of the Schuman and Son door. Paul stared for an instant, not believing he could have miscounted the floors and picked this one out of habit, and then he dashed away down the corridor. At least they didn't have to catch him *in* his family's rooms.

He hurled himself around the corner, knowing he was out of the cop's sight and had a clear run to the building's other stairs—

"Sorry, sorry!" he heard the cop say, as well as the grumble of someone he must have bumped into. The voices came from far back, *well* short of the corner.

Paul slowed; his pursuer hadn't sounded very desperate to pursue. He stopped and Opened his hearing again and heard the cop turning back and the fire door creaking open again.

"Come *on*, boy, he's going for the other stairs! Dispatch, I need…"

No-no-no-no… Paul dashed for the far stairs, the only way off the floor that the first cop couldn't watch from his vantage point at the central stair. If the second cop was any faster at getting there than his partner thought he was…

Paul wrenched open the fire door and saw an empty staircase.

Quickly, he eased the door shut and moved up the stairs, three quick strides as quiet as he could make them, to get out of sight. He could hear the other officer pounding up from below, then stopping to watch the door, unaware that his target had slipped past.

Paul pressed himself against the wall and moved on for the next floor, silent now.

"…on its way. You better be right, Willie!" he heard the cop's radio squawking.

Softly, move softly on these damn metal drum-pads. But I can't waste any time. Paul picked his way upward as quickly as he dared until at last he could ease open the door above and slip into that hall.

One chance now. Paul scrambled back up the corridor, retracing the route he'd run below—but instead of opening the door, he slammed his finger on the elevator button next to it. If he'd read the urgency in the cops' voices correctly, they wouldn't have someone to cover this third way down. They were counting on him blundering into them, thinking he wouldn't risk getting trapped in the elevator, until their backup arrived and cornered him.

If, *if* he was right…

And if the elevator didn't take all ten minutes to reach him. He stalked back and forth, mind racing. So two cops were watching the office—how much did they suspect he'd done? Had they even let Greg out, bail or no bail? How close was their backup? Why had he been foolish enough to come back here, and why, *why, WHY is this elevator stuck?*

Then came the impertinent little chime and the doors rolled open. Paul dove in and mashed the button to start down. If only he still had time…

And if the cop he was descending toward wasn't making the elevator stop to be searched. A surge of cold fear swept through him.

He only had a moment to flatten himself at the doors' side, tensing to attack…

But the car never slowed. It moved on past 4, then 3, 2 and 1, and opened on G. And Paul marched out into the lobby, eyes searching the scattered people for any unmentioned third officer he might be walking right in front of…

Finally the winter breeze brushed his face, blowing freely along the street. He turned to let it carry him along as he mingled with the other people walking, letting every step take him farther away from where the police would be driving up.

I didn't have to stake everything on speed, came the angry thought. He realized now he could have gotten out of the elevator again, below the cops' floors, and crept down the stairs and out the back door. Or he could have kept going up, picked an empty office, and hidden there until they gave up—

Enough! He shook his head, hard. At least he was out, he hadn't been spotted too near his family, and the police had seen so little of him that they might get sick of throwing manpower after phantoms.

Or they'd assign even more bodies, if they believed he really was this elusive, and this dangerous.

On shaky legs, he stepped into the lobby of the next large office building, and then tried the next, until he found a bank of phones. *I could at least ask Lorraine if Greg is out… no, I can't risk the police noticing the call, too.* He glared at his hand, frozen halfway toward reaching for the phone.

Was it the police that worried him, or some lingering thought of Lorraine and Quinn? Or just hearing her husky voice again?

Crazy. Still, he did need to know about Greg. *I'll make it quick.*

For an endless moment, he heard her phone ring, and he feared he'd reach nothing but her messages. But then: "Hello?"

He kept to the words he'd planned, and almost managed the right casual tone. "Hi, Lor. Got a minute for your cousin?"

She'd once told them all she had no family; had it been him or Greg who'd joked about her being lucky, so long ago?

She hesitated, but only for a moment before he heard her answer. "Not... much time. How are the kids?"

"Okay," Paul managed. So, they could talk. But did he really have to speak in trick statements? Would a judge actually let the police bug her line?

"Let me see," she said. And then a faint hiss through the line, as if...

He Opened, diving into the faint buzzes and beeps against his ear. *"Greg's been bailed out, but they're watching him,"* she whispered. And then, her normal voice exploded in his enhanced ear: "JUST ONE OF THOSE DAYS, YOU KNOW?"

"I get it," Paul said, and he felt a tightness loosening in him, even as his head rang. She really *was* trying to make contact with him, and she'd figured out a way, just as she'd tried whispering at his escape. "Anything I can do? I mean, if it helps to talk?"

"I... guess it's just things we have to deal with ourselves. Unless..." and her pause cued him for the next whisper. *"Unless you get this right. Please, nothing crazy like Greg!"* In her normal voice she finished, "Just think of us."

"I will. I always am."

—Dammit, why did that slip out?—

"And be good to your husband," he added quickly. "I know he'd do anything for you."

"Thanks. And," she added with a hint of warmth, "I know you'll be alright."

With those words in his ear, Paul waited for any further message. But she didn't speak again. *Do I really have anything to add?*

He hung up and turned quickly away to head for the street again, in case the police had somehow bothered to trace even that call.

Maybe, maybe he'd never hear her voice again, not if he did this right. The thought even brought a certain relief.

Nothing left to lose. My God, how did I get to a place like this?

* * *

Somewhere on his walk through the darkening streets, Paul gave up his last hope that he was ready to spy on the police themselves. Not that night, not when he was still weak and they were still on alert from his other escapes. Not when he wanted them to give up hope, or at least their hope that Greg was connected to him. It would be better, and safer, to go get Greg an ally.

So he headed to Bennet's office again, watching every corner and window until he slipped safely inside the empty building. But instead of a long search through their files, he dug out one address... with the libraries closed for the night and his laptop gone, he couldn't even locate the Councilwoman's home without an extra stop.

All the way uptown, he sorted through the arguments, hints, and dangers their confrontation might wind through. This visit couldn't be like the one he'd paid to James Koenig, just hammering away at one idea to keep an enemy off-balance—and this one had to *work*, when he was up against the woman who'd helped defeat his plans with Koenig.

Bennet's neighborhood was upscale, well beyond Lorraine's and Greg's, though the elaborate houses still didn't have much room between them. Paul moved past in the street, just slowly enough to probe the place. The last thing he needed was to set off calls about some unsavory stranger lingering around at eleven at night.

Small though it was, the house's alarm system was tighter than most; Paul could feel the radar tingle of the motion sensors on his skin.

But it had something else, too, waiting out on the street, the other piece of the key he needed.

Paul crouched down in the snow in the thickest bushes up the street and waited, listening to the quiet. When at last he heard the approach of what passed in this neighborhood for a high-speed car, he strode out, timing his walk to cross in front of Bennet's just as the car swept by him. As it did, he flung one of her recycling bins up onto her tiny lawn and darted up along the side wall.

In moments, he stood out of sight of the street, against the wall with his feet straddling one of the motion sensors, listening. His hearing traced Bennet inside, going to the front window, no doubt staring at the toppled bin and the departing car.

"No, no, it's nothing," she was saying on the phone. "The alarm was just kids knocking things around, I guess. Thank you."

She sounds tired, worn out. He could hear it in her step as she walked across the room and worked what had to be the reset for the alarm—but he was already inside the radar's sweep, and he knew the back had no other alarms.

He took his time, disabling the sensor at his feet and then picking the back door lock. Bennet was still sitting down, scarcely moving.

Paul crept inside, moving through the corridor as he reviewed the arguments he'd worked out. *She has to listen.* He heard her just around the next doorway… he Opened his sight and maneuvered until he could catch her reflection in the glass of a framed picture on the corridor wall.

She was sitting in her library, listlessly swirling brandy in the snifter in her palm, with no promising papers to lure her away from, no late-night phone calls. *Nothing but the two of us.*

Just then, she downed the drink and reached for the bottle beside her. *How many has she had? How much longer can she stay awake?* Paul flexed his breathing and throat to add menace to his voice, and boomed out, "You've had enough to drink!"

The glass crashed to the floor. She fumbled at the table for—

"Put the phone down!" Paul snapped. Her hand froze as he added, more quietly, "I said, put it down! If I wanted to hurt you, nobody on Earth is close enough to stop me."

She pulled her hand back, her flushed face going white in the glass. Paul almost flinched back so his eyes couldn't align with that look of horror, but instead he clenched his fists and went on.

"Better. Yes, I can see you, Erin. I saw you years ago, with the city funds."

She reached for the phone again, more slowly now.

"Leave it! Step back, now," Paul warned.

She halted, then pulled back, getting awkwardly to her feet and leaning on the chair.

"What else do you *want?*" she gasped, almost too low to hear before her voice rose. "I helped them, you know I did! But you... you can't simply be one of the activists."

"Can't I?" Paul laughed coldly, feeling a few pieces fall into place. So it *was* that very blackmail threat that had been pulling her strings at the press conference. That knowledge let him play the role. "Why can't I be?"

"Well... you're too good at this." She stood a little straighter now, glaring at the doorway toward him with more shrewdness than Paul liked. "You knew about me. You got the lab evidence. You're here now. But you must know what you got on the lab will never really stick, no matter what I do. And that detective thinks you're part of all kinds of other cases—he's just not sure which ones."

"And what does he think?"

"Why don't you go spy on *him?*" she snapped as she took a quick step for the doorway to look out. Ready for it, Paul glided back and turned into the kitchen, out of her view.

And he growled, "I'm asking *you,* embezzler."

He heard her stumble back a step, and lean against the wall. "He, he didn't say much. I don't have many police contacts, and I couldn't push without drawing attention—*please* don't ask me to, I dropped the hints about Greg but I swear there isn't much I can do to get them off your trail, Paul."

"'Paul'?" and he laughed again. "Oh, let them chase him." *Have to keep her off-balance, about who I am and everything else. But, did the blackmailer order her to keep the heat on Greg?*

Bennet didn't answer then. He could only hear her leaning against the wall. He wished he still had a mirror in position to watch her.

"But…" she said slowly, "your voice, the distorter…" She stopped then, the tipsy thickness almost gone from her voice now, replaced by suspicion.

Paul hollowed his voice a little further, reaching for more menace. "You think I always sound the same?"

"But," she said again. "But, how do I know you're the same…"

"I'm *not,*" Paul growled. "I'm the *other* untouchable blackmailer who knows all your secrets!"

He heard her stagger back another step along the wall. "Sorry, I'm sorry! I won't ask again!"

While she's shaken— "No… I *am* someone different. And I want your help."

"But you, you said…" Was that sound her sliding down the wall now, unable to stand? "How do I know—"

"You know I'm going to help you," he said. "Either believe that or believe you're trapped between two enemies who would *both* throw you to the wolves. Which do you want it to be?"

"I… you…" Slowly, he heard her get to her feet again. "What do you want?" she asked.

Finally. "Tell me about him."

"All I had were phone calls. No number, and the voice came through a mechanical distorter. The caller knew about me, and yesterday he wanted me to support Animal Alliance against LifeLab. I thought…" She stopped.

"Thought what?"

"I thought it might even be Greg, trying to take the business from Ian, somehow. Until Greg showed up yelling for answers."

She sleeps with my brother and doesn't know him at all. Well, she's grasping at straws. "So that was yesterday. And the other calls?"

"One call, this morning. He said to press all charges against Greg. He said that, if I made enough trouble there, he might not call again."

"And you believed him?"

She didn't answer, but she didn't have to. After all that, of course she'd had to hope.

"Well, you have one new order," Paul said at last. "Stall. Let the heat die down about Greg, as much as you dare. The police can go after his brother if they want."

"But—" And now she only sounded surprised, not shaken or afraid. "But, aren't you—"

"I'm nobody who's worried about Paul Schuman," he said, and that was true enough. "You can trust me or not, or fear me, but either way, it should be for the same reason: this is what I do."

It would have been so much easier if the police had just given up. But of course, Paul could see them still watching his family.

He'd hoped he could think of some way to track down the blackmailer. But here he was, still standing in the snow, staring across the parking lot for glimpses through the convention center windows at his father, Greg, and Lorraine at work. *Still waiting for an idea.*

The surveillance hadn't been hard to spot, not after he took a bit of time to place which figures and sounds were staying in one place or pacing back and forth rather than having real business of their own. Half the time, he could spot them from the way they grumbled on their radios about the job… but again and again, they said "useless" and "endless" without giving him much sense of how many burglaries they thought they could tie Paul to, let alone how long they'd keep pressuring Greg.

Lorraine could read it, if I asked her to. Maybe she already has.

Instead Paul trudged forward up the row of cars, trying to look like just someone heading inside as he passed a uniformed deliveryman on the way out. He kept his features calm even as he fumed, *I've been here too long already.*

If only there were *some* way to trace the calls to Bennet's phone that wouldn't involve digging through a dozen specialized computers—some way besides the one he couldn't risk. Once again, he tried to think of the other clues. What blackmailer would demand supporting Animal Alliance and persecuting Greg? Who could have found out about Bennet's past?

As he walked, he caught another glimpse of Greg through one of the center's windows. He seemed to be looking toward where the police might be, when the businessman they were showing around couldn't see. And Greg kept a sheltering arm around Lorraine, and she leaned into him, supportive as she'd always been. *How could I believe she had some secret with Quinn, even once? Or imagine her with me, ever?*

Paul looked down, scuffing his feet through the slushed-up snow. If the police were showing signs of giving up on his family, he could just leave—leave Lorraine and the Alliance case and the whole city. But here they were, and he'd promised Bennet—not that he really owed her in the same way he did his family.

Why didn't I just expose her embezzling myself, to disarm the threats and take the pressure off Greg? But then, the thought of leaving a blackmailer free twisted his stomach.

Maybe he should look at the police, at Detective Reid and the rest, to see how much they'd really push Greg. But if Reid ever glimpsed Paul out-spying the cops themselves, he'd *never* let the case drop.

Inside, one of the officers whispered, "And this guy broke into *how* many places?"

"Don't talk stupid," one of his partners said on their radio.

Can you please talk stupid, give me anything about how bad you'll make this for Greg? But they said nothing more, and he knew he couldn't, mustn't ask Lorraine.

Paul reached the side of the parking lot and loitered near a van, visibly checking his pockets, to give anyone watching him time to forget he'd already walked across the lot once. There had to be an *answer.*

And he still couldn't shake the worst thought of all, how these sudden threats with Bennet's secret followed right after Lorraine discovering it. Even the blackmailer's voice distorter could have been to hide a woman's voice.

Just the thought of matching wits with a mind-reader made Paul shiver, for all its absurdity. From the days of her engagement to her secret struggles now, the one thing he knew about Lorraine was her devotion to Greg… even after Greg's affair. *No, I'm only letting the suspicion haunt me because it would mean she might leave him. Or that I could stop wishing she would.*

Or maybe it was just because he couldn't drive out the image of anyone, even Lorraine, letting Arthur Quinn talk to her secretly.

Savagely, Paul shoved the papers and keys he'd pretended to look at back in his pockets and started trudging out across the lot again. He had *nothing*, only those phone records he couldn't crack and some wild guesses. *Maybe I need to take a look at Bennet's secret, to see how that end of it got exposed, or retrace the events, or see what Vernon knew. —Sure, either stir up the most unpredictable man in this whole mess or take weeks recreating the past when the police know my face!*

Passing another window, he saw Greg inside whirling to stomp toward a businessman sitting with a newspaper. "You looking at something?"

The man wasn't even one of the police. Paul couldn't see Lorraine near them, and it came as no surprise that Greg boiled over most when she wasn't at his side. And Paul realized he could do *nothing*.

But if Lorraine has drifted away, that means I have a chance to slip in to see her—

He wrenched his eyes away from the window, raising a fist but stopping short of banging angrily on a car roof; with his luck it'd set off every alarm in the lot.

Maybe I should consider the other side of things, look into why anyone would use blackmail to tip the debate against LifeLab. Lorraine could find that, but if she's keeping secrets about Quinn…

"Just got a call!" The cop's urgent tone pulled Paul out of his thoughts. "Someone snooping around upstairs. Abrams, go—"

Paul stopped in his tracks, staring at the center's windows and its waiting door. The police only sent two men up to check, but would he ever get a better chance?

Crazy! Paul turned and headed for the street at last, before they got around to widening their search. As he did, he listened to the cops shifting around, as his father—not letting Greg try it now—assured the uneasy clients that there was nothing going on.

And Paul could only kick his way along the slushy pavement, at a too-conspicuous pace that brought him walking past one pedestrian after another. He couldn't seem to settle down.

The police were still leaning on his family—and now they'd gotten a tip that he might be *inside?* It was either a coincidence or someone trying to tighten the screws at random.

Is someone actually using this to chase me? Or were chasing Paul and Greg red herrings to hide someone targeting the lab, maybe a rival like he had told Koenig… Or Lorraine, or it was all Quinn's scheme?

Paul scowled around the street, at the back corners and the glass towers full of secrets he'd spent too long learning. And now, when he should be saying goodbye to the city, he had to stop the police harassing his family.

Maybe, if the police took tips on their stakeout, he could wear them out with false leads? Or break in somewhere else while Greg was in full view of them? But those wouldn't be enough.

His neck tried to twist back, to turn him back to the person he needed—*no!* Even though it seemed so obvious that it wasn't, he could never *know* this wasn't her work. Maybe she was under Quinn's influence. *Or maybe it's just me, trying to stay near her.*

A crosswalk light brought Paul up short, and he looked around the city again. His eyes could pick out people whole blocks away or see skyscrapers well beyond that, but that was nothing against the miles of offices and motivations behind wall after wall. *Is this how my suspects feel, when their lies are ruined by someone who appears out of nowhere?*

Somewhere, someone is doing this. Paul had no clue how they'd done it and could only vaguely guess why. He had to deal with the nagging fear that Lorraine might somehow have a reason, or that Quinn had found a way. And Quinn had his tie to Lorraine, too…

Too much. Paul couldn't bear to think of her as an enemy, but he didn't have to go near her to be sure.

The light turned green, but Paul spun around and marched back toward the convention center. *I have to pick a path, so I'll go with my instincts and pick the most sinister one I know. Quinn.*

Just like a Schuman, Lorraine would have said.

* * *

As Paul had thought, noon brought a small crowd pouring out of the center's front door. And as he'd hoped, his family left within that crowd. *Maybe they're hoping I'll use it as cover to contact them.* They did split the police attention some, as Paul's father went one way and Greg went another with Lorraine and the bulk of the cops. It gave Paul a chance to slip up past his father and slide a note into his fine coat pocket.

That done, Paul moved quickly, keeping the crowd between him and the police until he was far enough away to break into a run. He had to get into position.

He made it, reaching the far end of the parking lot, far opposite the BMW, just as his father sat down in it. Paul Opened his sight, locking his gaze on that familiar face and tracking how his father's eyes moved as he settled in.

Just as the eyes glanced straight across the lot, Paul waved. His hand didn't rise above his shoulder. It was just a small motion from far away, nothing that would catch an observer's eye—unless that eye was passing right over him at that instant. *Look, look back, Dad!*

And he did look again, and Paul waved again and saw his father stare across at him. Paul brought a hand down and patted at a pocket, and his father looked down at his own pocket and pulled out the note:

Just whisper—I've set it all up. Tell me about Quinn.

Paul Opened his hearing just in time to hear him gasp "How can you—" in a weak, throaty sound.

He's never sounded so tired before. But then, nobody's voice was impressive when heard from an inch away, mixed with all the usual stomach rumblings and clothes rustlings. What mattered would be *what* he told Paul about his old enemy.

"Paul. Stay away, go far away and keep running," he said, the slow, intent words he might have used for a man on a ledge. "I swear, we can deal with this. You just find somewhere safe."

Paul scowled and motioned to his pocket again, to remind his father about the note and its request. *Don't you get it? I can't let this destroy you again! First that hospital fax and now this!*

"I said *leave*, can't you hear me? Go!" Then he sagged against the wheel and let out a long moan. "But you *can't* hear me. More of those cheap bugs, Greg said. Right. Come on, please, just catch a word or two. Go. Go. Just… stay away from that devil."

His voice died away then and he stayed hunched over, not even trying to look up again.

Huh? Paul watched a moment longer, trying to pull his thoughts together. To make the trick work this far, and then have it just fall apart from someone's sheer doubt… *But why should he believe in me after I've kept him and Greg so much in the dark?*

And to see his father just slumped there—

Paul spun away. This had to end.

*   *   *

"It's only how the payments keep going up. And, well, I'm not sure I can follow what this page says."

"I see," Quinn said. He still sounded unworried, even helpful. "Well, there is this one."

Paul heard a rustling then, a slightly louder sound, as if Quinn had brought out a larger sheaf of pages.

"Um…" the young man said.

"Think about it. I'm sure she'll still be there when—"

"Look, just let me think!"

Paul gritted his teeth tighter yet. Every minute a client for Quinn's real business was there, Paul wished that last time he'd hit the "furniture store" window with something a lot bigger than a bottle.

His fingers clenched to do it now, anything to break the stream of petty gullibility that trickled into the loan shark's office. He'd heard no sign of Quinn blackmailing anyone, not chasing after anyone's weakness, but just letting people walk in with simple dreams and undersized pockets. The leech hardly needed anything more, the way he always seemed to have the right word to nudge people, just enough, off the edge. And the victims… Quinn must have made plenty of loans to desperate gamblers and other unpleasant people, but today, everyone seemed to want help with ordinary, honest goals—if they weren't simply looking for a sofa.

I can even picture Dad coming here as a driven young man. Paul knew his father had struggled for years afterward to actually do enough business to avoid the loan's web of barely-legal penalties. *Well, I can picture his first time here—but for the second, who knows what that damn fax did to him?*

But that slow suffering of Quinn's clients was all Paul had learned by listening in. With part of the afternoon gone, all he'd done was stand in the cold listening to sheep searching for the slaughterhouse. *I'm not a single step closer to knowing if Quinn was pulling Bennet's strings, or what he did about the hospital and Lorraine—*

"Councilwoman."

Quinn was now alone in his Spartan inner office, and Paul almost missed the word, but he could not miss the metallic echo the voice distorter gave it—

"You were told to push for an indictment against Greg Schuman. You have twenty-four hours." And the cell phone clicked shut.

Paul sagged against the cold brick, straining to hear more, trying to picture the movements behind Quinn's sounds and where he was in that little room. Was the hidden panel opening? Did Quinn set down the tiny phone that could end lives? No, he only headed back out to the floor.

So there it is. Paul pulled himself away from the wall, but felt no warmer. Of all the schemers in the city, the danger *was* their oldest enemy, as ruthless as he'd been told… crushing lives every day, but also spinning a whole different kind of web.

And now this man had snared a key leader in the city, when he wasn't bullying the Schumans for escaping him. Or did he want even more?

What does it matter? They might start charges against Greg any time now, I've got to—

First things first. He needed more ammunition.

*   *   *

It didn't seem right, somehow.

Paul stood in a simple house. It had good security, but much less than Quinn's shop. It was in a decent neighborhood, but with none of the ambitions Greg's had.

The house was furnished with ordinary, classy tastes, as if Quinn really *were* only a furniture dealer. Soft chairs, good but mundane landscapes hanging on the walls, a variety of books and foods—it was clean, but there was no sense that a wife or child had ever set foot here. *It's almost as bland as Quinn's face.*

He detected no hidden spaces anywhere. Paul had moved all through the house, methodically tapping and lifting every surface until he thought his fingertips would never stop tingling again.

He looked carefully at the padded brown easy chair. Was *this* how a man with whole pages of secret fortunes lived? *Either Quinn buries his money in the yard or not a penny of how he spends it seeps into his home… and what might that mean?* Paul felt an urge to tail Quinn a while, to trace down some real leverage that he might need to take his enemy apart.

But he had no time—not with the coils tightening around Greg. *I haven't had time to do anything right since the LifeLab files went wrong.*

Instead, Paul opened Quinn's one computer and removed the hard drive, not caring how awkward he was at it. *Now I'm actually stealing— or holding it hostage, anyway. And I just don't care.*

It was only his first move.

* * *

The sun was already below the rooftops when he returned to the shop, the hard drive stashed away. Paul watched a little longer, letting his tactics line themselves up in his mind. Two customers drove up, conducted their business inside, and drove away while he planned.

One was a woman who'd soon be trapped on the loan shark's lists—if Paul couldn't hit hard enough.

He walked away and found the phone on the next block.

"Officer—I saw them unloading, sneaking it inside Quinn's Furniture—it looked like *dynamite,* they said they'd blow—I think they saw me—"

And he let the receiver drop and ran a few steps in the snow, in case the cop on the other end had good enough ears to hear the crunching sound. *Let Quinn ignore that!*

The police cars howled up the street in minutes. Paul hung well back from the space they cleared and the front ranks of the gathering crowd. The outer fringes gave him enough people to hide among.

Still, that crowd's frightened babble reduced Paul's hearing to erratic snatches of what Quinn said to the cops: first an authentic "Get everyone out—" as they cleared his building. That soon shifted to a sly "I can't believe anyone would…" and "Please call… as soon as you know what to ask."

And somehow, instead of taking him in for questioning, they let Arthur Quinn simply walk away down the street as the police continued searching his shop.

Paul watched him move into the thick of the crowd, and dove in after him, struggling to keep his focus on him—Quinn's unobtrusive way let him walk without distinctive footsteps to pick out, even when he was walking fast.

Six doors up from the shop, Quinn stepped off the street and between the buildings. Paul slowed to stay with the others on the street, keeping his hearing on Quinn. When Quinn paused in the back alley and moved around a moment in the crunching snow, Paul fixed that spot in his memory.

As Quinn moved on up the alley and back toward the street, Paul stumbled forward into the alley, still maintaining his connection to Quinn, afraid he'd slip away or turn back and catch him. But Quinn only kept going, and Paul reached the dumpster he had paused at. Because it seemed he had spent too long there to just toss something inside, Paul looked down underneath it.

Tucked into one wheel, already soaking in the snow, was a note. Paul drew it out, checking again that Quinn was far away before he opened it.

RRU-MNO-MNY LLE-OOE-RYS WWI

Paul stared at the twenty-one letters of code, then crushed the useless paper in his hands. Unless, he could wait here to catch whoever picked it up—

No, no more waiting. While Quinn is still rattled by the police...

Paul trotted back to the street, looked around, and spotted him again: a man in his fifties, ordinary suit. *The most ordinary man on Earth.*

Paul adjusted his wool cap to pull the full ski mask down over his face, glad that there were *some* things winter did help camouflage. He walked faster, slowly gaining on Quinn until he drew up just behind him and said, "I think you dropped something."

Quinn turned, saw the masked man and the note in his hand... and his face just *stopped*, right at the instant when surprise should have swept over it.

Instead, Quinn turned and walked on again, not even hurrying. Paul ran a step to move beside him, close enough to speak freely, even though there were people around. Quinn's pace didn't change.

Paul leaned a little closer, and hissed, "I can warn the police, or your clients. I can get any of your drop-points," and he waved the note, "and then…" He leaned in, looking for a reaction in that bland face. "I can give them the cell phone with your prints, the one that called Councilwoman Bennet and threatened her."

And Quinn *sighed,* drawing the sound slowly out. "Ah, poor Ms. Bennet."

He still didn't really turn to look at Paul; he just kept walking. Paul used the moment to flick a probe behind them in case Quinn had a bodyguard following, but Quinn said nothing more.

Have to keep the pressure on him! "Do you know how many dozens of ways I can hurt you, or confuse you, or cripple your 'business,' while you can't even find me? One phone call just shut down your office with a word and your name. The next one can have them believing you're *making* the bombs," and he leaned right in to glare at Quinn's still features, "because I'll be sure they find some."

"Next to where my records used to be?" Quinn sounded almost calm, and he never glanced toward Paul as they walked.

Fists clenching, Paul said, "Just move the initials two letters forward? Was that supposed to be a real cipher? Suppose I give the police the pages and their key," he added, not admitting he'd already lost the records.

"A list of initials? What would they investigate on that?"

"How about how the money figures on it are funding your 'bombs'? I only have to suggest that and you spend the rest of your life in their binoculars, until they find something real. Then I give them the phone you called Bennet from—"

"A phone you don't have." Even when he interrupted, Quinn sounded unconcerned.

"Don't I?" and Paul stepped around to block his path. The traffic had thinned out so nobody was close enough to interfere. His eyes locked on Quinn's. "I see two alleys here just waiting for me to disappear into after I grab it. Or I could pick any time I want and find you again. *Any time.*"

"You know, I believe you could, Paul."

And with that, Quinn actually stepped to the side and resumed walking at the same unhurried pace, and Paul fell back into step beside him.

Quinn went on "You've shown you can get to almost anything if it helps you protect Greg, or Ms. Bennet—although, can you tell me how exposing my dealings with her would keep *her* secrets?"

"Like they'd believe a terrorist's claims," Paul spat back. "Besides, you think I'm doing this for her? I'll play that card or not, when I want. But *you*," and his whisper sharpened like a blade, "your blackmailing stops. *Now.*"

"But I've barely started." And Quinn waved a dismissive hand, as if it scarcely mattered either way.

"You mean lately? Enough people walking in to just give you their money?"

"Business, of course."

"On the edge of the law, you mean. I know those tricks. But the blackmail ends, or…" He leaned closer, trying to make the man just *look* at him. "Or they get your records. And your cell. I find new ways to hurt you each day. I wonder how well a furniture shop burns? And all the while, I'll keep looking for the dirtiest deals you've ever made and just who to tell about them. So think of all that, against bullying a city councilwoman—how's that look on your balance sheet?"

"So all you want is Councilwoman Bennet? But you just said she wasn't your real interest."

Quinn *knew* this was about Greg, but Paul didn't have to admit it, and he couldn't lose momentum. He growled, "I said this is your whole life at stake, one piece at a time. Call her, *now!*"

"Well… I could give her a call, as a concerned businessman," Quinn said slowly. Then his head turned toward Paul: "After all, you aren't recording any of this."

I should have been—wait, how did he know that—

"So I should weigh my business against whatever use I can find for Bennet. Or," and Quinn's voice grew a little colder, "I could invoke the clauses in your father's contract and legally bankrupt him. I could increase the pressure on your brother, and his wife… well, I think you're presenting more targets than I am."

At once, while the chill was still sweeping through him, Paul shot back, "What targets? People I haven't seen in two years?"

"Until you took on the police to protect them. Why else are you here arguing with me?"

"If I wanted to protect them," Paul said, trying to hollow out his voice and give it a new level of menace, "all I have to do is remove you. Any time I want."

"Yes, you could," and Quinn stopped walking. "How about right now?"

What did I walk into—Paul looked around at the surroundings he'd lost track of, expecting to see a police station or worse—

And stared around at an empty side street, all but deserted.

What kind of trap is this? He flicked a probe out behind and around the alleys for guards, just a fleeting listening for footsteps, but as he did, he knew the danger wouldn't be there.

"Here we are." Quinn spread his arms, motioning to the stillness all around. "I've just threatened everything you love. So, *can* you kill me?"

Paul glared at the man, who was twice his age, then Opened his sight to search the lines of his clothes for hidden weapons. A moment later, he dropped the probe and took a step closer, to arms' reach.

"It's easy," he told Quinn. "I know all your hiding places, so your secrets won't blow up after you're gone. Or, I could give the police your records and—"

"The ones you already lost?" Quinn asked with a smile.

He knows that too!

Before Paul could continue, Quinn went on. "But why bother? Here I am. Just break my neck."

Paul's fists clenched, tighter, tight as iron. "I can. I have all your secrets, and you have nothing left—"

"Like the message under the dumpster?" Quinn motioned down to Paul's hand, and the forgotten note still crushed in it. "Try reading the last letter of each word, from the back."

For a moment, Paul couldn't force his fingers to loosen, but then he fumbled the paper around and reread it, then the message within the

RRU-MNO-MNY LLE-OOE-RYS WWI

Slowly, Paul's eyes turned from the three chilling words, back up to the man who placed it.

"A bomb threat, Paul, and so I run right to show you one of my hiding places? You think you're the only one who's read Conan Doyle? But still, maybe you *can* sniff out any insurance I left. You do keep finding what nobody else can. So why *not* just kill me?"

Paul's eyes locked on that face, the lines around the icy eyes and mocking smile. His fists rose, almost too close already to swing at the enemy… the smug schemer he'd hated before he was old enough to know what money was, the man who held his family's life.

He could almost feel Quinn's breathing, in and out. If he could just reach over and *stop* it somehow…

His hands sagged to his sides. *I can't turn assassin. I can't even steal!*

"Of course you can't." Quinn laughed softly, and drew back half a step, a more normal distance. "But since there's so much you *can* do…

did you still think I was interested in ordinary Greg, or an old grudge with your father? Did you even ask yourself why I bothered to push the police against Greg?"

"But…" But, Paul knew who Quinn had really been trying to flush out.

Those eyes bored into him now, pinning him in place with what they knew. "All your work, and you still have no money, no reward, and now your family's in more danger than ever. It's time to give them some real protection, and share in a little of what you've shown you deserve. You've been reckless, giving out story after news story until anyone could look and see someone was behind them. But still, you have real talent."

"What—" Paul could feel his life, his world slipping away with each word.

"Yes, you do. Ever since you started, with the hospital and your family—"

"What did you do?" Paul snarled. *The whispers together, my memories—* "You were there, Lorraine said you were just making an offer, but what did you do that night? *Tell me!*"

Quinn sighed. "You still don't know? Sad."

"Tell me!! Or I'll use every trick my power has to—"

"*Your* power? Do you really think it has a chance, against mine?" *He… he couldn't…*

Paul staggered back a step, but those eyes wouldn't let him move. If the power did come from seeing someone else's… and Paul had seen Quinn… *No, it's not right, it can't be—*

"Here's the offer," Quinn said. "Your family's safe, and you start to learn some of your power's real uses. Unless," he frowned, "you can't manage to do me a favor first. If you can't, I just might tell the police why their burglar always gets away."

"You wouldn't dare," Paul gasped. He found he couldn't get a full breath. "You'd give away your own secret too—"

"Me? I haven't been leaving my mark on secrets and scandals all over town. Besides, I don't have a whole family to lose. Starting with Ms. Lorraine—"

"No!" The word burst out like a reflex. "Leave her alone!"

"Make me."

And Quinn folded his arms and narrowed his damned eyes, and Paul fell back another step. *If Lorraine can see into a mind, what can Quinn do?*

"Poor, poor Paul," and for the first time Quinn sounded warmer, almost sympathetic. "You can turn around and go back to scavenged food and wondering who gets arrested first, and for what. Or you can go to the lab."

"Lab?" Paul stammered.

Quinn smiled. "You got into LifeLab once. This time, I need real evidence of how they abused their animals, enough to start a prosecution. And bring it to me by tomorrow. Don't forget, Bennet could pull together an indictment of Greg at any moment."

Paul could only say, "The lab… why *them* again? What did they do?"

"Because I asked you to."

And Quinn turned and strolled away. Paul started after him, but his legs shook and his knees barely had the strength to stand.

My God. My God, no…

D r. Lloyd Gardner stirred, half rolling over in his bed once again; his wife only huddled on her side, unmoving. And Paul only froze a moment and followed their breathing, still deep in sleep, before he finished swinging the door closed.

On the way out, he paused at the front closet and took down a long winter coat that would go better with the scientist's keycard than Paul's much-worn jacket. It looked warmer too, just the thing for long nights… *but I'll get this back to you, I swear.*

He grimaced as he stepped outside. What good was his code now, if he really had to go through with Quinn's mission, and then whatever came after that? *Please, let there be some way…*

*   *   *

LifeLab looked the same as it had the last time, although it was shrouded in snow now. Just a broad square of a building a little apart from the next factory along the street. They hadn't even added a fence.

But the differences wouldn't have to be visible, even to Paul's senses, as he watched it from up the street. This time, they knew someone had stolen their records once. Even if there weren't more cameras, the guards watching them would be more alert.

He looked longingly at the roof. Once, he'd been able to get a rope up, just between the camera blind spots, and never had to use the list of employees he'd gathered. When he hadn't had to plan and do it all in one night.

The big false beard all but *squirmed* in his hands, a corner always peeling away from his cheek or trying to stick to his fingers when he layered on more sticky gum to hold it on. But even that would be better than walking under those cameras with his own face showing. The stolen coat didn't hang right, either; it was too tight across his shoulders.

Can I really do this? Give Quinn the leverage he wants, and more evidence to control me, maybe even embarrass Sarah Gomez all over again? And yet, he knew that playing along was the only way to keep his family safe.

And still, still, he saw nobody come in or out, giving him no chance to guess at how alert the guard at the front desk was. Troubles or not, they'd all had two weeks to begin relaxing again. And a few lights did glow inside, so it wouldn't be too unusual for someone to come in at this hour.

But the waiting! He scuffed his feet in the snow. How long could he wait, how long hoping wildly that there'd be *something* in the lab he could use against Quinn, hoping to learn just a bit more about the guards before he risked everything?

A snowflake touched his cheek. More drifted down, and for a moment, Paul shook his head at the sky in simple frustration. Then he realized that standing out in the snowfall wouldn't just annoy him, it would make "Dr. Gardner" show up soaked, as if a well-off scientist had had to walk to work.

No choice, no more choice here than anything else now, he thought as he marched into the parking lot.

The anger was good, he realized, since anyone coming in at this hour would be fuming. He hunched his shoulders as grimly as he could in the tight coat, swiped the keycard, and stomped in through the doors.

A slight, balding man in a blue uniform glanced up from his little paperback and saw the bearded stranger. Time slowed…

Keep the card clenched in hand. No, not so obvious! I still have to hide its picture from him. The guard's pale eyes watched him, alarm buttons waiting in front of him. *Don't look at him, just keep walking past as if I…*

Paul swung the door open and stepped through. He slumped in relief, but then caught himself; the corridors still had their cameras, so he couldn't draw attention. He walked on, Opening his hearing as he did to make sure the guard wasn't bringing up reinforcements behind him.

He made his way through the silent, beige-painted corridor, trying not to look up at the cameras where others might be watching him. He was just one shape among a dozen empty screens… The rooms he passed sounded all but deserted, but still he fought the urge to keep his footsteps from echoing.

At last, he reached the maintenance door and stepped through, out of their sight.

This time, he didn't need to sag in relief. He just hurried through the empty room to tuck the winter coat out of sight and pull on one of the gray janitor uniforms he'd seen on his last visit. He added a cap and a pair of their plastic gloves, perfect for avoiding fingerprints, then used his scissors and the mirror to snip half of the false beard away—the guards had to forget that he'd gone into the room and a "janitor" had come out, so they couldn't both have the same rabbi-sized beard.

And he sank down into a chair, waiting again, this time for them to forget he'd come in here. Opening his hearing, he found himself wishing he could stretch that time, before… sure enough, he heard two men moving in his direction, wheeling along what could be a huge janitor's bucket.

Grabbing a mop to complete his look, Paul darted out the door again, walking as fast as he dared until he could reach the first turn and get out of their sight. The building layout was coming back to him now as he picked his way toward the stairs he needed.

At least he didn't hear many people, and it wasn't too difficult to steer clear of the few in the halls. He walked with his head and his cap tilted only a little low, trying not to think which move might be the one that would make the guards look twice at the screen that showed him.

Quinn is sending me here to test me. That has to be it. Getting "evidence" on the Lab would be easy with all of Quinn's power and cunning, maybe even just with power like Lorraine's to pull out the right thing to say. *Oh God, how long before Quinn picks up that she's worth using, too?*

Paul's fingers clenched on the mop. *I have to play along. She didn't think meeting with Quinn years ago mattered. Did he somehow* make *her underestimate him?*

Or even, could Lorraine somehow be working with him... *but I can't let him hurt her!*

Footsteps sounded around the bend ahead of him. Paul walked a bit faster, eyeing the stairs up ahead, hoping the footsteps would turn away but knowing they wouldn't. Paul couldn't run or hide, he couldn't do anything to attract the unseen guards' attention, but he also couldn't let this person up ahead ask who he was... he could only move a little faster, a little faster, until at last he ducked up the stairs and out of view. When the feet moved on past him below, he let himself gasp in relief.

On the second floor, he had only to step out and walk ten paces to the main room, to the vast grid of cubicles he'd used last time. Light spilled in from the corridors at the edges but the space itself was dim, although he saw one corner office door still bright. *Some sleepless manager still at work.*

But that door stayed closed, and Paul saw they'd added no cameras to the room itself. His stride shifted to a silent glide, even as he entered the chin-high cubicle walls and crouched below them. Two aisles down was the first work station on his list.

When he reached it, he leaned the mop awkwardly on the desk and dug out his notes as he powered up the computer. *Never thought I'd be nostalgic about spending most of a day curled up in the sub-ceiling with a James Michener epic and a dentist's mirror.* But at least then he'd *had* time to—

Footsteps, from the corridor he'd entered, were already starting into the room. *Why didn't I keep my hearing Open once that computer started humming?* Paul flicked the monitor off, reached under the table to twist the computer to point its power light toward the partition, and grabbed the mop as he slipped away up the aisle.

Too close! Paul had only scrambled a few steps before ducking into another cubicle, and as he squeezed in, the damned mop tapped on the chair. The slip sounded like a gunshot to him, as he Opened his hearing at last to track the approaching guard.

Guard, yes—something about the slowness in those footsteps spoke of a man glancing up and down, not just ambling toward work. Paul crouched lower, wondering if this was the man he thought he'd dodged on the stairway, who'd heard him after all. And now, how could he *not* hear the computer humming…

As the guard moved closer, Paul tried to shift in place, to face out instead of just staring into the cubicle with his back to the passing guard. But the long mop dangled one end too near the chair, leaving him no way to keep everything silent if he stirred. The guard was almost at his aisle, the computer humming louder than ever.

Is this my life now, stealing for Quinn and praying it saves my family?

And then, then, the guard kept walking on past the aisle. Paul kept every muscle still as the footsteps moved on to the room's far end, and out.

Luck. All his tricks, all the caution he could manage, and he still risked everything on nobody taking the wrong moment to give that second look…

Thick with sweat, Paul backed out of the cubicle and moved to the second spot on his list, switching on that computer's power but not its screen yet. At the third cubicle, he finally took the time to enter the password he'd seen its owner enter, weeks earlier.

Quickly, he dipped through the onscreen folder, expanding one layer after another and staring at the document names. Quinn wanted "evidence" that made the innocent lab actually worth prosecuting, while Paul just hoped he'd find some hint of how to fight him. But he couldn't remember how this woman had organized her work, so he could only look for titles that seemed more like experiments than administration.

This is no way to explore. Paul gazed at the column of cryptic names; he needed to get *everything*, any file related to experiments' length or intensity or anything else controversial. Instead he opened a Find File search, and began typing *results OR (pain AND regulations) OR…* When he'd cobbled together as many terms as the search line could hold, he turned it loose on the LifeLab network and flicked off the screen to move back to the other computers he could unlock.

Yes, he'd just copy everything promising and then get away and check if any of it was too dangerous for Quinn to have. He wouldn't even have to *click* on the files here and let the owners start tomorrow's work with surprising names on their software's Recently Opened lists. He could stop there and not risk entering the lab itself just for Quinn—

But that's not enough, not to give me any hope of finding a weapon against that monster.

Paul started a different search on the second computer, then returned to the first one he'd started and began exploring as fast as he could work the keys. This user didn't seem to have much about actual experiments, but he copied what he could to one of the several flash drives in his pockets. Most of the company network's shared folders wouldn't even open from here—worse, their *Trials* folder asked him for a password of its own. *That's new.*

Paul settled for giving that machine its own search to run, then moved back to the second. Its search was done, and he copied the long column of files straight to a flash drive and began exploring the company folders. But this user had even less access than the first.

And the lab was waiting; Paul knew he was stalling. Still, he gave the machine a new search and moved back to the third one again. He copied its search findings, clicked the *Trials* folder, and grinned when, this time, the user's basic log-in password opened the folder itself. He began clicking through it…

And stared at the St. Central name.

It couldn't be. But the file dates… Too many were the same month as Paul's lost night at the hospital, the same night his powers began.

The thought had barely sunk in before his fingers finished opening the largest file, and they trembled as he skimmed through it. The report's start and end summaries said nothing about strange effects on its test subjects, but it did deal not just with LifeLab's usual drugs but with a retrovirus, a tool meant to adjust DNA for one tiny bit of healing. But who could say what the full effects were of any virus?

Good God, could this really be it?

He dragged the whole folder and its subfolders to his drive, then spat a curse at the little warning window that said it wouldn't fit. He grabbed a few files, then started a search for *R91 OR senses OR telepathy OR unknown—*

And heard the footsteps again, just entering the room. *No no no no*—but his hands were already switching off the screen and grabbing his flash drive and the stupid, clumsy mop.

The footsteps had the same steady, searching pace they'd had before. Choking down more curses, Paul crouched low and crept up the aisle, keeping the bulk of the cubicles between himself and the guard.

When the guard started across toward his side of the room, Paul slipped back into the aisle the guard had just left… then realized it would walk him straight past the office that had the lights on. Instead, he scrambled back to his own side and out to the corridor before the guard came into view.

So close, so close—*close to being caught, or getting answers, or both?* Paul couldn't even let himself scowl since he remembered he was back under the corridor cameras again.

But maybe it was for the best. Under the cameras, he could only keep walking. He turned toward the lab section, trying to keep his knees steady.

After so long, after looking through all of St. Central and everywhere else, could this be it? Could it be some odd genetic virus from here that explained his power—and Lorraine's, and Quinn's, too?

But wait, if Quinn remembered any of it, why would he send me anywhere near something I could use against him?

Thoughts racing, he struggled to keep sweeping the corridors for sounds. He heard the footsteps ahead in time to veer up a side path toward the lab.

And Quinn, did he send me here to share in the secret, or is there something about the virus that left him so desperate that he'd even risk his rebellious cat's-paw finding out?

Schemes and blueprints stopped whirling in Paul's head when the lab section door came into view. He walked more slowly, looking through its glass into the well-lit space beyond. Machines churned and hummed, but at a muted level, and he could hear only one or two people moving in the whole area. There seemed to be no camera on the corner opposite the door, either. So maybe…

He opened a door across the hall from the lab and stepped into the tiny conference room. With no small relief, he propped the clumsy length of the mop in a corner, at last, and took out the key card. Now, it would be just his stealth and the answers, and the hope that the camera watchers didn't notice a janitor entering the lab.

He took a deep breath, stepped into the corridor again, and swiped the card in the door's card reader.

The door didn't move.

Paul shoved it again, fought the urge to rattle it, and swiped the card a second time. Still nothing. He turned away and retreated into the opposite room, hoping his time at the door had been too brief for anyone to notice.

So close, but the door won't let Dr. Gardner's card in! Why didn't I make time to learn to work electronic locks? But then, Quinn will probably force me to learn, if I can't break free of him tonight…

As Paul stood shaking in rage, he heard a motion outside. Footsteps, moving out from the lab and starting down the corridor. Paul flung open his room's door, but the lab door was already swinging shut again.

Stepping back out of sight, Paul tracked the footsteps of the lab worker down the hall and to the room he guessed was a bathroom. That left one chance…

Paul waited, stretching his hearing to one corner of the building and then another in search of the first sign that his movements had already raised an alarm.

This has to work! Getting the power's secret is the only way! But then he stopped short with another realization: *Quinn will read it in my mind. I'll have to think only about other things when I'm with him and hope that makes a difference… or stay away from him, or make a deal…*

At last, the bathroom door swung open again and Paul peeked out to watch a sleepy-looking black man in a lab coat walk back to the lab door and let himself in. As the door swung closed, Paul rolled a pen along the floor. *Please, let it move just far enough…*

The door shut right on the pen, and it held it open. And no alarms blared, and the scientist kept walking away.

Paul let him walk a bit farther and strained his Opened hearing so he could take in everything about the rooms beyond the door. Then he stepped out and strolled into the lab.

With nobody close to the door, he had a moment to duck to the side behind a table of instruments and match his glimpse of the room to what he'd heard. There were what sounded like a man and a woman working in the area, one of them heading up a corridor with several doors, several "islands" in the room he could try to hide behind, and only one camera looming in one corner, which would leave wide blind spots.

Opening his hearing as the woman entered one room, he caught the squeaking of a rat. Right, they kept rats on site, but not usually the pigs they used in their later studies. *Am I even at the right facility?* Paul pulled farther back into place, but not before he'd glimpsed another camera above that inner corridor.

He studied his corner of the room: walls of instruments, mostly metal boxes with readouts and controls that his months searching the hospital did nothing to explain to him. *And how long can I crouch in a corner before someone walks over this way, anyhow?*

Hold on, how did I get this far if they're working on what could be the ultimate spy tool? I've seen better security at—

The man moved away from his station, joining the woman in the rat room. Paul stepped out for another glance around, keeping to the side away from the camera. He could hear the two speaking, but he knew the odds against them saying anything useful in a random few minutes. Instead, he kept only enough attention on them to note if they headed outside again. Then he reached for the man's computer.

Costs, then *Timeframe*, then a folder on *Reports* that he opened, clicking on the latest file. But as he skimmed down, he saw only a reference to drug tests, not retroviruses, and none of the faint effects jumped out at him as related to enhancing the senses.

That was when the footsteps behind him moved closer to their door. Paul closed the report with one stab of his fingers and ducked back to his hiding place again, his nerves screaming from the close call.

This is crazy, me flitting around at the corner of their eyes! I'm lucky if I go another minute *without them needing whatever tool is kept just next to me!* Paul looked at the door, his only way out, wondering if he'd even get a chance to retreat.

Then he looked at the scientist again, an aging man who yawned as he tapped obliviously on the keyboard. And Paul had no more options, and no time—one quick grab from the right angle could overpower the old man and keep him away from the camera, leaving Paul free to do the same to the woman…

What do I know about knockout punches? But if I don't do something, Quinn's going to take it all—

As his fingers began flexing, the scientist stepped away again, ambling back to the rat room. Paul looked after him, noting that the corridor camera was too close to fully cover that room's door, while the room camera never came close. And with them both in the room together, he found himself wishing he'd hung onto the janitors' mop after all.

But there, waiting in a corner, stood another mop.

The sight was all he needed. Paul took a wide step around the room camera's view, seized the mop, and stepped out next to the door. Hanging back just out of the corridor camera above him, he reached out and *wrenched* the mop tightly into place across the corridor to brace the door shut.

He turned away at once, glad he wasn't hearing any reaction from the researchers yet. But it only took a few steps to dart back to the computer and slide his flash drive into place.

"Download to device not permitted."

No! Paul stared at the screen's security alert, his hands shaking with rage. As his ragged breath began to calm again, he removed the drive and brought up the email system, hoping the classic security hole still applied. Sure enough, the first files attached to his message and shot off freely through the net toward one of his old accounts.

As fast as his fingers could move, Paul gathered more folders together and flung their copies after the first. *Those scientists have phones. How long do I have before real maintenance workers come to let them out—or security guards, when they see the mop on their screen?*

And yet, he heard no sounds from his prisoners. For some reason, they still hadn't tried the door.

He emailed off the last folder, then took precious seconds to delete the Sent Message records and empty the Deleted folder, knowing their IT squad would end up digging out his address anyway. *And once the cops crack that, Reid can prove it was me on both this and the other cases I used that email for, like Sarah's—*

Still, his fingers wouldn't leave the keys. *A little more, a few more seconds...*

He dove back into the Reports folder, searching for anything near the time of his St. Central incident, and clicked open a file marked simply *Other.*

But all he found were more notes on the immune system. Even the complete listing of the retrovirus' effects had nothing about unusual powers.

He thumped the key to close it and dug out *Final,* a sick feeling growing inside him that all their "answers" would be as empty as the lab's security. No odd notes about the virus, no hints of other uses or special cases, no… *The cause was* never *here, I just saw a mention of the hospital and risked everything on the hope that it would be so simple!*

When the alarm howled, he gasped and whirled clumsily, as if his keyed-up nerves had been knifed in the back. The scientists shouted and hammered on the door so suddenly that he knew they only just noticed they were trapped. *So why…*

Paul felt his fingers leaving the keyboard and realized they'd reflexively closed the file. He took a moment to lunge across to the researchers' door and knock the mop loose with a kick—couldn't leave anyone trapped, though he *knew* it wouldn't be a real fire they'd spotted. Then he dove out the lab door.

A quick probe—

He clutched his ears, half deafened by the alarm's shriek. Only instinct started him walking to the right, away from what might have been footsteps. And walking was all he had, he realized. One floor up from the ground, with the cameras watching and his hearing gone, he had no hope left if they noticed him.

Ears ringing, feet fighting to break into a run, he tried to work out how far away those guards had been. Shouldn't they be already reaching him, unless they weren't running, maybe didn't know it was him? *Or their hands are reaching for my shoulder right now and I can't hear…* But he couldn't risk looking back.

Ahead, the stairs by the main room grew closer with every step. The building's layout flashed through his mind again, showing those stairs as the only chance he'd have of getting off the floor. Except… he braced himself and stretched his hearing into the stairwell, then winced as the alarm noise smashed through him again.

Was that movement or not? Every step brought the door to the stairs closer, but was he walking into…

He turned away, into the main room.

The moment he stepped clear of the damned cameras, he crouched down behind the cubicles. But as he did, he saw a guard across the room talking with an older man not in uniform. *That late-working manager in the office.* Paul crept closer, straining to hear without Opening.

"…not sure… full a… call about an in…"

Then the guard walked away, and Paul crouched inside a cubicle, trying to think. *"Call," they said. Did someone call them about me?* Was Quinn setting him up all along—while all he could think about was chasing the first wild goose he saw?

As if an escaped virus could really have given them their powers!

Gritting his teeth, he Opened the faintest probe he could, by the stairwell on the floor away from the alarms. Too weak, it barely caught anything but the clamor already echoing in his ears, but still he reached it downward. If the stairs were clear…

Faintly, he made out a footfall just at the bottom. Paul tensed to creep down and rush him, but he heard a second footstep nearby.

So that was it. *Trapped.*

As he let his breath out, someone shouted "What the hell—"

The man who shouted was running, running along the corridor. And yet, when his voice died away, he *stopped*, just standing there. Another man ran past the cubicles to join him, drawn by the shout.

My only chance. Not even checking if the guards had left the stairwell, Paul stepped out and moved to the corridor. A guard and the manager stood in it, staring out the window and down.

At an orange-red glow, the flicker of a fire dancing in the night.

Paul looked up, hating himself even as he risked taking the moment to Open and glance around the street. But he did see a single shape just close enough to have set the fire, ducking back behind a corner. *What's Quinn done now—*

But as she pulled out of sight, he saw the blonde flash of Lorraine's hair.

Paul froze, staring at the corner, sure his mind must be cracking. It couldn't, *couldn't* have been—

And I've lost enough seconds. He turned and yanked open the stairwell door, almost flying down the steps. In the next moment, he stepped out to the broad, open space below, glancing around to take in the several people at the far end, in a mix of janitor gray and blue security.

"Hey!" One of the guards waved him over. "Over here. Are you new—"

Paul walked slowly toward him, barely looking at the growing suspicion on the guard's face. Instead he glanced around at the room, the wide windows… the scattered cubicles and desks… the number of steps to cross the distance…

And in one motion, Paul lunged forward, snatched up the chair on his left, and twisted his run into a pivot on one foot that swung the chair around ahead of him, spun himself all the way around to build force, and ended the spin by letting the chair fly straight into the window.

In the instant his fingers released it, he felt a terror that he'd underestimated the strength of the glass. But no, the window exploded into flying shards, and Paul's arms were already rising to shield his face as he ran toward it. He heard the guard shouting and other shouts, suddenly clear, from the outside as he dove headfirst over the sill and into the night.

He tried to go limp in the air and then slammed down in a breath-crushing impact on the pavement. But the sheer *need* clawed him right up again, despite the pain, stumbling in the slush as he ran away. *There's too much I've got to know, to fix, to stop!*

Shouts rang around him and figures started toward him, but he dashed across the street and back into the alley. *They have no idea how blind they are.* Into the blessed, open night he ran, ranging around one corner and then another, his senses flickering out to lead him as the alarm faded away behind him.

He took a moment to snatch up his jacket from behind the trash where he'd hidden it, but he wasn't feeling the cold yet. The gray janitor's uniform even doubled as good camouflage in the snow and the shadows. So he ran on, tracking the guards' clumsy efforts to cover the whole neighborhood and riding the wild fear, need, exhilaration of just doing something he *could* do again.

What slowed him down was the car, the sight of Lorraine's green Toyota as he headed out from an alley. He turned to duck back up it again, but he heard feet in the snow along the street, even as he heard her moving toward him.

Thoughts whirling, he stopped to let her catch up to him.

She caught at his arm. "I've got the car—"

"You just firebombed a parking lot!" he hissed, pulling away. "It was just the empty lot, wasn't it?"

"Of course!" She stared at him in shock, then looked away. "Fill a bottle with gas, who hasn't seen *that* in the movies? I thought I could chase you out before you gave Quinn anything more to control you, and I knew you'd make it out…"

"Quinn?" The word slashed through Paul's thoughts, cutting away the lesser worries. Just the fact that she *knew*—

"I think he's on his way here. And the things I saw in his mind…" She stepped in and caught at both Paul's arms now. "You *can't* think we got our power from him—"

"Why were you really with him?" he spat. "How long have you been in on this? You said that talking with him *that night* didn't matter, you even said you didn't spill the fax that showed us as blackmailers. But what have you really done—"

"Stop it!"

Something in her low, fierce words and her grip on his arms brought him up short. He froze and watched her staring at him, her blue eyes looking away, then into his, then away again.

Then she looked back. "Paul, Quinn didn't even know about the power. He never had it. He lied."

What… Paul could only stare, stare at the unflinching face before him, as his mind reeled.

Impossible, the whole world was wrong now—Lorraine was lying, she had to be with Quinn, but that was crazy too—Quinn tricking him, or Lorraine, *both wrong, impossible, why can't I let go of either? Nothing makes sense now!* He felt his knees wobbling and wondered if her grip would have to hold him up.

"Anyway, well, I heard the alarm," she was saying. "I thought adding a fire could at least help you get out."

Still dazed, Paul stumbled back a step, out of her grasp. "You said that Quinn might be coming here. So just get away, before he sees you."

"But…"

Paul ran. His legs still worked, even though his thoughts couldn't catch their balance. Quinn's threats, the family's fax, the false leads on his power… all the questions gave way before two whole worlds of wrongness. *Why would Lorraine lie like that? Or is it true, did Quinn even trick me into revealing—*

That car. It passed him on the street, then slowed and turned back. Paul tried to dash away, but just the unhurried way the car turned made him pause and look back at the simple tan Honda as it glided toward him. The driver was no guard.

Quinn drew nearer, driving against the way traffic would have flowed by day, to bring his open window alongside Paul. Paul fought the urge to glance back to see if Lorraine were still—

I barely got out. I barely got out. He had to keep thinking that, in case it hid his other thoughts. *If that makes a difference to mind-reading. I should have asked her before—I barely got out. I barely...*

"So you got away," and Quinn smiled, the so-ordinary lines in his face spreading with actual warmth. "I hoped you were good."

The way he said it... Paul took a step toward the window. "You *did* call them. You sent me in there and then tipped them off!"

Quinn had betrayed him. He'd guessed right! He concentrated on *He betrayed me, he betrayed me—*

"And you passed the test." Quinn's smile widened. "As we agreed, I'll let up all the pressure on Greg. And there'll be bigger rewards once we make our case against the lab. So, about your evidence..." His hand reached out the window, waiting.

"Here." Paul dug out the flash drives he'd copied, struggling to think only *he betrayed me,* but he couldn't hold his thoughts away from that smile before him and how much he wanted to put a fist through it.

He held out the evidence, and Quinn reached to take it. Paul flung out his will: *Show me! Show me whatever his thoughts are. I HAVE to be part of them...*

Quinn's jaw dropped open in pure amazement, and Paul felt the motion as if his own jaw were moving, too. But he held the link, and the next moment, he realized Quinn's face hadn't moved at all.

And yet he saw it move again, an astonished gasp, and something else… a nervous shifting of Quinn's eyes as he looked for answers he couldn't see. And then, when the eyes focused on Paul, Paul could feel his own eyes wanting to stare back, to measure, to use.

The motions blurred hazily across Quinn's face. *But they aren't real expressions!* They were something else, some inner sense of lingering surprise, of ignorance, of Quinn's drive to find the answers and control them—

Quinn's fingers reached toward him still, twitching from sheer greed for the money they'd bring.

Then those fingers took the flash drives from his, and Paul felt himself only watching, saw Quinn's real face looking back at him with a curl of curiosity in his eye. Or in his real expression anyway, the one *masking* the thoughts Paul had just seen.

"Now we'll see what these are worth," Quinn said. "You go get your sleep. Come see me tomorrow at one."

Just like that. He thinks he can call for me any time, always keeping me off balance. "Right," Paul managed to say.

Quinn's smile grew wider yet, wide and warm, as if there were any human feeling under it. "You've made a great start, Paul. You've proved that it's worth keeping your family off-limits, with results like these. In fact, why don't you think about what kind of reward you want next? Your horizons are expanding, and you'll need to cope with those possibilities."

"I will."

Is that how he does it? He drops hints that imply he's talking about "our" power, without saying any details, since he doesn't know what the power is.

So far.

"And when you do come—" Quinn added, and his car's engine stopped revving and idled again, just as Paul thought he was driving away. "When you come, bring back the hard drive you took from my house."

Quinn didn't even sound angry. *Because he's winning—or thinks he is.*

When Quinn's car turned the corner and vanished from sight, Paul finally took a dazed step forward. Quinn *couldn't* read minds. He couldn't blur memories, hear whispers, or anything at all! *There's still hope. I can still beat him. And I might prove that I got my power for a reason.*

And now with *new* power to read thoughts—

Except, Quinn had something that might be even stronger. Using no power at all, he'd used sheer cunning and intimidation to goad Paul into blurting out his one great secret, a secret Quinn hadn't even *known* about!

Paul felt back in his memory, trying to reconstruct all of that searing, horrifying moment:

"…every trick my power has to…"

"*Your* power?"

It must have taken less than a second, for Quinn to come up with his ultimate lie in the middle of Paul's shouting.

Paul's hands shook and kept shaking, even as he clenched them and tried to keep them still. How could *anyone* fight a man who thought so fast?

He stumbled on down the street. Now Quinn just knew too much. He had too many ways to hit Paul's family, and in a few days with Paul, he'd probably figure out everything about the power, too—*because I told him.*

Realizing he was shivering, Paul pulled on the jacket he'd recovered. Then he scooped up a bit of snow and tried to dissolve the adhesive on the false beard, but the treacherous thing only clung more tightly to his chin.

I did it again. My family's trapped and it's all my fault! He spun around to look down the empty street. *Why won't this beard come off? I took on Quinn to protect my family and stop a blackmailer, but this time... this time I hurt them by letting the blackmailer win.*

The beard ripped loose, taking layers of skin with it.

In the hospital, he'd rejected blackmail and punished them all for it.

Paul's face burned in the cold air as memories tore through the old haze. Greg's papers, the evidence his brother had gathered to pressure the hospital, how they'd crinkled when Paul had stacked them together... Greg's fax, the one thing that tied Schuman and Son to knowing the hospital's schemes, how he'd seen it at the bottom of the stack... his fingers moving to draw it out, then pushing it back in and sweeping them all into the envelope together.

I did it. I blamed Quinn, even Lorraine, but Dad was right all along. To punish his family for blackmail, he'd betrayed them. And so, he'd pushed them into Quinn's grasp from the start.

Paul slumped against a building. Looking down, he saw a bit of blood dripping to the snow. His face still burned, he'd forgotten. *I tried so hard not to remember, but it's all my fault, then and now—*

"Hey!"

He whirled to find Lorraine's car at the curb. He hadn't noticed.

Whose side is she on—but, am I fit to be on anyone's side—

"Get in!" She leaned over and swung the passenger door open for him. "The police are still out there."

"But... you..."

Too much, too much! Paul found himself lunging toward the car, stopping just short of the open door and leaning down.

"Are you working with Quinn or not?"

"*What?* No!"

Paul's will was already lashing out, sinking in, joining. And he saw, *felt*, the face behind Lorraine's face take on one expression: A tight scowl, a curled lip of true loathing, glancing away toward the absent Quinn... and a little bit of disgust at him, for being bastard enough to ask.

Paul let the link drop at once, but the scowl tightened on his own face now, for what he'd just done. *An hour ago, I thought mind-reading was obscene!*

Worst of all, Lorraine's real face only frowned at him a moment before softening into sheer, innocent confusion.

"I'm sorry." Paul heard it come out as a groan, but as it did, other words came with it, and his thoughts fell into place. "We... we have to stay away from each other. Quinn's too dangerous. I can't do anything except line up the biggest threats I can find against him and then stay out of town so he won't think he can use me..."

"No..."

"I have to, Lorraine. I can't let him suspect what you—"

"No!"

Lorraine burst out of the car, stepping around it and advancing on him. Her hands reached out, but she stopped just short of coming into reach as she snapped, "I thought you had a life here! I don't know why you'd live in hiding like this, but it *is* a life, and a purpose. And you're going to let him chase you away?"

"Purpose?" Paul flung out a laugh as a barrier between them. "Life? I tried to bring out the truth, but I kept getting it all wrong. And now Quinn's planning to use me against anyone who can pay him."

He started to laugh again, but he broke off when his torn mouth burned at the motion.

A moment later it faded, and he sighed "You know, I let myself believe there *was* a reason I got this power, that something or someone wanted it to be *me* who had it." He shook his head. "Well, you had a better reason than I ever did, to stop that break-in or just to stop me from throwing away what I had. And I'm sorry I was too big a fool for you to—"

She *kissed* him.

Blinding moment, searing warmth and a whirl of faint perfume, so much right against him from such a soft touch…

Then it was gone. Paul saw her stumble back, slip, and half-fall into the snow as she staggered away. She never looked back at him, even as she scrambled into her car.

She was mumbling something. "Sorry, so sorry, sorry…"

"Hey… don't…" It was the only thing Paul could get out.

"I'm *sorry!*"

And she sped away, the forgotten passenger door swinging wide and shutting with a slam that mingled with the engine's roar.

Somehow, he managed to get some sleep. Even lying in the attic, his jaw burning from the beard's glue and his lips from the kiss… he knew he wouldn't be able to face Quinn without some rest. And at last, stretching his senses far enough, he managed to drift off.

He even woke on time, and returned to town hours before his 1 p.m. deadline—though when he realized he'd never set up an alarm clock, the thought of telling Quinn, "So I overslept!" gave Paul a rueful smile.

Even now, he couldn't keep from drifting toward the Schuman office on the way to Quinn's. Just a glance, to see if the police had moved on and if he could test one thing before the battle of wits began. *Sure, keep telling yourself it's not about saying goodbye, or having some chance of seeing Lorraine.*

But his careful look around the lobby didn't show any of the police surveillance he'd learned to recognize. Instead, he strolled across to the far stairs and moved softly up them to the opposite end of the corridor from Schuman and Son. When the corridor was clear, he moved out to the empty suite next to it. The lock was so common that one of his keys opened it at once.

Then he had only to walk through the wide, empty office space and study the wall. Even without hearing the patterns of where people walked, he knew how many steps of the wall were opposite his father's office. Leaning against it, he Opened.

The room was unoccupied just now, the wall screening its stillness into almost a void of silence. But Paul pressed his hands harder, stilling his breathing and making himself hear the faintest hums. There was the phone at his father's desk, of course, but he also probed slowly along the room, down each wall. This room was where Lorraine had explained Bennet's secret, and she'd *never* have gone to tell it to Quinn. But if Paul could just get one last confirmation for himself that Quinn had still needed to…

Buzz. A tiny hornet of electronic sound on the far wall.

For an instant, Paul thought of the framed picture of their Animal Alliance rally, the one his father must have rushed to get in place the next day. Quinn could have arranged to slip a bug into that, or whatever the thing was on. Maybe after Paul raided his office, he'd tried bugging a dozen of his enemies in hopes of…

Stupid! Paul banged a fist on the wall. Quinn probably hadn't even been *thinking* of the Schumans until Paul started blaming him for things, *and he'd* never *had power like me and Lorraine.*

He just had everything else.

So now I know. Paul turned and walked away, not looking back. Closing the suite door, he marched off down the corridor, leaving the firm behind him. At least the police weren't hounding Greg any more, but Paul knew he could never apologize for that fax, for driving his father back into Quinn's grip then and making it worse now. Better to just stop Quinn. *So just keep walking, and—*

"Paul?"

He heard his father's footsteps behind him. *I just had to bang on his wall, didn't I?* But still, the easiest thing was just to keep walking, not try to face him. The stairs waited just ahead.

When the stairwell door closed behind him, Paul lunged forward to catch the banister and vault upward, keeping silent even in the metal-and-concrete echo chamber. A moment later, he crouched above the stairs' turn, surprised he'd made the full effort to hide his trail.

Below, the door opened. He heard his father pause where someone would look and listen along the stairs for the person he was following.

Did I go up, or straight on down, Paul found himself thinking. *If he realizes I'd choose up, because he sees tricks are all I think of now, I can still wait for him and…*

The footsteps started down.

*   *   *

Another doomed customer walked into Quinn's Furniture, and Paul fought not to bang on the brick corner he crouched behind. With almost two hours left before he answered Quinn's summons, he still had no real idea how to break free.

Yes, warning the victims about Quinn's loansharking would hurt him… Add that to the threat Paul had tried yesterday, to brand Quinn as a terrorist, now tied to last night's raid on LifeLab…

Except the clues there would only point to Paul—and to Lorraine and the fire, that she'd started to keep Paul from digging himself in deeper. *And I could only fixate on her talking with Quinn two years ago! And I kept hearing Quinn's words from that night, all to distract myself from remembering who'd really betrayed the family.*

At least Quinn's old words didn't seem to echo in his ears any more. *Now that I know what I did, all to hurt Greg for dabbling in blackmailing—and now I'm turning blackmailer myself—*

Paul broke off that train of thought, as not helping. What he needed now was not just to stop Quinn, but to find and remove the pressure he could put on the Schumans…

Paul had bluffed about rooting out Quinn's hidden files and resources before, but it was the only real answer. It would take time to find them all, but at least Quinn couldn't actually read minds, and now Paul could—if he was careful.

But Paul had felt Quinn's sheer greed. *He will always want more, and the more he realizes my power's more than a delusion that inspires me...*

A car glided in among the parked shapes, a gleaming blue BMW.

Even before he Opened his sight, Paul knew. He stared helplessly, praying his father wasn't going in to face Quinn...

And he *didn't.* Instead, he sat in the car. As Paul watched, he saw his father's lips moving. Was he talking to the *car?*

"Please be listening!" he was saying. "Just leave Quinn alone. Come on, I'll say it as many times as I have to..."

Paul shook his head, dazed. *After I left that note, he still thinks there are bugs somewhere in the car.*

And maybe there *were!* How many devices might Quinn have scattered around? Paul strode forward before he knew it, stepping through a gap in traffic to cross to the BMW.

From the first honk in the street, his father looked up, and Paul at once held a finger to his lips. His father looked startled, but stayed in his seat as Paul approached.

Remembering the camouflage he'd used when riding with Greg, Paul turned the corner of his shirt collar up to his ear and slid out the edge of his sweater cuff as he extended his arm into the car. Waving the "concealed device" around, he Opened to listen for any irregular buzzes among the tangle of humming wires...

Long seconds later, he turned the collar back and stepped around to climb into the passenger seat. "Now we get away, in case he's watching. The car has no bugs."

As his father turned the key, he said, "Except for yours."

"Well…" He knew he should say he'd already removed them.

"Paul…" Ian Schuman's voice hesitated, sounding embarrassed. He kept his eyes on the road as he continued. "How much did you hear?"

"Um," Paul began, but he couldn't find the words, not with his father's strange, awkward expression, always facing away from him.

"Try to remember, it's been more than a day since I heard from you. So yes, I tried and tried to get more messages to you, and never knew which ones you might be… well, I hope you didn't catch only the wrong parts. Yes, Paul, I swore at you for being stubborn, and I shouldn't have done that. But you stopped the police from watching Greg… ahh, this isn't about how much you've given or taken from us—"

He started to turn toward Paul, but then stopped and looked past him. Paul followed his gaze and saw Lorraine and Greg at the curb ahead.

What? They're all *out looking for me?* As the car pulled over, he realized they had a right to.

The two climbed in behind him, Greg first, putting him right behind their father when Paul turned to regard them both. But Lorraine sat just behind Paul, and he could barely see her without stretching all the way around.

The car pulled away again and drove at a leisurely pace down the street.

"So, you're the reason the police *finally* left us alone?" Greg leaned forward, frowning as he mentioned them.

"I guess, in the end," Paul nodded. He didn't want to explain the price he might be paying. "It was my fault in the first place."

From the corner of his eye, he could glimpse Lorraine's face in the mirror, looking worried and a bit drawn. He resisted the urge to sneak another look.

Greg said, "Well, then we—"

"Just a minute," their father cut in. And, looking right at him at last, he asked, "Paul… how much did you hear?"

He's not demanding or encouraging, not leading. Dad really is embarrassed at whatever he thought he said to me—but he's not letting the others stop him from asking. How much could he have said, when he thought he'd found the only way to talk to his son?

Silly question. Looking at his father, he gave the only answer he could: "Every word." *Or all the ones that mattered. Now.*

And that drew a smile like Paul hadn't seen in years. The car itself seemed a bit warmer, a little smoother as it glided along.

"But really," Paul went on, "you know I can't stay in town."

Behind him, Lorraine asked, "So you're just leaving?"

What's she thinking? Why is her voice so expressionless? Still not looking in the mirror, Paul continued "I'll do everything I can to make things right here. But my staying here won't be safe, for any of us, ever."

"That's not true," his father said. "You've already calmed the police down. We can have every lawyer in the city on this. What have the police got, anyway? A few burglaries that still don't have real evidence?"

"Um." Paul tried not to squirm in his seat. Whatever clues they had now, a suspicious detective like Reid had seen too many signs of what Paul could do, and he'd keep looking. *And now, what would the police do with last night's lab raid?*

"Why the silence?" and Greg sounded angry again. "More of your secrets?"

Seems like it. Paul felt for an answer, and glanced around—

Did that car in the mirror just duck behind that van? Are we being…?

Greg snapped, "I'm sick of it! Your lies, and yours, too, Lor!"

Paul jerked his head around. Greg was scowling at both of them now, and Lorraine sat frozen, more expressionless than ever. But Greg *couldn't* know about their power…

"Yes, both of you," he was saying to her. "You've been part of his secrets from the start. 'A deal,' you called it, for him to find out about the break-in and all of it. And I keep apologizing for starting all the trouble. But this 'deal'—just what did you *give* him?" He sneered the word into pure ugliness.

"What?" Paul shouted, fighting the seatbelt to lean back toward him. *How* dare *he, especially after he'd had his affair!*

But that kiss…

Their father broke in "Greg, you're joking—"

"Don't you take her side! She's been lying to me since this started! She's been working with him to track this down, cutting me out of it. And, she keeps going off to meet *him*—"

"That is enough!" their father bellowed. "Now, Lorraine?"

That car, behind us…

Slowly, coolly, Lorraine said "There *was* no deal, Greg. It wasn't a trade. All I did was ask him to help us, and he did. Like a brother."

"A brother who helps 'us' by keeping you away from me?"

"It kept you from rushing off and getting arrested," she said, and some heat began to grow in her words. "At least, until you found out."

Greg raised a fist—

"And," Paul cut in, "you still haven't noticed Detective Reid following us."

"*What?*" Greg twisted in his seat, staring back at the white Taurus a few cars behind them. "But they stopped!"

"He wouldn't dare!" their father said.

They don't get it. Reid might not have as many reinforcements now, or Bennet and Quinn driving him, but after all Paul had done he'd never stop.

The car slipped forward to squeak by under a yellow traffic light. Paul saw Reid stop behind them, and shot his father a grin.

"Dad, turn here."

"Why? Do you want to…"

As the car slowed for the side street, Paul unsnapped his seat belt.

"Hold on…" Greg began.

"And check your office for bugs, Dad! Those aren't mine!" Paul added, ignoring their stares. As the car was still slowing, he stepped out to the street.

He lurched but kept his balance, and stumbled forward along the building's side, moving at a quick trot so he could get out of sight behind it soon. He could hear the BMW glide on and start to gather speed again. By the time another car rounded the corner, he was walking slowly through the back alley.

So, no more pretending. He'd protect them, but they couldn't even guess how much he'd stirred up. And now that he'd lost too much of the time left before he had to go to Quinn, his only option would be to just go and bide his time—

"Hey!" And Lorraine trotted in from the street, with the shaky, determined stride she used to make speed in the heeled boots she wore. *Her face…*

As she reached him, he said "You're getting better at finding—" *What am I saying?* "What's Greg going to say about you going after me?"

"How do you know he's not looking, too?" she answered with a smile.

Paul looked away from that flash of teeth and kept walking, even though she fell into step beside him. He said, "He won't be, not when he's mad. I know my brother, and you shouldn't have. He loves you, remember? Even getting jealous proves it."

"After cheating on me?" But she sighed, a long sound that let her shoulders slump. "I know him, too. And he *is* looking… partly because he's afraid Vernon will come by again to accuse us of blackmailing Ms. Bennet."

"Vernon?" Paul swung around ahead of her, stopping her. "What's he done?"

"He wasn't violent. We calmed him down. Greg and I did," she added, and started walking again. And, as if facing down an unstable thug were nothing, she went on. "The happiest years I've ever had were with Greg, you know. Even if he did cheat, and then try to throw it all away by threatening her." She almost sounded more bothered by the second than the first.

Paul nodded. "Bennet's change just startled all of us, after we'd had too many shocks already. Greg's not good with the unknown, that's all. Not many of us are."

Paul broke off and watched the woman picking her way through the alley beside him. *Why are you here, dammit? Why did you kiss me and then run off?*

But instead of asking those questions, he swallowed and said, "You need to tell him about your power."

She looked toward him, startled.

"I mean it. Say how you got it, and all about how you're trying not to use it much. I'm sure you'll keep your life safer than I did," he added with a sad chuckle. "Say I tried to train you—not that you needed much. And now you can just have a real life again… except…"

Wait, if Greg's jealous of her meeting with me, how's he going to deal with my power changing her?

Before he could warn her, she responded quietly, "I can't tell him, ever. Or anyone."

"What?" She had said it like it was a prison sentence.

"I read *minds*, Paul," and she looked up and reached for his shoulder, then drew her hand back. "Remember how you were when you first found out I could? You think he can *live* with someone if he's always worrying about whether I'm seeing one nasty little thought or another? Or starts thinking that I'm using it to make him love me?"

"What? You'd never—"

"He couldn't help wondering. It's what anyone would be afraid of… and I don't know how to make him understand."

"Well…"

But Paul's voice died away as they walked, because not a single idea was coming to him. Was this the fear she'd always have to live with now?

And I have to get this out. "I guess I'll find out myself. I figured out how to Open to thoughts too. And," he rushed on as her eyes widened, "I'm afraid I used it on you last night, I needed to be sure you weren't working with Quinn and I stopped it at once and I've hated myself ever since—" He stopped at last.

"Oh." And she looked away.

Wasn't that what she said the first night, when I told her the power couldn't read minds?

"I talked to Sarah," she said. "I asked her how much she thought you deserved to be hunted for trying to expose a cover-up… and then trying to do it all over again when that turned out to be the fraud. She said there was no excuse for what you must have done to get your story, but I think—yes, 'think,' I didn't peek—that she really respects you for how much you did."

"That's good," Paul said slowly, trying to cope with the subject change. "Did she say if she still had a job?"

"She's holding on to it. I think she's too good at it not to." Lorraine smiled.

"Well, she can do it without me. She's one more thing that's not safe for me to be around. And besides," and he swallowed hard, and looked right at her, "she's not the one I ever really knew that well anyway."

"Are you *still* talking about running away?" Lorraine's eyes flashed.

Did she change the subject again—or not? Paul thought, even as he said "You think Reid's going to stop? With what I am, and what I've been doing, all in secret—I'm everything the police are afraid of, and everything Quinn wants to own. The only reason I could operate was that nobody had put the pieces together. Now, if I ever want to do anything with my life again, I need to find some of that safety. If you're asking if I'd do anything different—"

"Why is it you always come back to giving up?" she snapped.

"I'm *not* giving up, I'm choosing the fights I can win! I can take on Quinn, somehow, if it keeps you away from him. And I can choose not to fight the whole city—"

Somehow she was facing him now, looking up at him. "You mean, you'll save us from Quinn, but you won't stay and fight for your own place here."

"Fight for *what?*" Paul shot back, then stopped. *Without you, there's—*

He looked at her, at her flushed cheeks and piercing eyes, looking back into him. *If I just raise my hand to touch her...*

"Then I hope you win, some day." And she turned, hair tossing like a shimmering curtain, and simply walked away.

Paul froze. His hand had just started to rise. His voice didn't seem to work, as the only one who had a clue about what he was walked away, her heels crunching in the snow.

He stayed frozen, until her echoes faded from the alley. *But... but still...*

He turned his head away. This was for the best. It was what she wanted and what he knew would keep her safe.

While he faced Quinn.

15

Closed for the afternoon.

It was a simple sign on the main door, but to Paul, the black letters on red glowered a threat at him. All the shops behind the door, all Quinn's neighbors, had shut down and cleared out in just the time since Paul had ridden away with his father.

He walked slowly up to the door he'd always gone around before.

Before he reached it, the guard he heard behind it trotted forward and pulled it back for him. Paul glanced at the big man in the pale blue uniform as the guard gave him a silent nod. Did he know Paul was the one who'd outwitted him a few nights earlier? Was that gun at his hip the one he'd used to shoot at the pigeons?

The guard only led him inside, walking slowly. Paul followed, their footsteps echoing in the deserted corridor and up the stairs. On the second floor, they passed a barber shop, a travel agency… *They all seem so ordinary, but their shutting down now means they're all businesses that Quinn owns—or had controlled, probably more to show me his strength than from a real need to keep our meeting more private. And* this *is who I have to outwit.*

At the end of the long walk, the guard opened the Quinn's Furniture door. He stayed outside, and as Paul stepped past him, for just an instant, a flicker of sympathy might have shown on the guard's face.

Quinn waited at the back of the room, at the desk beyond the maze of furniture. Clear across the room, he smiled, but he said nothing.

As Paul walked to the waiting chair, he noticed his LifeLab flash drives laid out on the table, and the steaming coffee pot on its corner.

Paul steeled himself, gathering his wits. He had to hide the details of his own secrets, and use his power to pull out Quinn's—and he had to keep Quinn happy, or at least off his family's backs, until…

Quinn sipped from his cup until Paul drew near. Then he said, "Right on time. And the streets must been cold—would you like a cup?"

I don't want anything from you. But that was no way to begin negotiations. "Why not?" Paul said as he sank into the chair—a simple, hardback chair, but more comfortable than most.

Quinn poured the cup, then just started to reach it out before he drew it back again. "You did bring my hard drive back, didn't you?" His smile never wavered.

"Here." Paul dug the little metal box out of his coat and laid it on the table, then took the cup.

"A petty question, I know, but it was a petty move for you to steal it. And I'm sure you found I don't keep anything important there anyway."

Important? He wants *us to talk, and think, a little about how we both keep hidden notes?* Paul raised the cup almost to his lips and Opened his mind to Quinn's, trusting the cup to hide some of his expression if his face tightened at the prospect of touching those ruthless thoughts. But all the power showed him was Quinn's lip curling in contempt, still savoring Paul's fruitless theft.

Paul needed to lead those thoughts closer to the secrets, and Quinn was still watching him, waiting for an answer. "Right," Paul said. "I've learned that myself, that the real secrets are too dangerous to keep around. But I've always kept track of names and numbers, just in case

I needed them again." As he finished he reached his mind out again; this time his own features felt like they only hardened a fraction.

"Of course," Quinn said, and his secret face melted into a slow smile, a sense of agreement, of common ground…

"I ended up keeping notes and codes," Paul went on, hoping he hadn't paused too long. "And now and then I gathered them into a hidden spot or two. Of course, I never needed to keep *blackmail* evidence nearby," he added, Opening on the last words. *Please, this time think of where you keep yours…*

But as Quinn smiled "I guess I have a few more options than you," all Paul saw—

—was a cold, gloating smile.

"But you did so well getting these," Quinn added. "There's so much LifeLab data, it would take weeks to really sort it out—or did you already have it from when you broke the story the first time?"

Paul frowned, as Quinn smiled faintly, eyes watching him for hidden signs. Paul felt his fingers heating up around his coffee cup, but he had to muddy the trail of just what powers he'd used to get the files, so he said "Yes—"

Wait, the files have dates! It's a trap!

"But," he managed to add smoothly, "I didn't have the full package then."

Quinn sipped his coffee. "And how did you get the rest in just a few hours?"

"I…" Paul hesitated, scrambling to think of how to evade it. An endless, desperate second later, he could only say "I got it, that's all. A bit of planning, some stealth, some hacking—how do you think?"

"I think you did pretty well. Even the escape, except for being so loud." And he took another sip.

Paul's fingers tightened on the cup in his own lap, almost too hot to hold now. Was that it? Would Quinn let it go without more questions or threats? But of course, he was pretending to have the same "delusions of power" he thought Paul had, and he didn't know which powers to hint at having. Yet.

Suddenly Quinn added, "But less hacking than the rest, right? It's never that convenient for you."

One word, he'd seized on one word of Paul's. *Does he suspect I barely know anything about cracking the machines themselves?*

"Still, you've dug out so many secrets, and kept your own. You even found Crusader Bennet's weakness so fast."

No, that was Lorraine! Have to distract him— "Not that fast, it built on the groundwork from everything else." But, did Quinn's eyes shift faintly, did the distraction itself draw his attention? Paul started to Open, but Quinn was speaking again.

"And you used all of it to protect your family. Is there anything you wouldn't do for them?" Now his face was blander than ever, smiling against the sharp-toothed words.

"I don't know," and Paul heard an edge in his voice as the cup's heat seared deeper into his fingers. "Nobody's ever tried to find if I had limits there. And it's a bad way to start a partnership," he added, Opening.

As Paul said the last word, Quinn's smile stretched before his eyes, tight with cruel satisfaction. But with the same calm voice, Quinn's real mouth said, "And yet you never took a partner. And there's nothing you hate more than blackmail—why is that?"

Right, his bug heard me tear into Dad about Bennet's secret. "What do you mean?" he asked, trying to seem puzzled.

"I mean, why would you spend years fighting to know everyone's secrets, and *never* put them to the obvious use? It's not often I meet someone so convinced about his own rightness—especially about burglary."

Paul watched Quinn's steady gaze, not looking away as his fingers burned. *I will* not *talk about what is left of my purpose, not to this creature.* Taking refuge in the pretense Quinn had to keep up, he said, "Like I said yesterday, I don't remember. And you said you did." He reached for Quinn's mind…

"And then you burned up a parking lot and ran away from a lab full of cameras that recorded every line of your face above that absurd beard," Quinn said, as blandly as if discussing the snow. "For all your dedication, you need something more to hide you now, and to protect your family. Don't you?"

He's making me say it. "Yes," Paul growled.

"Well, then it's time to head back to the Lab."

"What?" Paul started, felt the cup shift in his lap and almost splash its searing liquid onto him.

"You've made LifeLab nervous. It's time to make them *more* nervous," and Quinn reached down and opened a drawer in his desk.

As he looked away, Paul finally set the coffee cup down on the table, flexing his burned fingers in relief and realizing he'd never had a chance to take a single sip.

"Since you like disguises so much, I thought I'd give you a better one." Quinn handed over a bundle wrapped in brown paper that flexed like clothes in Paul's fingers. "You'll go in as an agent for Keyhole, a security company I've… done some business with. It should be an easy role for you. You simply talk your way in, plant what's on this," and he handed over a flash drive, "in their computers, and that's the last you'll have to see of that lab."

Paul stared at the flash drive in his hand. *He wants me to plant evidence. He's not just using their secrets, he's making new threats. Who knows what he'll do? I have to say something.*

"You think I can just walk in…" *Wait, I can't admit I normally use stealth instead of wigs.* Paul sighed, knowing he'd just have to make it work. He reached for Quinn's mind…

Quinn stood up. "And I think you should start. Oh, look at the center of the package."

Paul glanced down, squeezed the bundle, then dug past the wrapping and the fine suit to…

Stacks of money, thick ones, what must be thousands of dollars, maybe more. His fingers closed around a wad almost on their own and drew it out, his instincts burning to throw the bribe in Quinn's face…

"What are you *doing?*" And Lorraine swept into the room, her face white with something like terror that made Paul flinch and drop the cash. The guard trailed behind her, looking shamefaced as she marched toward Quinn. "What are you trying to turn him into?"

Get out of here, Lorraine! But as Paul gasped in a breath to chase her away, he felt Quinn's eyes behind him, watching them both for their weaknesses. He froze.

Quinn actually sounded offended as he asked, "Just what are you saying, Ms. Schuman?"

"*Saying?* You've threatened my family, bullied Paul, tried to lock up my… it has to stop!" She leaned over the side of the table, her eyes wide.

When Quinn answered, he spoke slowly, uncertainly. "I'm… not sure what you think I've done. Paul, let the lady sit down," and he motioned to him in his chair.

Paul jumped to his feet. "Nobody's sitting. We're leaving right now!"

"*Are* you?" Quinn slowly swung his gaze from Paul to Lorraine. "Didn't you come here to sit and talk?"

She scowled at Quinn and then turned to Paul, eyes fierce with the full force of her worry, anger, hurt pride… Paul stepped back, knowing it was useless. From the corner of his eye, he saw the guard leave the room, dismissed.

As she sat and Paul moved behind the chair, he belatedly remembered he had a free moment to focus, so he Opened to Quinn's thoughts again. He saw Quinn's inner eyes flick just past Lorraine to the back of her chair, then down to something out of view behind his desk. *Of course, no wonder Quinn gave us both that chair, in a room full of furniture. He's stuffed it with bug detection tools to be sure so he can talk freely.*

"So, just what do you think I've done?" Quinn was asking.

"Don't lie to me!" she burst out, as if she could barely control her own words any more. "How many years have you been pushing the Schumans around, or wishing you could? And now you think you can hold some hostage against the others with your frames?"

"Frames?" Quinn asked, laughing lightly. "The facts are clear that Paul has…"

"Has *what*? What do you think he's done that's so awful you're paying him money to dig him in deeper?"

She's questioning him. *She's trying to draw out and read his secrets, too!* But the thought barely made a ripple in the growing chill moving up Paul's spine, the helpless urge to just drag Lorraine away from the schemer's presence before—he couldn't imagine what.

"You mean, breaking into half the mansions and offices in this city?" Quinn asked. "The police know he *has*, Lorraine, however much they can prove so far. What did you want, to beg one of your clients to hide him? What were you thinking?"

"I…" Lorraine stopped, her hands twisting together in her lap. Her voice was weaker now, desperate. "I thought we could pay you, or do something you needed, whatever it took. Just… why would you give Paul to the police, when you're holding all the cards now?"

"And you have no cards? Then I can play mine whenever I want, can't I?" He suddenly, deliberately glanced from her to him. "Paul, don't you have work to do? Now?"

Paul stared at him. Did he really think anyone would walk away and leave Lorraine with—*wait, nobody would normally. If I left her, it would only prove I'm trying to hide how much I…*

He opened his mouth.

Lorraine sighed. "You do? Then I guess there's *really* no point in my coming." And she stood up and gave Paul a look of scorn that stabbed right through him, even as he felt part of himself unknot in relief.

Behind them, Quinn said, "I hope I'll see you again, Ms. Schuman." The door opened and the guard stood waiting, having answered some hidden buzzer. "You can show them out. And be sure Paul does what he's agreed to."

Suddenly Lorraine turned and took a step back toward Quinn. "*Please…*" she began, and then hung her head and started out.

Paul wanted to take her arm, but with Quinn watching, he could only gather up Quinn's clothes and money and trudge out after her.

As the guard shut the door behind them, Lorraine broke into a quick step away, and Paul moved to catch up, his knees suddenly weak with relief. The guard was still a few steps behind when Paul reached her side and hissed, "*Why* would you—"

And she spun around, away from him and started back to Quinn's door. Paul started after her, but the guard stepped in his way just as she banged on the door and called, "We're not finished!"

And Quinn opened the door, as if he'd been waiting for her all along.

For one long moment, Paul saw her step inside, her mouth stubbornly clenched in her pale face, Quinn's welcoming smile... before the guard moved in the way.

Damn, damn! I can't show him she's my weakness! Paul turned and started away, Opening as he did to catch any final whispers Lorraine might have for him.

All he heard was her mumbling, "Please, please can we talk..."

A hard hand shoved him forward and the guard growled, "I said, let's go."

And he *went*. He stumbled forward and kept walking, not letting himself look back. Not with this guard, not with Quinn watching for that sign of weakness. He could only keep thinking, *it's Lorraine, scared or not, and she knows what she's doing.*

So why did leaving those two alone scare him more than the guard's gun?

* * *

The parking lot felt different. It wasn't just the daylight or the rows of cars, but the many gaps in those cars. Although the police seemed to be gone, Paul had a sense that last night's excitement was far from over. And no visitors could have missed the boarded-up window where he'd made his escape.

And now Paul had to walk up, trying not to glance back at Quinn's guard in the car or tug at the suit that didn't quite fit. At least the wig and the glasses stayed on, as if they were meant for him. *Just trust Lorraine. Give Quinn what he wants until she finishes whatever she's planned with him.*

Still, when the guard beyond the door looked up and studied his face under that wig, all Paul could think about was how hard he'd always worked to avoid trying to out-talk people... and how much he wished she were beside him now.

The guard buzzed him in, beckoning him to his desk. Paul walked slowly toward it, using the moment to listen beyond him and catch the several voices arguing over the lab's security. When he touched the guard's thoughts, his inner face looked much like his ruddy visible one—neutral, but narrowed a little in caution. Paul's tie still felt too tight.

And can I really leave Lorraine alone with Arthur Quinn? Her, Quinn, her—

Forcing his thoughts away from that, he rushed the last two steps and slapped the business card down on the desk. "Michael Weiss, from Keyhole."

The moment he named the cover company, he saw the little *ArmCo* logo above the guard's shirt pocket. Not a LifeLab employee, this man came from his own security firm, a rival. Two strikes against Paul already.

"Do you have an appointment?" the guard asked, just a hint of a smile in the ritual words.

"You should have called *us,*" Paul snapped back.

Lorraine, with Quinn… their voices together in the hospital, how I'd strained to hear them… In mid-breath, the shifting memory tore free in his head and began to fall into place.

The guard was starting to frown.

Desperately, Paul fell back on the subject he knew, speaking as fast as he could point his hand around the lobby. "You see the angles on those cameras? If someone crept in and moved to the side, on the screen it would barely show as a motion, so you're not doing what you need to make the observer *notice* that screen among all the others if that happens. And I'd lay money there's no sensor on the door to remind him, either."

"There's *me,* right here," the guard said, his face flushing even more. "And the door itself…"

Lorraine's voice, and her dying mentor's too… Fighting to hold down the whispers, Paul flung back, "Your intruder got a key last night—"

"How did you—"

"And any single guard might be distracted, *or bribed,*" he went on, just a bit louder.

"Are you implying—"

"I'm 'implying' that if an agent of your firm won't let ours get in to make our case, LifeLab can wonder why!"

The guard scowled at him, and Paul fought to keep his thoughts on that red face, the slow motion of the hand to the phone…

Not seeing, hearing. The St. Central corridor. Quinn's insinuations about if they'd pay or not. Paul crouching behind the corner, straining to hear who was talking to him…

How he'd strained, *needed* to hear. He'd been amazed and frightened and so certain he *had* to…

His world wrenching open, Opening—

The guard was speaking on the phone again, lips moving without a sound.

No, not just from the need. What had he heard from Quinn? Both "They won't pay" Curtis' bills and "I'm sure they'll pay"? Both! First Quinn had argued one, then actually conceded the other, after…

After Lorraine's voice, and Curtis', insisting *We'll find a way,* and the tugging, shimmering certainty they'd both infused into their words, to *make* him accept…

"Mr. Weiss?" Somewhere far away, a man was saying, "The director wants to see you."

Lorraine…

Paul felt his eyes going wide, unseeing. She'd had the power long ago. It had been her voice influencing Quinn. No wonder she'd begged off his offer of lessons to control it. No wonder she'd always insisted on keeping it secret, only cared about what kind of life she had despite it. Why didn't he know…?

The footstep, the echo of his own shocked step, how Quinn's words of acceptance had begun to burn with *presence,* Lorraine's and Curtis's wills raising up Quinn's voice to hide their own voices from Paul… him stumbling away with his Open mind spinning…

"Sir? Who did you say?"

Did I say her name, aloud? "Sorry, sorry," Paul gasped out, hand on his forehead. "Guess I'm not ready to get back to work." Muttering something about calling later, he spun around and managed to walk almost steadily toward the door.

It was better than the exit he'd made that first night… how he'd run, so afraid and furious at what he'd heard human beings do, what he'd *done,* how just maybe the mind-controller's voice had been Lorraine's own… still lying to him, from the start… *No, no, she does care, doesn't she? Is she trying to work off her own guilt at what she did to me? Or is she…*

Somewhere in the parking lot, he caught his balance, stopping for a moment between the cars. The next moment, he walked on again. Whether Lorraine was a schemer to stop, a woman to protect, or just a force more than able to deal with the problem herself, he had to find her. *I can't follow petty missions when she's alone with the enemy. At least, with the one I know is an enemy…*

He'd forgotten Quinn's bodyguard until he saw empty space where his car had been. Mind still racing, he trotted along the street, searching for a cab. At least Quinn's suit and money were good for that much.

As he climbed into the cab, one last truth fell into place. *It really was seeing the power that did it.* That and, how easy it would have been to think these were things *someone else* did, that the whole life he'd spent not bending the world to his will had to mean it was something different about those people... *and yet somehow I'd* believed, *right down through my senses and thoughts and scrambled memories down to my soul, that if they could, I could too.*

Nobody chose me to have this power. I gained it because I chose *to believe.*

* * *

From sheer habit, he left the cab a block from Quinn's building and slipped along the alley behind it, not knowing what angle his guard might be watching. As he drew near, he could hear that the place was still silent except for one man outside the shop's door... and the two voices inside.

"Then Curtis helped me set up a business, teaching computer use for people on the go. And then... I guess I'm not a businesswoman, but it helped me meet Greg."

"He must be grateful."

"Well, I've tried to be good to him." Lorraine fell silent then.

Down in the alley, Paul felt his fists shaking. *What's she doing? How long has she been just chatting away with the enemy? Did Quinn put something in that coffee to make her careless?* But no, if he tried that she'd have read it in his mind long before she took a sip. *I've got to stop thinking of her as a novice...*

She went on. "I know your loans have taken a lot out of the family. But at the same time, I've seen the firm keep growing and thriving, and your money's been part of that, too. And we've always been able to be happy together, the four of us—or the three of us," she added.

Paul scowled again; did she think Quinn wouldn't notice that she'd counted Paul, and what that hinted?

He stumbled around the back corner of the building, wishing he dared stop listening and just run the last steps to the fire escape. But then, what good would it do to barge in, anyway?

"Happy, even after Greg had his affair?" Quinn sounded sympathetic—or close enough to it to anger someone just the right amount to keep them talking. "You seemed so determined to stay with him, to *help* him, even after you found out."

"I… don't really understand why he cheated," Lorraine said with a sigh. "But I know he loves me. Besides, when I saw our front door kicked in—right after the accident he had—I went a bit crazy. I would have done anything to find out what was going on."

"I guess you got your wish."

Paul's eyes went wide. Was Quinn hinting… was he sounding Lorraine out about how much she'd done herself, and whether she'd had ways to learn Bennet's old secret herself? He'd heard her announce it in the office he'd bugged…

Paul looked up at the fire escape, and froze. Quinn's window now had bars over it. *Of course! Did I think he'd just leave it free after last time?*

"I begged Paul to help me," he heard Lorraine say. "I guess it worked, because he did find the answers. But, I think along the way he broke into your office just out of pure suspicion."

"Is that how he put it?" Quinn asked, as if her being an accomplice to burglary barely mattered to him.

"Oh, Paul only told me what he wanted to tell," Lorraine muttered, brushing it aside as if it had never occurred to her to ask for more. "But he seemed… oh, he can't have had an easy life since he left us, and that was all of our faults. But since he came back, I think… sometimes, I think he's… dangerous."

"Dangerous?" Quinn asked. Paul could imagine how his bland face would just hint at real concern now, to push Lorraine on.

She was telling him what was safe to hear—but, why? Could she really be searching his mind, in just her few seconds between speaking?

"I've seen a bit of how he gets what wants. And he…" Lorraine's voice grew hesitant now. "He thinks he has some kind of 'power' that helps him. And he let it slip that he thinks *you* have that 'power' too, and that it means you'll always be a threat to him."

"Always? I see," Quinn said, and Paul noticed he didn't claim or deny anything about this power he didn't know much about. "What do you think he'll do?"

"I couldn't guess. But I know it can only add to all the dangers here. You're trying to use him, he's looking to outsmart you, and you think you can force him to make a deal—but do you really think he'll stop fighting you some day? And now all of us are trapped by all these secrets!" she finished in a desperate rush.

"I hope you're wrong. The last thing I want is a war."

"Nobody wants that. All I want is for our lives to go on, and Greg to come back. But none of them would even hear about talking to you. You're the one in control, you have all the cards, and if you just don't push anyone to something desperate… well, I'm sure you know better than to push too hard."

For a moment there was silence. Paul tried to think. *Can I get past the guard inside, get closer? But really, would that make any difference?*

"I… I also know about flattery," Quinn said after a moment, and Paul wondered if he'd shaken off some pressure of her power. "Still, I agree. We both want things calm. Unfortunately, as you said, Paul doesn't see it the same way. Whoever wins or loses, he seems to have a real hatred for learning to play the game at all," he added with a sigh.

"I guess he does," Lorraine said slowly. "I don't understand why."

"Are you sure you don't? Remember, he already ruined the family's deal about looking after your friend Curtis. Yes, he tried to do it without blaming all of you, but his recklessness still led the newshounds right to you."

Paul gritted his teeth. *Reckless* was right, and Quinn didn't even know how much Paul had really done to his family. What he'd babbled in front of Quinn's bug was bad enough; at least he hadn't said why he couldn't remember more.

Lorraine was saying, "But, we were the ones who drove him away. Family should be better than that."

"Maybe you could have been. Or maybe," Quinn went on in a softer tone, "he wasn't angry so much as trying to justify what he'd already done, by trying to expose secrets everywhere."

"You think it was guilt… about us?" Lorraine asked slowly, as if reaching for a lifeline she'd never known was there.

Like she never knew I was running from her power, too! Quinn sees too much, but she hides too much, too well…

"Maybe," Quinn said. "And it could mean that, if he saw now that he could help the family most by *not* making trouble…"

"It's not that easy. Remember, he's been doing this for years."

"And you've been part of the family longer than that. You may want to decide if it's worth persuading him. As you said, it would be better for everyone if he were less hostile." Quinn paused and added, "Except…"

"What?" Lorraine asked. Paul had a sudden sense of a fish biting into a hook.

"Except, you said you felt guilty about him yourself, but still you wanted to get things back to normal. And yet," and Quinn's voice sharpened, "you've been helping his schemes, again and again. It would have been so easy for you to stay back and leave things to him. But… here you are, coming to me."

"What are you saying?" She sounded a little angry, or defensive. "I needed his help, and we all owed him. But the sooner things settle down…"

"After all the secrets Paul has found over the years? But, did he find them alone?" Quinn pressed.

"*What?* Of course he did! Do you think I was secretly helping him for years? That's crazy! Why would I do that? When would I even have the *time?*"

"Exactly," and Quinn paused. "I'm sure you let him go, back then. But now, something has changed, and it's drawn you into his world."

No, she just found a chance to see if my power was giving me a good life, the same as I thought I owed her for giving her the power! Or maybe, she...

Somewhere outside Quinn's door, Paul heard an odd thump, something heavy against the floor.

Lorraine was saying "Of course, he was *gone* and then he wasn't, and he found out—"

"Yes he did. But *you, you* discovered our Councilwoman's secret all by yourself."

He knows! Now he'll never let her go either—

"What..." Lorraine said slowly.

"'What am I saying,' you mean? Only that you did impressive work, finding her one weak point from old records and talking with one person—"

It was a loud *whoosh*, a mechanical cough of air cutting through the rising voices. But Paul had heard it before, in the same room, and the sudden silence in its wake could only mean a gunshot—

Paul strained his ears against the stillness. *Is she hit? Why did I let this go on? But how, who...?*

And shouldn't there be a groan or a body falling by now, if anyone was hurt...

Then, at last, a sound. Footsteps from the door, and a shout:

"*You* did it! Say it!"

The voice was Vernon's, wilder than Paul had ever heard him as he charged across the room.

"Say what? What have I done?" Quinn began, before the sound of a fist slamming into flesh.

"Admit it!" Vernon yelled.

Got to get in there. Paul tried to run for the building's front door, but his legs moved clumsily now, and he couldn't let go of his hearing.

"Say it! You had the files, right behind the brick, right where Lorraine said!"

Lorraine? Talking with Vernon? Paul strained to hear more as he pushed to run faster.

His blind step went wrong, his balance swayed, and his feet slipped in the snow. But even as he felt himself toppling, he tightened his grip on the sounds inside.

"So don't you think some friend of yours can still send out your poison if you're gone! Admit it! You tried to blackmail Ms. Bennet!"

Struggling to his feet, Paul heard the crash that might be a man thrown against something. What was Vernon doing to him?

Then, in a weak but steady voice, Quinn answered. "Why should I tell you anything? You've already killed my bodyguard just for being in the way—"

"He's not dead!" Vernon broke in, a little too quickly. "He'd be fine if he hadn't tried to draw that gun on me. *You're* the one who should suffer for trying to destroy Ms. Bennet. Admit it!" His voice gave way to more punching sounds.

The door didn't open, and Paul released his hearing to dig out his lockpicks and Open to his touch, trying not to think as he twisted the metal in the lock. *Did Lorraine really know Quinn's hiding place before she came? Why did she bring Vernon into it? What's she doing?*

His fingers couldn't stop shaking. He concentrated, forcing the trembling picks to feel out the last tumbler and shift them all. The lock turned and he rushed into the empty corridor, his eyes going for the stairs and his hearing reaching beyond them.

"Talk! How did you find out? Why did you think you could get away with attacking her?"

Then Lorraine's voice broke in, shaking but saner: "Slow down, please! Don't you see, you've already won? The moment you looked behind that brick and got his evidence…" Then she paused a moment, then added "Unless someone has orders to go to some safe deposit box…" And now Paul heard her take a steadying, mind-probing breath.

Lorraine was *reading* Quinn about that second stash, and betting any third one would be right on his mind too! *She doesn't need my spying or her verbal fencing now*—those few brutal seconds had given her everything she needed to disarm Quinn.

But not to stop Quinn himself…

Paul froze at the top of the steps. Quinn's guard lay in the corridor, in what looked like a whole pond of dark blood.

Alive, Paul realized as he knelt by the unconscious man. The bullet had hit his arm, the blood looked awful with all its red but his heart was still beating decently. *Vernon must have shot his gun arm and then finished him with a punch.*

A few slashes of Paul's tiny pocket knife cut strips from the guard's shirt, enough to slap on as a crude bandage against the worst of the bleeding. When he finished, Paul found himself glancing at the guard's empty holster and around the floor, but Vernon must have taken his gun.

Was I just thinking of shooting someone? Besides, Vernon is part of whatever Lorraine's plan was… and that's even more ominous…

Almost hesitant now, he looked up at Quinn's shop and reached his hearing toward Vernon's voice.

"Admit it! Say it! Say—he passed out?" The thug almost sounded surprised.

"I guess he would," came Lorraine's queasy answer.

"Don't you let up on him. He's destroying your family too. He's got to be stopped!"

"Do you really want to do that? If it's traced to you, and the Councilwoman—"

"Ms. Bennet doesn't know. I had to spy on her to find out why she was acting like that… why wouldn't she *tell* me?" he added, with almost a whimper of pain.

"I don't know. Unless…" and she broke off.

"What? Tell me!"

Slowly, Lorraine said "She might, she just might be trying to keep you from doing something like this. To protect you."

"Protect me?" Vernon repeated, with amazement slowly warming in his voice "You really think she could care that much…"

Lorraine's guess hadn't calmed him at all. Or—*My God, is she encouraging* him, making sure he's devoted enough to kill?

Something cold stirred in Paul's mind. Maybe, maybe there was no other way to stop Quinn. Their enemy *knew* Paul could get at anything, and that Lorraine could too in her way, and that they'd always defend their family. Whatever they did to threaten Quinn, he'd never stop gathering his own threats to control them… *unless we remove Quinn himself.*

Paul stared at the doorway ahead, the simple, oversized door hanging half-open, and felt the coldness clutching at him. *Am I really thinking…*

Then Quinn's voice, weak but clear, said, "How…"

Vernon cut in. "Shut up!"

"How did she find these papers?" he wheezed again. "Found them… brought them to you… when her husband had been closer to Bennet than anyone—"

"Watch your mouth!" Vernon thundered.

"Watch *hers*," Quinn said in a strangled gasp, his voice gathering strength now. "She's trying to keep you from thinking. She said she found… some papers tucked behind a loose brick, you said? Just right there for you to take?

"And you, Ms. Schuman. You went and asked for his help… why? To protect your husband's *mistress*? You think we wouldn't guess your husband was the only one who'd get a look at Bennet's secrets, and that when you learned them, *you'd* use them against her?"

"Me?" Lorraine scoffed. "Then I suppose I ordered her to have Greg arrested…" She stopped, seeing the trap.

"Destroy the cheater, control his lover, the perfect revenge. Think, man!" he said to Vernon. "She put her own papers there for you to find, then told you…"

Why am I just listening? Paul tore his mind free of the voices and crept toward the door. Even when Vernon shouted, "*You!*" with a whole new level of venom, Paul only let it mean he was distracted. He peeked around the corner and into the office.

Vernon was shaking Lorraine by the throat—

Paul looked away before the red rage started blurring his vision, then ducked into the shop to crouch behind a sofa. He crawled along it, leaning around the end to see the big man still just shaking her, and then risked a quick dash past the open space behind a set of chairs to reach a cabinet. One piece of cover at a time.

Don't listen, I can't listen, just Open to my movements and keep them silent. He felt every tremor of the flood of fear rocking his arms and legs, every clumsy step in Quinn's fine shoes, but if ever in his life he moved softly it *had* to be now…

At least their voices helped drown out his movement, but he'd give anything for them to be quieter, calmer.

"He's lying," Lorraine gasped. "I never—Vernon, believe me, I'd never hurt—"

"Believe *you?*" and a body crashed against a wall.

Only two beds left to crawl behind. Stay low…

Somewhere, a world away, Greg gasped "Lor?" as his feet pounded into the room.

"*Listen* to me…" Lorraine gasped. Paul's attention wrenched toward her voice, drawn by her *power*, distracted…

But Vernon only gasped "What…"

Paul drew his legs in, ready to lunge.

Then the gunshot.

A single, hard *whoosh*, from Vernon's silenced gun. The sound froze Paul in his crouch, froze him for the endless moment before he heard the body fall, and the shocked cry:

"Dad!"

Finally, Paul could turn his head. Through the outlines of a chair set, he saw Greg standing over their father, saw his father's arm spasm against the floor and then grow still, saw the stain of blood seeping out from his side. The next instant, Paul's hearing leaped across to share his breathing. It was weak, fading, but not yet gone…

As he pulled his sense away, a footstep brought his gaze back to Vernon. He saw the big man stepping backward, swinging his gun between the dazed Greg and Lorraine, where she crouched against the wall. He looked around wildly, his gaze passing too near Paul—

"Don't!" and he turned the gun straight toward Lorraine. Vernon's voice was tight now, and Paul saw the weapon trembling.

Lorraine slowly drew something out from her coat. Her phone. "Don't shoot! Please, if we don't call for a doctor *right now…*"

"Shut up!" Vernon lashed a fist out, and the device clattered away along the floor.

"Don't!" Greg shouted. "The cops are already coming."

"Liar! You're both liars!"

The gun swung between them, shaking as it did. Then it settled on Greg.

"But you lied to *her!* You made her think you cared, and then you let your wife find out!"

Lorraine gasped. "No, he didn't…"

"Leave her alone!" Greg said. "It's only Lor. She can't hurt you."

"Greg didn't know…"

"Stop it!" Vernon howled, waving the gun wildly. "Let me think!"

"Then think of the papers," Lorraine said. "You know I had them, all those things about Ms. Bennet's secrets. So it must have been Quinn, or me…"

Paul recognized Greg's sudden shift to silence before he saw the gun swing toward Lorraine, and he knew his brother would never allow this. *My last chance…*

As Greg's first footfalls drew Vernon's gaze back to him, Paul lunged. With all the speed he could risk, with all his focus on quieting the first two steps before the last rush.

One step, silent.

Two. And Vernon looked around, but how—

In the endless instant the gun began to swing around, smashing down just as Paul closed under it—

Raw pain slammed into him, sent him spinning away, crashing down along something all too solid. Head swam, ribs burned—

Somewhere, a woman screamed. His brother called a name. Another, deadlier voice shouted *Don't!*

Prying his head up, he saw the giant level the gun right at Lorraine. And Vernon's head swiveled back and forth, between Greg so far away, Lorraine where she stood frozen, and Paul as he tried to wrench himself up from whatever he'd sprawled over.

How can I reason with him, reach him? Paul Opened to his thoughts.

Vernon's face seemed to leap across the room, appearing before him. He caught one glimpse of the clenched rage, felt the pain and desperation tear through his nerves. He fell flat, curling in a ball trying to get away from the pain, so much fear, drowning…

Except, a sound. A desperate voice, a woman's tone, echoing with something more.

"Not them! It was me who tried to control you… and I did it because I can. Because I know what you're thinking."

Some deeper voice tried to cut it off, but it went on.

"You think I'm lying again. You think I never stop lying, and you don't care what I say. You'd give anything to be out of here, back to Ms. Bennet… yes, just to Ms. Bennet, and it's always 'Ms.' Bennet to you."

Paul dragged himself away from the compulsion in Lorraine's words, the pure *listen to me!* He flung his hearing away, to the one thing that mattered.

His father's wound, still dripping, his father's gasping breath. Wheezing, but breathing. *There's still time…*

"Yes, I can see it all. You and she can never have secrets I can't take. Are you going to trust me, or—"

"Witch!" Vernon swung the gun up, finger already tightening on the trigger. Paul dove forward, knowing those steps had to carry him a world away—

Vernon jerked once, and fell where he stood. The thunder echoed as Paul scrabbled to a stop, almost slamming into where the big man lay. He turned and saw Quinn lowering the pistol—such a tiny thing, too small and well-concealed for a silencer.

A sudden thought flashed: *How long has Quinn been waiting?* And yet he'd acted now… to save a mind-reader he still meant to control.

"There," Quinn grunted, and he looked right past Paul. "He's down, but alive, Greg. He'll never stop coming after your wife now. And he's already shot your father. My gun only had room for one bullet, but before the shot brings the police…"

He motioned to Vernon's fallen weapon. Greg was already stepping toward it, moving with trancelike slowness.

As Greg bent for the gun, Paul glanced over and saw the demon's smile peek out across Quinn's face.

Paul kicked out and the gun slid across the room.

Greg stared up at him. "What are you—"

"Think! You touch that and he'll *own* you!"

The soft voice answered, "Where was Paul a minute ago, or ever? When I just saved your wife's life…?"

Just as Paul turned, he saw a red hole sprout in Quinn's skull. The loan shark dropped without a sound.

Slowly, Paul looked back, past Lorraine, past Greg…

His father was already slumping where he lay, Vernon's gun falling from his hands.

"Dad!"

Paul didn't know which of them said it, but the next instant he Opened and:

"He's still breathing!" He dove across, Greg closer and in his way. Paul had to shoulder him aside, trying to think of his first aid rules again.

First cover the wound, every drop of blood matters— He caught odd damaged smells from the stomach but he could feel his father breathing.

And, *I kicked the gun that way, did I mean to…*

Right at his ear, Greg said "Come on, what next?!"

"Please!" Lorraine gasped, across the room. "He's been *shot*, here on Drake, at Quinn's Furniture, he's dying!"

Not dying, not quite! Not if they hurried—

"I'm so… sorry…" he heard Lorraine say.

But his hands struggled to hold in the blood, and then motioned Greg to keep the pressure on as Paul leaned in to begin mouth-to-mouth, all the while Opening his touch to feel the heartbeat rippling within the flesh, still strong, but a little weaker every time, a little slower. Whatever Greg was saying he couldn't hear it, couldn't hear anything.

Not a sound, until a firm hand drew him aside. He heard the trained voices speaking and sagged on the floor, finally feeling the pain in his ribs and all the wracking struggle to keep going…

Now the EMTs closed around his father, measuring, injecting, lifting him onto the stretcher. And he heard the blessed, blessed words: "He's holding…"

Paul looked around and saw other teams struggling to help Vernon, ignoring Quinn. He stumbled after the stretcher, Greg beside him, but couldn't keep from looking around. *Did Lorraine go outside to guide them in? Where is she now?*

When they reached the street, it was empty. Onlookers, yes, the ambulance and police cars gathering, but she was gone.

And the police were moving in.

As the team hauled his father to the ambulance, Paul let them draw ahead and he faded back. Greg made enough noise, fighting to join them in the ambulance, but Paul took a moment to Open and trace Ian Schuman's breathing. Weak, but steadier now.

Then he slipped away up the corner, before the police looked away from the stretcher. At least Quinn's suit and wig kept them from noticing their fugitive just yet.

Out of sight, he glanced down at the jacket, and saw it was as bloody as his hands. He shucked it off and wiped his hands on its inside as best he could, and the cold air stabbed into his chest.

His fingers touched Quinn's money, still tucked away in the inside pockets. The wad had been too big to hide anywhere else… Paul flung the jacket away, cash and all, glad to be rid of them.

Opening his hearing, he found the alley empty. Nobody chasing him, nobody…

He trotted up the block, then out to the street again, already shivering without the coat. The ambulance was speeding away, and Greg seemed to be gone with it.

And Lorraine had done what she'd wanted. Quinn's threat was gone. Somewhere in the city, she was probably closing in on some safe deposit box she'd sensed, his last threat…

He looked up and down the frozen street, knowing: *She won't be coming back.*

She'd leave the city, just as he had said he'd have to. All the secrets she had lived with, but she'd only wanted to live safely with Greg… *or with me, I'll never know.*

Now she was alone, on the run, wracked by guilt and not sure how their family could survive what she had dragged them through. *She's just where I was two years ago, but with so much more power…*

He searched the streets. The cars seemed to mock him, gliding on their way, not caring. The cold wind rose.

Where, where would she go?

www.kenhughesauthor.com